The Boy Who Found Salt

S. Pitt

Firsthale

Author's Note.

The Boy who found Salt is a story of environmental change and the capacity of human beings to adapt and survive. Being a kind of myth, it is not set in any particular place or time.

The Boy Who Found Salt

Prologue

The land was mostly flat. Its earth and rocks were red. Where rivers flowed, green grass and forests flourished; in the centre was a sea of fresh water and around the edge was ocean. The salt waters of the ocean teemed with life, with corals and fish and great whales and the land had its own creatures, eaters of leaves and devourers of flesh. Birds flew over land and sea but there were no men to watch or hunt them.

This is how it was in the Ancient Time, long ago.

There are many stories to explain whence the first men and women came. Some say a great spirit made them from dust, others that they came from the stars, or crawled from the ocean or out of the little pools that form where water upwells from earth. But there are many kinds of people, each with their own tales, and though they may look strange to one another and speak different tongues, some things are the same for all. Where there is clean water to drink and plenty to eat and shelter, that is good. And where these things are lacking, it is bad and the people move to where they can find them. And this is true for all people and through all time.

Although many tales tell of one man and one woman alone at the beginning, this was not the case in the great flat land. A few dugout canoes and reed rafts came from across the encircling ocean, families journeying from island to island until they reached an endless coast. From here there was no need to island-hop though there were still islets of sand and coral offshore where fish swam in great coloured shoals and turtles laid their eggs alongside giant birds taller than a man. The families hurried along the beaches, eager to know what kind of place they had come to and who dwelt there. For it seemed impossible that so vast a land could be empty.

What drove them to their journey? The lands they left behind were green and bountiful and good to live in but a hungry, fierce people had come there. These invaders smeared themselves with charcoal to make themselves invisible at night and attacked the camps of the first people, the Old Ones, killing everyone they found and drinking their blood to make them strong.

Terror of these Night-Stalkers forced the Old Ones to flee. For they were timid, hunters rather than fighters, long-limbed and light-footed, shy and quick, skilled with spear and fishing-hook, lovers of dappled forest and sparkling water, fearful of storm and dark. And though their craft all landed on the same stretch of coast, they dispersed quickly. In their hearts they guessed that the Night-Stalkers would follow them even to this new shore, and they wished to find their own places far from strife and fear.

But the wide flat land held its own terrors for the newcomers. It was full of huge beasts that hunted them with fang and claw, of snakes and lizards and gigantic birds that could not fly, though none of these were as frightening to the Old Ones as the Night-Stalkers. And sometimes it happened that families would come across one another in their wandering and once their tales had been exchanged and their common roots discovered, they travelled together, for in numbers lay safety. And after a few generations they invented words and customs unique to each group and new languages evolved: thus disparate tribes came into being.

Yet the new land, though vast beyond the comprehension of the Old Ones, was not boundless, nor its bounty unlimited. Some of those that had journeyed into the interior instead of following the coasts came to a great expanse of water. At first, seeing it from a distance, they took it for the ocean but when they reached its shores and tasted it, the water was fresh. And so they camped there and since the inland sea was full of fish and birds that came to feed, there was plenty to eat and the people felt no need to move on. At first, when others arrived, there was enough for all: the newcomers were welcomed and rumour of the Night-Stalkers became something to scare children with, no more substantial than a shadow. But as the Lake Folk multiplied, food became scarce. The great beasts that had roamed the land before people came were all gone now and the smaller, quicker animals which had replaced them grew shy and elusive or fled to places where no men were. And the fish stayed in the deepest parts of the lake so that the people were forced to make boats or rafts of reeds and sticks in order to catch them and many drowned in the attempt.

Then the lake and the marshes which surrounded it became a bad place in the minds of the Old Ones. Because with the fish of the shallow waters gone, birds no longer flocked there in great numbers, so there were no eggs or chicks to eat. And worse, without the fish and birds, stinging flies multiplied until they formed swarms like black clouds which made life miserable for the folk living on the lake shores. Then the rains failed, not only upon the lake itself but in the wide land beyond so that the rivers which fed the inland sea flowed sluggishly and became choked with mud and weeds, then dried up. And the reeds surrounding the lake grew brown along the edges as the mud desiccated and cracked around them and as the cracks widened, the brown spread towards the spines of the leaves and they clashed in the hot wind and died. Gradually a rim appeared around the perimeter of the lake, a little line of bare mud between the dying vegetation and the water and as the dry continued and the sun beat down, flaying the land with heat, the rim slowly widened, for the level of the lake was going down. Then that mud also cracked and dried to dust and when the wind blew, it picked up the dust and carried it across the lake and then failed so that a red-brown scum settled on the surface, smothering the life beneath.

The Lake Folk looked helplessly at the drying mud and the dust that veiled the sky, turning the sun red as blood, choking young and old alike. Now they were hungry and as the lake shrank, so its waters turned foul with the rotting bodies of dead fish and the corpses of animals which, going to drink, became trapped in soft mud at the water's edge and died. A brackish taint came to the liquid which had once been clear and was now turbid with slime: many of the people sickened and some died. Yet the remainder were loth to leave lest the lands beyond the lake were even less hospitable.

One day a child saw something glisten in the drying mud, white and tiny as a star in the night sky. Next day there were more and soon a white crust formed. It sparkled in the sun but when a brave man tasted it, it was salt, bitter as bile. Thenceforth, every day as the water retreated, so the white crystals sprang on the surface of the drying mud and a foul stench spread over the lake for the salt was poison. Then the people knew they must move or die. The strongest and bravest, men, women and children, gathered their possessions and set off again. Four generations had lived and died beside the lake since the Old Ones first reached its shores and there was much grief at this parting. The memories of men are short and those that remembered the flight from the Night-Stalkers were long dead so that in the minds of their descendants the inland sea was the centre of everything.

But not all the lake-dwellers left at once. The less bold and those families with old or sick folk among them clung to the hope that the rains would come because to move meant certain death for the weakest, either from the rigours of the journey or from starvation if they were left behind. They watched the little paths between the dead reeds with dread lest those who had already left returned starving and defeated but days passed and none came. And so, convinced that a better place lay only a little distance away, more departed. Soon only a few remained, digging pits in mud which had dried to a rock-like hardness to collect pathetic puddles of brackish water, eating the lizards that crept out to bask on the glistening shore though their flesh was tough and salty. And every dawn they looked upwards for the tell-tale wisps of cloud that presage rain but the sky was a clear, merciless blue, and then they looked along the empty paths and sighed, wondering what had become of their friends and kin and how long it would be before they were forced to follow. For with each day that passed, their lives became harder.

Chapter 1.

A man called Mingar belonged to the Lake Clan. He was tall and had once been strong and fleet but soon after the birth of his first son, a tree branch fell on him when he was out hunting. His companions carried him back grieving for he lay limp and still as the dead and, some remarked after, it might have been better he had died for when he woke it was as if some vital part of him were missing. His back was twisted so that when he walked, his body jerked as if a string had been threaded through the ball of his right foot to the nub of his left shoulder. And where he had been swift in action and quick to laugh he became timid and silent and so, as he had once been held in high esteem by his peers, now they began to mock and scorn him.

In vain did his kin try to restore him to his former self: relating tales of his past lest he had forgotten who he was; dancing and singing to entice his old spirit back: his wives prepared his favourite foods and lay with him all together. But none of these things worked. He smiled sadly at the entertainment; he picked at the fish and fruit set before him (for the accident happened before the start of the Great Dry); he stroked his wives' heads tenderly, then rose and left them to squabble and scold. And later, when the first families left the failing lakeside, he watched them go and refused to speak of them afterwards, as was the custom with those that had died.

Now it happened that the child who first found salt crystals in the mud was Mingar's son. He was bold and generous in spirit as his father had once been but Tark was too young to remember that time. Most of Tark's close friends had long since left the lakeside camps. The boy had begged to go with them but Mingar always refused.

'When a man's body fails, he learns to use his head,' he shouted, 'and I know the rains will come. Then it won't be the fools and cowards that ran away who'll be laughing. They'll be back, you'll see, and they'll envy those who stayed.'

With that Tark had to be content but time passed and none of his friends returned. Then he grew more frustrated though he did his best to hide his feelings because of his mother's and foster-mothers' sorrow; with the few of his friends that remained, he was lively and good-natured as ever. But as the drought continued and the lake-waters grew foul, sickness stalked the salt-flats and many died. And Tark's faith in his father was shaken irrevocably.

One day, great clouds appeared on the horizon. They towered high and blocked out the sun and the people left their shelters of mud and sticks and animal hides to watch and beg the rains to fall on them. But then a wind, drier and hotter than they had felt before blasted across the plain and it bore the smell and taste of smoke. And a pall swallowed the clear blue sky that the people had come to hate and rolled along the ground, a suffocating reek that brought with it a blinding terror. For there was no distinguishing the roar of the gale from that of fire and soon the lake-folk struggled after the hordes of panic-stricken creatures fleeing past them onto the hard-baked mud that would not burn. And when they reached the soft clay which rimmed the polluted waters of the lake, some rushed on, craving the cool wetness that lay beyond, and they sank into the mire and were trapped and their cries were lost amid the noise of the burning.

The smoke turned day into night but when true night came it was lurid with flame and the flames was reflected by the smoke so sky and land were red and there was no glimpse of stars or moon for the people stranded on the salt flats. And the creatures that had fled with them huddled together, even hunter and prey, hunger forgotten in the greater terror that had driven them there. As they sat or crouched or lay on the glistening salt (which reflected the lurid surroundings so that it looked as if they huddled in a pools of gore), so their thirst increased until they were desperate and began the perilous journey to the lake. Soon, instead of treading on mud and salt, they found themselves stepping on the sunken bodies of those that had gone before and this added to the horror because some of the trapped creatures were still alive and squirmed and cried or begged for help as they were trodden still deeper into the mire: there were people among them.

When at last they reached the edge of the former sea, the lucky few drank. The water was warm and foul-tasting and seemed opaque and thick as oil but they did not care. Some waded deeper to cool themselves for by now the air seemed to burn the lungs at every breath but many drowned, being too weak to swim. And all the time, the walls of smoke encroached on all sides, roiling and shot through with sheets of flame as the dry reed-beds burned.

Then, seeing there was no escape, even the bravest bowed low to the ground hiding their eyes from death, and the mud-stink numbed their senses so that they were hardly cognizant of the gradual lifting of the darkness. A red dawn came which enhanced the bloody appearance of water and salt and all the refugees crowded on the flats shared the same hue since all were coated with mud. And because they were still, from exhaustion or despair, the living were indistinguishable from the dead. When the land beyond the shore was revealed at last there was only a smoking waste where before there had been trees and it was black beneath the reeking sky.

First to stir were the birds. Sensing movement in the air above, they began a desperate preening to cleanse their feathers of the clogging slime so that they could fly again. Their activity roused predators which, now the danger was over, were consumed by hunger. They rose from where they crouched or lay to stalk the weak and vulnerable or to tear at the corpses which littered the flats, forming a grotesque tide-line around the lake's perimeter. And though there was flesh enough to glut them all, being quarrelsome by nature they fought over the choicest pieces and their noise woke the people from their stupor.

The men struggled to their feet and rubbed stinging, bloodshot eyes to try and make sense of what they saw while the women tried to comfort their children by putting them to the breast though by now none had any milk to give. After a little, the children turned away from their futile sucking and cried weakly while their elder siblings emulated the men, standing and rubbing their eyes, then staring silently across the wasted land.

As Mingar stared at the devastation, Tark's heart shrank. Through the terrors of the night he had helped his mother and little sister. His father had been like one stunned or unmanned and, had his other wives not dragged him away, would have stood in the midst of the settlement until the flames engulfed him. And so despite the weariness that slowed his thought and made his limbs seem heavy as clay, the boy dreaded his father's reaction to this new blow. Every time Mingar had refused to leave the dying lake, his whole family had felt ashamed, Tark most keenly; now, seeing how some of the men knelt broken in the mud, he felt the old familiar tightening of the stomach. He knew no-one else cared what his father said or did but that did nothing to dispel his apprehension.

Yet Mingar did not fall. He stood swaying slightly and slow tears made tracks in the filth that caked him like a second skin. His eyelids were so swollen from smoke and thirst, his eyes appeared as bloodshot slits. He licked his lips and when he spoke his voice was cracked and harsh as the ruined land.

'Now it must rain,' he said.

'Aiee!' The cry came from Eeli, Tark's mother, who was sitting close by. In her arms lay Tark's sister. Although the child was five years old, she was small and weak and spent most of her waking hours crying. 'Ah, you are mad, my love. We cannot stay here. Do you want us all to die?'

Never before had Eeli disputed her husband's will for while among their people it was the right of any woman to speak and many were counted among the wisest, she was mild in word and action and seldom raised her voice. Mingar looked at her in surprise and for a moment his fists clenched. Then his other wives, Draa and Myee began to wail, in anguish at his words and from fear that he would punish Eeli.

'Silence!' shouted Mingar. 'What chance do you think we'd have in that?' And he waved his arm towards the reeking shore with such violence that he lost his balance and staggered, recovering himself only by grasping Tark's shoulder so fiercely, the boy winced.

So passionate was Mingar's outburst, it drew the attention of all within hearing. Even the most despondent raised their heads and when they saw the cripple, his hand on his son for support, his wives and children at his feet, some smiled to themselves and their despair was replaced by contempt. They struggled to their feet and gathered round the family. Soon a crowd of about forty men, women and children sat upon the mud, their faces full of expectation, not in hope that Mingar would somehow save them but that his intransigence would justify their own weakness.

When the crowd had settled, Eeli scrambled to her feet, the child still in her arms. Her visage, like her husband's, was gaunt and caked with filth but her gaze was fierce as she looked first round the ring of faces, then at Mingar.

'All this long time we have waited for the rains and they have not come,' she said. 'Yet we have been patient because we, your wives, love and respect you, Mingar, despite the scorn of others. But this is too much. Stubbornness and pride have blinded you to our suffering, ay and that of your children. Now there is nothing to eat save what we can scavenge, and that will not last long. Do you want us to die? We're already starving, or have you not noticed?'

With these words she thrust the child towards Mingar. Already the little girl exhibited the protruding belly and stick-like limbs of the malnourished.

Mingar looked at his daughter with indifference. 'There will be more children,' he said. 'This is my final word: we stay.' And he took his hand from Tark's shoulder and turned to limp away.

The boy watched him go, appalled. His mother's face told him what he already knew in his heart: that with these words, Mingar had condemned them all to death. And yet he, Tark, was only a child, powerless to intervene. All he could do was clench his fists and will his father to turn, to change his mind. In vain.

'Stay then, but you will be alone!' To the astonishment of all, Eeli spoke again and her voice was loud and clear. The men stared, astounded, while the women murmured together in admiration and agreement. Tark was gripped by fear, thinking that his father had no choice now but to inflict some dreadful punishment upon her or else lose face before his people wholly and irrevocably. Yet Mingar did not pause. He limped on across the mud and none could tell if he was deaf to his wife's cry or had chosen to ignore it. They watched him in silence and each wondered what Eeli would do:

whether she would run and beg his forgiveness or wait weeping upon the flats until he relented and came to find her.

'Come.' Eeli took no notice of the crowd. Beneath its mask of filth, her face was calm and resolute. She gave the child to Tark while she helped Draa to her feet. 'We have listened too long to our fool of a husband: we should have left when Tark first found salt. We will take our children and journey to the green place where our kinsfolk are. Better to risk death on the way than wait here until it claims us. For if we stay, that is what will happen, surely as day follows night.'

'I will go with you,' Draa said, 'for you are right: there is no future for us here. But it is no small thing to desert a husband. What of our duty to Mingar?'

'What of his duty to his wives and children?' retorted Myee, who being youngest of the three, was the most impulsive. 'He has neglected us for more years than I have fingers on one hand. If he decides to stay, it is not our fault.'

At this, a murmur arose from the crowd and the men looked at their own women and children in sudden doubt lest they also rebel. And then, as some of the women stepped up, clamouring to join the three, a man who had been listening quietly but attentively at the back, pushed forward and shouted for silence.

This man's name was Tani. He was a little older than Mingar and a wasting sickness had afflicted him in youth so that he was little more than bones covered with skin. Like Mingar, misfortune had embittered him but he made no attempt to contain it. Now, shaking with a palsy that was part of his condition, he spat at Eeli, cackling horribly when she recoiled.

'Look at them!' he mocked. 'Such brave women, planning to abandon a crippled husband to save their own skins! Who would trust them to find the way? And if they manage to cross the wasteland, who will welcome them, knowing their crime? And this lad' - he pointed a bony finger at Tark – 'he started it all: shouldn't he be punished?'

Tark opened his mouth to protest but Tani's glance silenced him. Everyone was staring as if they had never seen him before.

'I didn't!' he stammered and then his tongue cleaved to the roof of his mouth for Tani's lips had curled in a smile more dreadful than any curse.

'Are you threatening my son?' Head held high, Eeli thrust her way between the two. 'You're more foolish than Mingar if you think Tark is to blame. If you'd found salt by the lake, would you have held your tongue, fearing what lay ahead? Yah, you and Mingar are two of a kind, blind to the truth that stares you in the face. Tark is more a man than both of you together.'

The boy felt a thrill of pride yet the danger was not over. Many of the women applauded Eeli's speech but the men shook their heads and Tani's eyes narrowed. Ignoring the women, he gestured once again towards Tark.

'Even so a hen plover will sacrifice herself for her chicks,' the thin man sneered. 'What else can be expected from a woman? Yet I say to you, the rains will fall again if we make them welcome. Long have I thought upon this and talked with wise spirits and this I have discovered: we have lived here years beyond count, taking what we wanted yet giving nothing in return! Now the land is rejecting us, like a father who casts out a son who comes empty-handed to the hearth. And so we must redeem ourselves through a gift. Yet how? What do we, who have lost everything, to give?'

He paused and raked the silent, apprehensive crowd with glittering eyes. When none dared answer, he gave a short, harsh laugh.

'Have crows stolen your tongues?' he jeered. 'As rain falls and soaks into the land, so our offering must sprinkle the earth. And hearing it, the clouds will relent and free their water. If we hold back, so also will they and then we shall die. Yet those lacking courage to stay are free to leave. Only the faithful are welcome here and they will see how the gift is rewarded!'

So cunning was this speech, none comprehended its true meaning. They stared dumbly and Eeli's brow creased in thought but guileless as she was, she also missed its significance.

'Ha – he talks of giving as if we have anything to spare!' Draa exclaimed at last. 'When did we last eat properly? We have nothing to offer our children, let alone to feed the earth. Let us leave this madman to his dreams and go from this place ere our strength fails utterly.'

With that, she took Eeli's arm and began to lead her away but Tani's voice stopped them in their tracks.

'Go then, and your bones will bleach along with those who went before!' he cried. 'Only make sure you leave the boy behind. He brought woe upon us: he shall redeem us. The clouds, seeing his blood drip into the dust will have pity at last and Mingar, whose sacrifice this is, will be proved right after all!'

'What do you mean?' Eeli's frightened gaze went from the fanatic's face to her son's and back again. 'You can't – '

'For the good of all,' said Tani, meaningfully. Quick as a snake, he lunged for the boy. But Tark was quicker. He twisted away from the thin man's hands and ran.

'Catch him!' Tani's cry rang in the boy's ears but he had already pushed through the crowd and the salt flats lay before him. Only one figure was to be seen upon that wide shore, limping steadily towards the blackened ruins of the village: Mingar. But even as Tark considered begging his father for protection, he remembered that Mingar had denied his children and swerved to avoid him, half-blinded by tears.

Any pursuit was, however, doomed to failure. Tani screamed at the men to catch the boy but they were hampered by many of the women who joined Mingar's wives in blocking the way. All were, in any case, exhausted, lacking strength to run any distance while the boy, fear-inspired, was already far ahead. Soon the men stopped, gasping for breath in a cloud of dust and ash raised by their own feet and still the women yelled imprecations until their throats were so dry, they were choked into silence.

'Are you satisfied?' Tani stood hands on hips and surveyed the panting, beaten crowd, the distant figure of the fleeing boy, and the plodding form of Mingar with sardonic eyes. By now the sun was visible as a glowing red orb in a bronze-coloured reek of dust and smoke and as the people licked cracked lips with thirst-swollen tongues, they tasted the thick, metallic taint of blood. 'If the rains do not come, the fault is yours, Eeli.'

The shock of Tani's decree and Tark's close escape had drained the last of Eeli's strength. Wearily she turned to face her tormentor.

'Say what you like, Tani,' she said. 'I am tired. But you will not have my son.'

Her voice trailed into silence, she swayed and sank to the ground. At once Draa and Myee bent to help her away but she sagged between them and with the little girl to carry and their other children clinging on, they had not gone far before they were forced to stop.

'So the earth has chosen after all!' Tani's voice, though dry and harsh, was triumphant. 'How fitting that it should be a mother. For we all come squalling from between a woman's legs and, in the end, we all return to dust.' And he advanced with terrible deliberation upon the little group of women and children, the crowd following close behind.

From the rim of sandy mud which had marked the lake shore before the start of the Great Dry, Tark watched the groups converge. Though they were tiny with distance, he could identify each individual for he had known them all his life. He saw his foster-mothers put the children down and bend over Eeli as the skeletal figure of Tani menaced them, then the crowd swarmed and the women were engulfed: he could not see them any more. There was a sudden tumult, a flurry of limbs, a shrilling scream that seemed to tear the stagnant air asunder, frenzied yells like the raving of mad dogs. Dust and ash rose in a boiling cloud beneath milling, stamping feet: it rose waist high, to their chests, then obscured them completely but it could not silence them. Their shrieks, wails and howls, which no longer sounded human, made earth and sky shudder.

Tark sank to his knees, trembling, bathed in sweat. He pressed his face into the dirt and waited for the noise to stop but it seemed to go on forever.

The boy woke to an eerie silence. For a blissful moment it seemed that he had been in the throes of a dreadful dream but his body ached as if he had been beaten and there was a foul-tasting dryness in his mouth. He lay still for a while then, unable to bear the oppressive quiet any longer, opened his eyes.

The salt-flats appeared empty of life save for a single spot far out towards the lake where a mass of carrion birds heaved and squabbled.

Tark sat and stared. The birds were congregated about a dark blot on the pale surface of the flat, a surface that, from a distance, looked smooth but which was, in reality, churned to a treacherous paste of salt and mud. From their frenzied flapping and noise, they had found fresh meat. Then he leant forward, retching. He knew what they were feasting on.

When the spasm was over, he sat up as before but his eyes no longer saw the birds. He thought of how his sister had weighed like stone in his arms, how he had resented the charge and his mother's presumption. Now he would never have to worry about either of them again yet he felt nothing. It was as if his head had become a hollow gourd. Even the memory of how Tani had wanted to slay him could not stir him. He was too tired to mourn, to be afraid, to do anything but sit under the louring sky and wait for fate to overtake him.

Slowly, inexorably, the sun climbed and its rays penetrated the layers of dust and smoke. And little vortices formed and the suffocating blanket began to break and lift. Then the wind awoke and it carried the reek higher. Water condensed around each grain of dust, every particle of smoke and the droplets coalesced and clouds formed. And when a drop of water grew too big and heavy for the warm air to support, it fell to earth, sometimes knocking into and melding with others on the way to form great raindrops which splattered on impact and made little craters in the dirt.

At the first touch of rain, Tark thought burning embers were falling again for he could not tell if the little pricks of pain were due to extreme heat or cold. He tried to ignore them, to sink again into the mindless oblivion of his stupor but they persisted, increasing in intensity until he flinched for they were small and hard, like the flakes of stone the Night-Stalkers were said to use upon their war-spears.

When he opened his eyes and saw the falling rain, touched his skin where the layers of filth were turning into slime and washing away, breathed of the rapidly cooling air and heard the clamour as birds, animals and people found their voices and rejoiced, a consuming rage filled the boy and he beat the moist earth with his fists and howled his anger and grief to the world, a cry that was lost in the tumult rising all around.

'Hush, Tark, quiet little one.' The voice was gentle, calm, arms enfolded and rocked him: he thought he must be dreaming and gave himself wholly to the illusion. Here was safety, security: he was in his mother's arms and the rest, all the horror and despair, had been no more than a nightmare. He relaxed and settled his head into the hollow of her shoulder but something was not quite right, the shape of the bones was different to what he had expected, and the voice, as it continued to soothe him, seemed, despite the hoarseness caused by dust and thirst, lighter in timbre than he remembered.

Lightning seared across the sky. Even seen through closed eyelids, it startled the boy; the woman's voice was lost in an ear-splitting crack of thunder. Then the rain lashed down with even greater fury so that he clung to her, needing warmth and reassurance. But this time she took hold his shoulders and pushed him away. And he opened his eyes and saw that it was Draa.

'Aue,' she groaned when she saw the shock of recognition in his face, 'Eeli is dead,' and he had to force stillness on himself as her fingers dug painfully into his shoulders.

How long they knelt thus, Tark never knew. The rain sluiced down and water washed around them while his eyes took in every detail of her face. It was battered and bruised, one eye swollen shut, her lips split and her nose twisted, but his thoughts were slow and it took an immense effort to form words and say them: 'What happened?'

Draa groaned and shook her head slowly from side to side. 'It was Tani. He led them into madness. Men, women and children, he drove all into a frenzy of fear and hate, saying that Eeli and her children were to blame for the disaster and only their blood could appease earth and sky and bring rain. And Eeli said nothing, she sat on the ground with her head bent over her little one and that only made them worse. They called on her to deny it and still she would not speak. And Tani said this was proof of her guilt and they swarmed over her like ants and when Myee and I went to help her, they knocked us down. Aye, Myee they slew along with your mother and sister and they would have killed me too save that Tani dragged me aside. 'Mingar deserves one woman,' he said, 'he can share you with me from now' and then he told me to run before he changed his mind.'

Her voice trailed into silence and she lowered her eyes, unable to bear the fierceness of Tark's expression. For her words had woken something stronger than fear or grief: the desire for revenge.

'Ah, please, no,' Draa moaned when she recognized his intent. 'Tani will slay you if you go near him again. You must leave now, if you want to live!'

In an effort to comfort her Tark forced himself to take her hands in his though he yearned to find a large rock or broken branch he could use as a weapon, then seek out Tani.

'You're only a boy,' she wailed. 'And now it's raining, don't you understand? Go!'

'Why?' He thrust his face almost into hers and felt a moment's triumph when she recoiled. 'My father is a coward: who else will avenge my mother and protect you?'

'Fool!' She pulled one hand free and caught the side of his head with a sweeping blow he could not evade. 'That's how much chance you have against Tani and the rest! Think! He told them that if they shed blood, the rains would come, and see: they killed and the blood soaked into the dirt and it's raining! But that was not the sacrifice he intended. It was your blood he called for: you heard him with your own ears! Do you think he will be satisfied with this? No, not until the lake is full again and the land is green, and the rain is already lessening.'

Eyes streaming and cheek smarting from the blow, Tark looked out across the flats and saw that this was true. The veils of rain were thinning, revealing broad pools where there had been only salt. Far out towards the lake the carrion birds had been replaced by four-legged scavengers which fought each other over every scrap. Tark shuddered and swallowed convulsively, then turned his eyes away.

'Tark, listen,' Draa said urgently. 'The others believe in Tani now: they will have no mercy. You cannot hide here. Go now, while you can!'

There was no mistaking the passion in her voice and gaze. And suddenly Tark's bravado vanished. Where he had been ready to take on Tani and challenge him, now he realized the truth: he was a boy, small even among his own people and weak from hunger and shock. He looked at his hands and saw that they were trembling, had to fight an urge to fling himself into his foster-mother's arms and weep.

'Ah my love, my little one,' Draa murmured in pity. 'If there was any other way! But there is none. Run now and hide before the rain clears and if you wait by the Black Tree, I'll bring food and anything else I can find that you might need.'

It was in his mind to beg her to leave with him but from her resigned expression he knew she would refuse and that to argue would only upset her. Without another word, he rose and plodded away through the ankle-deep water now flowing towards the lake. He did not look back and thus never knew how she watched until the curtains of rain and still-rising smoke and steam veiled him from her sight.

The Black Tree stood at the intersection of two paths. It had been an early casualty of the Great Dry and had since been struck by lightning in one of the dry storms that were common in the hottest part of the year. By the time Tark reached it, his legs shook with weariness but at least he had slaked his thirst. Away from the salt-pans the floodwaters, though tainted with mud and ash, were drinkable.

The tree, which had been blasted so that only the lower section of the trunk remained (from which a single branch outstretched like a grasping hand), appeared unexpectedly in the murk and the boy stopped in his tracks, heart thumping wildly, mistaking it for a person. Then, when he realized the truth, he hissed between his teeth and hurried on for part of the stump was hollow and he longed to curl up in its shelter and rest.

When he reached it, the hole was crowded with small animals which fled at his approach. He scrambled gratefully into the tiny space and curled up on the thick bed of leaves that had collected there. It was not dry but at least, for the moment, it was above the rising water. He closed his eyes and fell instantly asleep.

It was dark when Tark awoke, so dark that at first he thought he was blind. Usually, even on a cloudy night there was enough lambent light to see shapes: the rectangle of the hut's doorway, the humps of neighbouring shelters beyond, but this darkness was complete, as if night had grown opaque. Tark lay motionless, listening for the slightest untoward sound. Soft, furtive footfalls in the mud made him stiffen, fearing some predator or carrion-eater had scented him, until he realized the sounds were not made by a four-legged creature at all.

'Tark, are you there?' Draa's whisper instantly dispelled the boy's alarm though how she had found her way in that suffocating darkness, he could not guess.

'Draa!' He scrambled out of the hollow and his body was stiff and painful: he gasped and so she found him.

'Ah my son,' she murmured, reaching out to lay a hand against his face. 'You did well to hide. Tani has sworn to drain your blood in the lake bed so the rain will come and fill it. And your father went to the ashes of the hut he shared with Eeli and lay face down in the dirt. He has not moved or spoken since. Maybe he waits for death but one thing is certain: he will not intervene should Tani catch you. Therefore you must leave as soon as there is light to see by.' She paused, then added quietly, 'And know that my heart goes with you, along with this'

She sought his hands and pressed something very small and hard, like a kernel, into them. There was a fine string threaded through it. It was smooth when he put it to his lips to feel its texture and cold as stone but he could not identify it.

'It is a very rare and precious thing,' she said. 'A shell from the shores of the island whence our people came long ago. It has been passed from mother to eldest daughter since the ancient time. Eeli kept it hidden for it is a woman's thing, but now you should take it for your wife in remembrance of us and of what has happened here. Put the thong round your neck to keep it safe and do not forget your mother and foster-mother and sisters, nor Draa who loves you still. And Mingar too, because he is your father.'

Numbly, the boy put the string round his neck and settled the tiny shell against his chest. Then Draa bent and thrust a bundle into his arms. 'Take this,' she said and now her voice was hard and urgent. 'It will fill your belly for a day or so and at first there will be plenty of meat to find, after the fire. But after that you must live by your wits for I have no weapons to give you: all were lost. Go now and maybe one day we shall meet again.'

Now that the moment had come at last, Tark was unprepared for the final, irrevocable step that would take him away from all he had known. Every time families had left the lake he had wanted to go with them but to set off alone into this new desolation was more daunting by far. He stood with one hand clutching the little shell, the bundle of meat hanging from the other, and felt utterly alone though he could hear Draa's soft breathing and feel the homely warmth of her.

'You must go!' she said, and he saw a faint lightening on the very rim of the horizon, a diffusion of the darkness into grey. 'Quick, Tark, dawn is coming! And when you find the rest of our people, tell them what has happened to us. Then, even if we die here, our story will live on. Do you understand?'

He nodded, for all speech had left him. Already the light was spreading into the sky: he could just make out Draa, a slight, dark figure against the silvery backdrop of floodwater. She raised one hand and he never knew if she meant to hit him again or it was a gesture of farewell because next moment she spun on her heel and splashed back the way she had come.

Even when she was lost to view, Tark stared after her. He felt weak and empty, lacking the strength of will to act. When he finally turned and plodded past the Black Tree, it was more an execution of her desire than his.

Chapter 2.

Dawn came swiftly despite the murk that hung over the land, a meld of drizzle and smoke that made a grey, featureless pall. Water moved sluggishly round Tark's ankles as he trudged through it, his only guides a faint lambency in the cloud that marked the position of the rising sun, and the direction of the flood which was flowing towards the lake. There was no landmark that he recognized for all had burned, nor was there any change in the horizon. A flat line where flood met weeping sky, that was all, and the monotony of it seemed to seep into his brain, dulling grief and fear until it was only the lack of anywhere to stop and rest that compelled him to keep moving. His head was bowed, the bundle dragged at his right arm while his left hand clutched his mother's talisman, not in hope or remembrance but simply because it acted as a kind of anchor to hold him in the living world. He walked in a daze which even hunger could not penetrate, hating the heaviness of the bundle he bore whilst being incapable of realizing that it contained food and would lighten each time he took from it.

By the time the sun reached its zenith, Tark could go no further. The rain had diminished to a thin drizzle but the flood was knee-deep and fast-moving. Every-so-often pieces of debris, broken branches or the bodies of animals, struck his legs or tangled his feet and freeing himself sapped the boy's strength until he could no longer summon willpower to place one foot in front of the other. He stopped and, almost for the first time since setting off, looked around.

The monotony of grey-brown floodwater and dirty sky was broken by blackened stubs of trees, the remains of a great and ancient forest. They formed sad ranks whose lines marched to the horizon in all directions. All were roughly the same height as the boy but their thickness varied greatly: some he could have spanned with his two hands, others were of such girth it would have taken the linked arms of many people to encircle them. The spacing between them varied also, the largest standing in clear areas Tark's whole village would have fitted into, others being crowded so closely together, they might have sprung from the same root.

Every stump was crowded with survivors of the cataclysm: lizards, snakes, mice, any creature small enough and with strength to climb and cling to the burnt timber. Above them circled birds of prey, those not already glutted from scavenging by the lake. Their screams rang in the boy's ears but he was aware of an immense silence between their noise and that of the swirling water. It was a quiet born of self-effacement as each of the clinging creatures tried to make itself invisible for, as during the worst of the fire, predators and prey were forced into close proximity, often clawing and biting at each other to reach the highest spot. Having achieved some measure of safety, they froze in the hope of going unnoticed by the winged killers overhead.

When he saw that fresh meat was to be had simply by plucking an animal from a stump, the boy was overwhelmed by bitterness against Draa. It was both unreasonable and irrational but that he had dragged the bundle she had given him so far to no purpose incensed him. He let go one side of the already stinking skin and let the meat fall into the water.

But as soon as this was done, he regretted it. He knew Draa had meant well, could not have known what lay ahead. Almost as an act of penance he bent and scrubbed at the bloody skin until it was clean, then tied it round his shoulders like a cape.

After that, he simply stood there while tears of weakness and self-pity welled in his eyes. Already his senses were growing dull and his will to act ebbing: the anger he had felt against his foster-mother had drained the last of his reserves, leaving him empty and exhausted. If he did not eat soon, he would die.

High above, a raven spied out the flooded land with merciless eyes. It saw the crowded stumps and swooped for a better view then, spotting the boy, veered aside with a startled croak for alone among the creatures of the earth it feared men, stone-flingers and nest-plunderers.

The raven flew off in search of easier pickings but its voice had penetrated the boy's stupor and roused him to a final effort. He scooped up a handful of the muddy, foul-tasting water and drank, then waded to the nearest stump. Past making any attempt at stealth, he ignored the panic his presence caused amongst the tenants who clawed and climbed upon each other in their effort to escape. In the end one lizard simply fell into the water, ousted by its peers, and he had only to catch its neck and hold it under until it drowned.

There remained the final bloody effort of getting at the meat without tools of any kind or even a flat surface on which to work, but hunger had awoken in Tark and he tore at the soft skin of the belly with his teeth and ripped the body open to get at the kidneys, liver and heart. The smell and taste of blood turned his hunger into a kind of frenzy: having swallowed the organs almost without chewing, he hooked out the intestines and let them drop, then tore off the skin and bit deep into the haunches, eating voraciously as his body began to appease its desperate need for sustenance.

When he had finished, the desire for sleep overwhelmed him. He tossed away the remains of his meal for some other creature to feed upon and looked round for a stump large enough to support him. It did not take long to find one but before he could rest, he had to check it for snakes for these were the only creatures he feared. This he did with great care and when he was satisfied, he climbed up. The other animals occupying the stump crowded to the edge but did not leap off from fear of drowning.

Simply to be above the floodwaters was a relief; to have a full belly and a cape to lie upon filled the boy with a kind of contentment, a sense of security that was entirely misplaced. He curled up in the hollow at the centre of the stump and fell instantly asleep.

It was dawn when Tark woke. Sullen grey light spread from the east revealing a heavy layer of cloud whose folds hung overhead like the belly of a monstrous toad. No rain fell from it but thunder muttered and reverberated through the still, fetid air like an incessant growling.

He looked at this lowering sky and clambered down from the

stump, dragging his cape with him. His whole body ached despite his long sleep but he knew he could not afford to linger. Now the rain had stopped, Tani might be on his trail.

The water was still knee-deep: while the flood lasted, he had a ready source of food. He plucked a lizard from the stump he had slept on, flicked it against the bole to kill it and tore it open with his teeth. So prominent had lizards become in the diet of the lake-side people he was well practised in the catching of them and chewed absently on the tough flesh as he walked.

Directly ahead, beyond the ruined forest, a dark line was visible. It was a ridge of sandhills. They were not high but the flatness of the surrounding landscape made them significant and the simple fact that they were upstanding from the flood filled Tark with relief for he longed to feel dry land beneath his feet again.

When he drew close he saw that the slopes were crowded with animals and birds, those too large and clumsy to seek refuge on the stumps and many that had been maimed in the fire yet still clung to life. All seemed stupefied by shock, hunger or exhaustion for they did not flee at the boy's approach and seemed oblivious to each other. Some raised their heads to stare at him but they soon relaxed, perceiving no threat for he was small, alone and unarmed.

Tark waded across the last stretch of floodwater and when he clambered onto the sand it was as if a heavy load were lifted from him for the water had dragged at his feet every step.

This relief was only momentary because the sand was covered by a film of dust and ash. Rain, followed by the movement of so many animals, had churned it to a grey paste which clung to the soles of the boy's feet and picked up sand grains as he began to climb until he appeared to be wearing shoes. He stopped to rub it off and it was then that he heard a shout: 'Yah! Look there!'

The cry was faint with distance yet the language was his own. Tark spun round and stared back the way he had come. In that landscape of black stumps and grey-brown water it was impossible to make out any pursuit yet the boy crouched instinctively, making himself smaller. If Tani was within sight (and he could barely believe his ill-luck if this was so, since the flood had ensured he had left no trail), he knew movement would betray him. And lest his enemy should be using the same tactic, he held himself still, only his eyes moving as he scanned the flooded land.

Tark was beginning to wonder if he had mistaken some unfamiliar bird-call for human speech when at last he saw them. Five figures, far away yet recognizable as men with spears. And as if fear had leant him a hawk's vision, he saw that the last of them was far thinner than the others and leant on a stick for support.

At the sight of his enemy, Tark hissed between his teeth. They were still half a day's walk from the sandhills given Tani's slow pace but the very fact of their finding him in so vast a desolation was a blow. For a moment he was overcome by a sense of futility for it seemed to him that all his efforts had been in vain. Almost he wished he had defied Draa and confronted Tani by the lakeside: it would have made no difference in the end.

Unexpectedly, the leading four stopped and huddled together as if uncertain of their direction and purpose. When he caught up, Tani pointed directly at the slope where the boy crouched but the others looked all around and two walked a few steps away, gesticulating wildly. It seemed that an argument was in progress.

In fact, to the hunters, Tark was invisible. His movement had alerted them for an instant but before they could be certain what they had seen, he had effectively disappeared, his filth-ingrained skin melding with the mottled greys, browns and red of the slope. And though they had followed Tani willingly at first, they had not expected the chase to last so long: they worried about kin left beside the lake while the swift cessation of the promised deluge had sown seeds of doubt in their minds. Two of them had even begun to regret the killing of Eeli, for she had been loved and esteemed by many for her kindness and wisdom.

Thus there was dissent within the group and this was to Tark's advantage for sensing revolt, Tani's prime concern switched from capture of the boy to maintaining his leadership. He turned from his scrutiny of the sandhills and began haranguing his companions, yelling and waving his stick with such vehemence, he staggered and almost fell.

Seeing this, Tark relaxed a little. If they had known where he was, he was sure they would have rushed to capture or kill him before arguing. Yet he was still far from safe. His dilemma was whether to risk moving in the knowledge that if they spotted him, they were still some distance away or to stay still in the hope they would not reach the sandhills before nightfall. Once they found his tracks the hunt would be over. He could outrun Tani but the others would catch him easily.

While he agonized thus, his eyes never left his pursuers. The argument was still going on and two of the hunters had moved to stand beside Tani as he continued to berate the others. But the dissenters appeared to have had enough: they turned abruptly and started back the way they had come, their weapons balanced on their shoulders as hunters were wont to carry them.

For a moment Tani stared after. Then he spoke to his companions who, without hesitation, cast their spears.

The lake people lived by hunting and fishing: there was no chance the two would miss. The boy watched appalled as the victims fell, pierced through the heart by the force of the throws. They lay face down in the floodwater, and were slowly carried away, drifting inexorably in the direction of the lake. The spears transfixing them stuck up like masts.

Tark hesitated no longer, certain now that if he were caught, they would kill him. He sprang to his feet and raced up the slope with as much speed as the soft sand would allow. Startled birds and animals fled before him, a flurry of movement that would, he knew, betray his presence to anyone who saw it. But he no longer cared. All that mattered was to put distance between him and the murderers. The breath rasped in his throat and his feet sank into the sand at every step but he forced himself on until he was over the dune-crest and beyond sight of his pursuers. There he flung himself down to rest. When he had recovered a little, he raised himself to look over the ridge, sure that his enemies must now be on his trail.

To his amazement, Tani and his companions seemed oblivious to the disturbance on the slope. They were busy towing their victims through the flood. When they reached a platform of debris that had jammed between stumps the killers climbed onto it, dragging the corpses with them. Only then did they tug their weapons free: this done, they jumped down and clapped each other on the back in celebration.

It was only as they turned again to the line of sandhills that Tark understood that by moving the corpses thus they had avoided any danger of the killings being discovered. Carrion-eaters would swarm to such easy pickings: within days nothing would remain of the two men but scattered fragments of bone. And the callousness of this shocked the boy for the killers displayed not the slightest sign of respect for their victims though they must have been kin. All the people of the lake were related, by marriage if not by blood.

But though sickened by what he had witnessed, Tark's mind was at last clear. He rose and fled down the slope. There was no need for caution: it would be some time before they gained the ridge. By then he would, he hoped, have found a safe hiding place for he knew that there was no chance of outrunning them.

As he jogged down the sandhill, he scanned the landscape spread before him. The floodwaters extended as far as he could see, the dune-ridge forming an isolated island. On this side there were fewer tree-stumps and they grew sparser with distance. Towards the horizon, where it was almost impossible to discern the grey-brown flood from the pall of cloud, there were no trees as all nor any rocky feature to relieve the monotony. And the very flatness of that region made it hard to tell distance: whether the edge of the ruined forest was several days' walk away or an hour's.

But at that moment Tark cared little about what might lie ahead: he had yet to escape what lay behind. He knew he had no choice but to leave the sandhills where it was impossible to move without leaving a clear trail, yet still he hesitated before stepping into the flood. By now the flow had slackened and the water was shallower but it was thick with mud and stank of death and decay. And flies buzzed and swarmed in dense clouds, descending so thickly upon the boy that they formed a kind of second skin. They crawled into his ears and nostrils, clustered in the corners of his eyes and whenever he brushed them away, it seemed they returned threefold.

Flies he was used to: since the shrinking of the lake they had plagued the villages yet there was something revolting in the sheer mass of these and so, as he splashed on, he flapped his hands constantly in a futile effort to drive them away.

Almost imperceptibly, the light faded. A deep gloom spread from the east. When he looked behind, Tark could barely make out the line of distant sandhills. He slackened pace and looked for somewhere to rest.

The water was now a mere film over the ground he walked, most of the flow being concentrated in channels eroded deep into the soil over years of alternating drought and storms. This made walking easier because at least he could see where he was putting his feet but piles of debris had been left by the flood. Some formed formidable barriers, heaps of burned and broken branches entangled with corpses. Tark was forced to skirt these, having neither desire nor strength to clamber over the stinking piles. They seethed with flies, rats, snakes and carrion-birds.

But the darkness soon became Tark's main concern for while it protected him from watchful eyes, it made finding his way almost impossible. No light from stars or moon could penetrate the heavy cloud layers and there was no likelihood of the situation improving until dawn. Apart from the hazards of falling and the ever-present threat of night-prowling predators, without stars to orientate by, he could easily walk in a circle without realizing it and find himself back at the sandhills with his enemies but a spearthrow away.

This he could not risk yet there was nowhere for him to rest for the stumps of trees in this region were too small for him to sleep upon. After searching in vain for a while (he did not even consider spending the night on one of the vermin-infested debris heaps), Tark realized he had no choice but to make a sleeping platform. And so he pushed down two of the weakest stumps, brushing off the lizards and other creatures that clung to them, and with these as the base, constructed a raised area just large enough to lie down on, filling the gaps with handfuls of leaves and mud, anything he could find that did not stink of death.

By the time he finished, it was so dark he could barely make out his hand in front of his face. He climbed onto the platform and pulled his cape over to cover himself, not for warmth but comfort. Then, almost instantly, he fell asleep.

The horrors he had endured took their toll: Tark slept through the night and woke long after dawn. He stared uncomprehendingly at the bruise-coloured clouds hanging overhead for it made no sense that it could be day when he had only shut his eyes for a moment. Then he sat up and looked round in alarm for while the sun was still obscured, it was full daylight and the hunters had probably been long on his trail.

Down on the plain however, it was hard to see far. The sandhills formed a dark line on the horizon but there was no other landmark and he knew that if Tani and his companions were stalking him, he would be lucky to spot them. The debris heaps provided plenty of cover and Tark's stomach clenched with apprehension: he might not even see the hunters before their spears stole his life.

While he slept, the floodwaters had receded, leaving a layer of wet mud over all they had touched. Now many of the creatures that had been marooned ventured off the stumps and pieces of debris which had served as refuge. But for some the mud was still too deep: they sank up to their necks or floundered as it clogged their fur or feathers. Even frogs and toads were hampered for there was a clinging quality to the mixture of clay and ash that made it adhere to the skin like glue and it accumulated even as the creatures struggled through it, ploughing deep trails behind them.

Seeing this, Tark was loth to leave the security of his platform. As soon as he stepped off it, he would leave tracks and once the hunters found them, it would be over. And despite a full night's sleep, his body was stiff and sore and cried out for rest, time to gather strength for the journey that lay ahead whether Tani was still in pursuit or not.

In the end it was this lingering weariness, a lassitude of the mind as much as his body that made up his mind. He would stay where he was and if his enemies discovered him, so be it. And as soon as the decision was made, he relaxed. He rolled onto his stomach and gazed back towards the sandhills, his eyes closed and sleep overwhelmed him.

Gradually, the pall of smoke lifted. Great holes formed in it and stars appeared. A keen wind arose and swept the last of the foulness away and now the stars blazed, bathing the scorched land in cool, silver light.

At the lakeside, the people were woken by the starlight which seemed brighter than they had ever seen. They came out from the crude shelters they had constructed from animal skins, sticks and bones, and gathered together in silence. Their feet made deep tracks in the soft mud left by the flood and these, shadow-filled, were stark against the pale surface, seeming more substantial than the ghost-like figures of the people who looked at the stars in awestruck wonder. Believing the spirits of their ancestors to dwell in the sky, it seemed to them that there must be some message in this blazing night, if only they possessed wisdom to comprehend it.

But two of the survivors did not look at the stars. Since the killing of his wives and children, Mingar had lain on the ground as if struck down. He had not eaten since before the fire and would not speak but from time to time Draa trickled a little water into his mouth. Now, weak with fasting, he lay in a stupor and flies formed a crawling blanket over his body. Beside him, Draa lay curled and her slumber was like a black pit which no light could penetrate.

The perplexed, wondering people looked at one another and each saw their anxiety mirrored in the eyes of the others. Without someone to guide and lead them, they were lost: Tani, who had taken control after the fire, was far away. They looked into the sky and flinched at the flickering brightness and saw no answer; they looked across the shining expanse of mud and water (for the floodwaters draining into the lake had partially filled it), and it was empty, and the vastness of the flat land and the vault of sky frightened them.

Then a young woman noticed Draa's absence. She left her husband and went to find her, for in former times they had been close friends. And suddenly the memory of how Mingar's wives and children had died returned to the people: without Tani to beguile them they were assailed by guilt and shame and wished their crime could be undone, even if it meant the rain had stayed away. As one, they turned their eyes from the sky and watched the woman crouch beside the sleeping pair. For an instant nothing moved: the people held their breath. And then the woman shook Draa's shoulder and she woke and sat up, rubbing her eyes, then stared at the star-studded sky like one awoken from a nightmare.

Draa thanked her friend who withdrew, from fear of Mingar and a kind of awe. For there was a serene calmness in Draa's face that seemed almost inhuman: her eyes were black and glossed by the starlight; her skin smooth as wind-scoured stone; her expression devoid of emotion, as if the cataclysm had left her alone unscathed.

For a long while Draa looked into the sky and then she turned her attention to her husband who lay motionless, face down with arms outflung.

'Mingar!' She bent low to his ear and whispered words of love and encouragement but he did not stir. Only the slow sliding of the shadows between his ribs betrayed the fact that he breathed.

'Mingar!' This time she hissed his name and shook him roughly at the same time. He groaned and tried to shrug her hand away but she would not be deterred. Hooking her hands beneath his shoulder and hip, she pulled him onto his back. He was so emaciated, he weighed little more than Tark would have done: she was shocked by his frailty. He lay awkwardly because of his twisted spine and his upturned face was skull-like in the pale light, the hollow cheeks and eye-sockets pools of shadow.

'Mingar - wake up – the stars are looking down on you!' Draa commanded. 'Open your eyes and live!'

Again Mingar groaned then his eyelids twitched. They were crusted with dried mucus and, seeing him struggle to open them, Draa was overwhelmed by pity. She licked a forefinger and tried to wipe the crud away but he lifted a hand to stop her. 'Leave me alone!'

It was so long since he had spoken, the words were hoarse and laboured: it was a voice of dust and ashes. Yet the very fact of his speaking was a source of joy to Draa: again she bent low and this time she licked his eyelids clean and he did not prevent her for it was an act of love.

'Open your eyes,' she said again and slowly the lids parted the merest slit. And seeing the stars, he let out a sound that was like the groan of a mighty tree before it splits asunder.

'Aue,' he moaned, 'why am I alive?' and he rolled his head from side to side as if in agony while his hands, which had lain loose and open on the ground, clenched with such force that the nails incised little crescents into the palms.

Draa sat back on her heels and watched him in his throes. All around she heard a quiet murmur for the people had slowly encroached upon the couple, drawn by curiosity and a kind of desperate hope. But though she was sharply aware of them (and her skin crawled beneath their scrutiny), Draa remained focused upon her husband. All her bitterness and resentment had been melted by compassion.

'Ah Mingar,' she murmured, 'do not despair. See: the smoke and cloud have gone and the Old Ones have not deserted us. And I, also, am here. Together we shall find a new place to live: it is not too late.'

He lay still, considering, and licked his lips. 'Fetch Eeli and Myee,' he said at last, 'and Tark, who is my prop and in whom my hope resides.'

At this a groan arose from all within hearing and Draa could not conceal her dismay. She stared at Mingar and an invisible hand seemed to tighten round her throat so that she could not speak. A dreadful silence fell and Mingar, sensing the sudden tension, raised himself on his elbows and looked round the ring of faces, blanched by starlight, stark with grief.

'Where are they?' he demanded. 'What has happened?'

'Aiee!' Draa's ululation shuddered across the flats and even the birds and beasts that heard it crouched close to the ground in fear for no such sound had been heard in the world before, even during the worst of the cataclysm which had convulsed earth and sky together. Three times she cried aloud and when the echoes had died away, a profound silence fell and the people looked up uneasily, certain that her anguish must have reached even unto the ancestors.

And where entreaty and compassion had failed to rouse Mingar completely, Draa's outpouring at last brought him to himself. He recalled turning his back on his wives and children, leaving them to the mercy of his rival, Tani, but he could not remember Tark's fate nor guess it, for while he had heard the tumult as the crowd closed upon Eeli and Myee, he did not know if the boy had been with them. For the first time in years he was pierced by anxiety for someone other than himself; he sat bolt upright and grasped Draa's wrists: 'Where is he? Where is my son?'

Draa made no attempt to pull away though his grip was of a fierceness and strength remarkable in one so diminished. Yet looking into his face, a visage more like that of an animated corpse than living man, her heart quailed.

'He fled,' she stammered. 'Otherwise Tani would have killed him too. He is gone.'

Mingar's features convulsed. He dropped Draa's wrists as if the touch of her had burned him and the onlookers flinched under his wild gaze.

'Tani then,' he demanded. 'Where is he?'

A kind of collective moan arose from the crowd and all avoided his eyes: none wanted to be the one to reveal the truth. For Mingar's voice was no longer weak, it was harsh and commanding, made all the more frightening by his obvious frailty. It was as if some great and terrible spirit were using his body as its mouthpiece.

'Tell me!' Ignoring Draa's stricken expression, Mingar lurched to his feet and now the illusion became even more powerful because he swayed as he stood and his head wobbled on the stalk of his neck like a dotard's.

'Tani: come out!' The people stood as if spellbound as he began pushing and shoving, trying to see where his enemy was hiding. None retaliated or even protested for deep in their hearts they desired atonement for their crime and in Mingar's visage they thought they saw their doom.

Surrounded by these awestruck, half-expectant faces whose eyes seemed to feed upon him rather than offer comfort or help, Mingar realized suddenly that his efforts were in vain. With a curse, he turned and they fell back before him until he came to Draa. And she stood calm and steadfast as a rock for alone amongst her people she understood how her husband's passion was rooted in regret and guilt and that his uncanny strength was fuelled by will-power alone. Yet she was careful not to betray this. Remembering how swiftly this same crowd had been incited to blood-frenzy by Tani, she no longer trusted them, guessing that their growing fear of Mingar might turn them against him.

'You then . . .' He stumbled to a halt an arm's length from her and the breath sobbed in his throat. 'Tell me the truth. Spare nothing.'

In faltering words Draa began to relate all that had happened from the moment Mingar had turned his back on his wives and children after the fire. At first her voice was weak and tremulous but as the tale proceeded, it gathered momentum and power until the words flowed like a torrent from her mouth, terrible and compelling. When she came to the killings, the crowd moaned and wept, all save Mingar who stood as if turned to stone.

'Aie – but though the blood of Mingar's first wife, Eeli the Wise, had soaked into the ground; though that of his second, Myee the Beautiful, formed streams across the salt which swelled with the blood of their children, Tani was not satisfied,' Draa cried. 'It was the blood of Mingar's son he wanted, for Tark had challenged him like a man and then escaped so the thin one's heart cried out for vengeance. Thus it was that he called for hunters, skilled in bushcraft and fleet of foot, those still with strength to bear spears, to step forward and then, with four companions, he set off after the boy though the blood of Eeli and Myee was still wet on the parched earth.'

Now Draa's telling had turned her recollections into an epic tale so while they knew it had strayed from the truth, the drama of it affected all who heard her. They gasped and swayed as she described the first drops of rain: warm and thick like drops of blood, and their shame and grief became a kind of ecstasy. Some moaned and howled while others rolled on the ground and bit at the mud but through it all, they listened still.

'The rain fell harder, as if to beat the raging earth into submission,' Draa continued. 'Ay, like a man hitting an unfaithful wife, only the rain did not relent. Water ran over the ground, pouring over the salt-flats, and streams melded into rivers and spread until, where we had been burning, it seemed we would drown instead. Tani and his companions were swallowed by the rain: of Tark nothing had been seen since he fled. And now the rain has stopped and the stars look down upon us, but neither hunters nor hunted have returned.'

So loud were the cries of lamentation that arose at these words, few heard the last of them. But Mingar listened and understood and his eyes narrowed with contempt as those whose hands and feet had dripped with the blood of his wives and children abased themselves before him. Then, meeting Draa's gaze, which was steady and accusing, the thought came to him that by failing to protect his family he also was culpable, for though he had not condoned the killings, neither had he tried to prevent them. And the din of the mourners seemed to beat upon him like the rain which, in his stupor, he had not noticed: he turned upon them in sudden rage, yelling for silence and, to his astonishment, they obeyed.

Then Mingar at once regretted his boldness. For the people looked at him with an avid hunger, not for nourishment or comfort but leadership. Confused and terrified by the cataclysm, they had believed Tani, even killing at his behest yet he had gone, leaving them bereft. Now, unwilling to take the responsibility of decision-making themselves, they looked to Mingar for help and guidance, forgetting that it was his intransigence, his refusal to leave the dying lake, which had led them to this plight.

Mingar understood at once what they expected of him. Silence had fallen but the tension was such that the very air seemed to shimmer with it. He swallowed and the sound seemed magnified; a woman shifted from one foot to the other and the rising impatience of the crowd filled him with dread. From Draa's tale he guessed they would turn upon him without mercy should he fail their expectations and yet his mind was blank and he did not know what to say or do. For all his anger was directed against himself.

Standing opposite him, Draa sensed her husband's indecision and the crowd's growing frustration. She knew that procrastination would provoke them to violence for they had been driven to the very limit of their endurance and were hungry and desperate. And so, recalling Eeli's courage, she drew herself up until she stood tall and straight and surveyed the crowd with a proud, almost imperious gaze that at once calmed them. For though she was thin and filthy as the rest, the starlight shone in her eyes and there was something awe-inspiring in her calm self-containment.

'Look at Mingar,' she said and her voice was stern and

reproving. 'Have you no shame, here under the gaze of the Ancient Ones? These long days and nights he has lain grieving for his wives and daughters who died at your hands, and for his only son whom you drove away. No food has touched his lips since that day: he is weak and likely to die. If you would have his help, you must redress the balance. Bring him things to eat and clean water to drink, make a shelter in which he can rest and regain his strength. Then, perhaps, he will forgive and consider what to do.'

This speech shamed and daunted the crowd but it also did much to mitigate their uncertainty. Cowed yet strangely comforted by her authority, they bowed their heads or spread their fingers in a gesture of submission and then they crept away, leaving the two alone.

Perceiving that the danger was past, Mingar sighed heavily and the effort of will that had kept him on his feet failed. His legs folded and he collapsed to the ground, becoming no more than a huddle of skin and bones at Draa's feet, a dark blot on the gleaming mud. So diminished was he by fasting, it seemed to her that she looked upon a child: it might have been Tark lying there. And as this thought came to her, so her resolve hardened and her purpose grew clear: somehow Tani must be found and stopped and Tark saved. For in him alone did the blood of Eeli run and it was the belief of their people that the very life of the clan resided in its children, for through them were the stories of their forebears preserved and in them the continuity of the tribe was assured.

To Draa, this unexpected realization of purpose came like a revelation, a direct message from the spirits, perhaps from Eeli herself. She looked up, deep into the shining cloud of the Milky Way, and a feeling of certitude such as she had never known before settled upon her. She and Mingar would conquer Tani, their enemy, and find Tark and with him restored to them, they would be whole again. And then they would journey together to a new green land where they would thrive and thus their lives would be fulfilled.

But though her eyes shone and strength flowed into her with this resolution, Draa knew she must use all her patience and wisdom to persuade Mingar to this course. Because being a man and proud within himself, while he would listen to a woman's counsel, he would only take it if it coincided with his own purpose or he thought it originated from his idea. But Draa, like most women of her kind, was especially skilled in the subtle manipulation of men, to guide his thoughts along a course which seemed of his own making but, in fact, was hers. And so she knelt beside him and put her arms around to hold him close and tried to ignore his trembling.

All power of resistance had deserted Mingar. He nestled into her like a child though his angular bones and harsh skin made it more like embracing a thing of sticks and leather than a human being. And perhaps it was this child-like, trusting, submission that inspired Draa (for afterwards she could not tell what had brought this song of all the hundreds she knew to her lips): she rocked him gently and began the ancient lay most beloved of their people, which told of the great journey undertaken by their ancestors, the terror of the Night-Stalkers and the finding of the great flat land that was to become their home.

Over countless years this song had been sung and gradually it had been embellished to celebrate and immortalise the great ones of each generation. And so now, seeing that her husband, though lying relaxed in her arms was yet awake (for his eyes were open and gleamed in the starlight), Draa inserted lines to suit her own purpose. In this version, the Night-Stalkers came with fire and storm to devastate the world; their leader was so akin to Tani in look and deed, they might have been twins; the one who arose to lead the forest-dwellers was, like Mingar, a passionate, proud man who had suffered much: he also had a twisted back and was, at first, embittered by his misfortunes, only when his people needed help, he stepped forth and led them across the treacherous sea to safety and they loved and revered him as their saviour.

As he listened to her voice, roughened by all she had endured, Mingar slipped into a reverie. Images conjured by her words formed before the backdrop of the star-hung sky and it was himself he saw in the hero's role, a Mingar crippled still but ennobled by his struggles not galled by them: a man steadfast, strong-willed and just. And as her song continued in verses never heard before, describing how the people had settled by a great lake where they lived happily for many years, he realized that even as she could alter the ancient tale of their people, so he could change their future if he indeed possessed the attributes of the Mingar in the song. And he willed her to sing on, to tell how after the drought and the calamity of the dying lake, the devastation wrought by fire and flood, one man, so akin to the leader of old that the great one might have been reincarnated in him, arose and led his diminished, desperate clan to a new land of plenty. And in his version of the future, they did not meet those who had abandoned the dying lake before them: these had perished in the Dry, regretting their foolishness in leaving, for than his own stubbornness was justified.

But the song did not continue so far. Draa sang of the cataclysm and the deaths of Mingar's wives and children, the flight of Tark from Tani, the Bone-man, and how Mingar lay fasting; she sang of how the rain slackened and cleared and the stars shone once more, the Ancestors looking down with cold, glittering eyes. And then she stopped and an immense, ringing silence descended.

It seemed to the two huddled together on the shining, stinking flats, that in that moment they were somehow isolated from all other living beings. They breathed self-consciously and each was aware of the other's breaths: the eyes of the Ancient Ones pierced them with their crystal-sharp gaze and they were afraid.

How long they remained transfixed, they could not tell. The spell was broken by the sound of muted voices and they saw figures approaching, tiny in the immensity of the night. The two felt a momentary trepidation, then as the people came closer, they saw that they bore food and water and their mien was humble. And Draa knew that now was the time, perhaps the only chance, for Mingar to redeem himself.

'Ah, my love,' she said softly, 'they are coming to pay homage. Be sure not to disappoint them.

Chapter 3.

It was dark when Tark woke but this was not the suffocating blackness of the past nights when he could not tell whether his eyes were open or shut. The cloud had finally dissipated and everything was bathed in starlight. He lay on his back and the stars blazed, then dazzled as his eyes filled with tears for under such a sky all that had happened seemed impossible. Then he wondered if his mother and little sisters were among the spirits of the ancestors looking down upon him but the stars flared and glittered impassively: his heart cried out to them and there was no answer. He was lost and he did not even know if Draa, who had tried to help him, was alive to see this sky, these stars.

How long he lay thus he could not tell but gradually his eyelids grew heavy: even grief and loneliness could not counter his body's weariness. It lapped at his consciousness like a tide and, eventually, blotted out even the blazing stars.

He woke with heart-pounding abruptness and sat up, staring round wildly. The stars had faded into a translucent pre-dawn twilight and a bar of paler sky marked the eastern horizon. It was faint still but enough to make bold silhouettes of three men approaching from that side.

Tark did not wait to find out what they wanted. Snatching up his cape with one hand, he scrambled off the platform and fled. And it seemed that his sudden movement startled the hunters as much as their appearance had alarmed him: there was a shout, then the whiffle of a spear. It passed an arm's length from the boy and stuck quivering in the mud.

After his rest, Tark was stronger than when he had left the lakeside but the light was growing all the time and though he knew he could outrun Tani, the other two were hunters, faster and with powers of endurance far greater than his. And yet as daylight spread over the land, it revealed a flat landscape of mud, transected by wide, multi-channelled torrents, all flowing back towards the lake. As far as he could see, there was no place to hide.

But the flung spear, though it had missed, left no doubt as to his enemies' intent. The breath sobbing in his throat, he ran on, skidding and sliding on the mud. The skin cape hampered him so he flung it aside. In this flat landscape it was impossible to see far ahead but he knew he must avoid the rivers for though they looked shallow, they were fast-flowing and even to attempt a crossing would slow him. And so whenever he saw a line of brown, churning water ahead, he veered away though this forced him into the wide hollows where salt had accumulated during the Dry. These were now covered with a film of water and red silt, as innocuous looking and deadly as any bog.

Tani's companions, the two hunters, were flanking the boy, loping easily at a distance for they were in no hurry and their plan was to exhaust Tark, then capture him: the spear had been thrown not to kill but to scare him into flight. Tani himself was far behind, dreaming of a triumphant return to the lakeside, the fugitive bound for the sacrifice that would bring more rain, enough to fill the lake. He, like his companions (and Tark), had no idea of the danger which lay ahead.

Tark was small and light. He had splashed his way into the centre of a great oval-shaped depression before he felt the ground give slightly beneath his feet. Even then he did not realize the significance of this: he ran on, warily, and with each step the ground shuddered and he was overwhelmed with a kind of instinctive dread. He slowed but it made no difference. The clay seemed to stretch and sink and ripples spread out, not only across the thin film of water which covered the surface, but through the mud itself.

Then, from behind, came yells of terror which turned to shrieks for help. So compelling were those cries that Tark stopped to look despite his fear of the pursuit. (Had he paused to think, he would have realized they could easily have killed him by now had that been their primary objective).

From the fate of many animals and people on the margins of the dying lake after the firestorm, what he witnessed now should have come as no surprise, far less shocked the boy. But the horrors of that night had been eclipsed by the slaying of his mother and sisters afterwards: the rest seemed like a nightmare, remote and unreal. And so now, seeing men struggle waist-deep in a mire of clay and salt, he was transfixed. He stood motionless, watching as the mirror-like surface swelled and rolled, felt that wave-like motion (which propagated not through the water but the ground beneath), rock him and realized suddenly his own danger for he was in the very centre of the pan where the crust would be thinnest and the underlying clay wettest and most treacherous.

'Tark – help me!' The closest of the two waved frantically. 'Tark – I was your father's friend!' He tried to claw his way out, his fingers ploughing great furrows in the mud but, inexorably, he was sucked down until only his head and flailing arms were visible. With each movement, he sank a little deeper.

Appalled, drawn by pity, Tark took a few steps towards the man though he knew he could do nothing to help him. Once stuck in a wet clay sink a man could only be saved if he had many strong companions who were on firm ground and possessed a rope and, even then, rescue was not certain. And the clay was quaking under his own feet: another step and he, too, would break through. He stood still, trembling, and watched.

Realizing no help was forthcoming, the trapped man began to rave but as he sank further his cries grew fainter for he could hardly breathe. His hands reached out, quivering, in a last effort to grasp something solid but he was clutching at air: with a horrible gurgling sound his head disappeared and he was swallowed completely, leaving only a churned dark patch on the smooth surface of the pan.

The other hunter, to Tark's left, was calmer or perhaps simply more resigned than the first. He had sunk thigh-deep but instead of struggling to clamber free, he had flung himself forward, arms outstretched, head craned above the thin film of water. So far the fragile surface layer was supporting him and he had not sunk any deeper. But he could not move, save his eyes, which desperately sought aid, and did not cry out, perhaps sensing that even to fill his lungs and expel the air in a shout would send him deeper into the morass.

The sun, which had risen almost unnoticed by the boy and his pursuers, was now well clear of the horizon. It flung Tark's shadow before him and he felt its heat upon his back. He crouched, for it seemed to him as if that pitiless light were deliberately pin-pointing him. And though he did not know it, he appeared so insignificant even within the oval of the salt pan, that the trapped hunter saw only a small dark shape that might have been an animal carcass or boulder and turned his eyes away, assuming the boy had been swallowed by the mire or, perhaps, had never been there at all, for a thin haze shimmered above the ground as the film of water evaporated and salt began to crystallize, white and glittering, on the greyish-brown mud.

Through the haze a third figure now appeared and the effect of heat and vapour was to enhance his thinness and magnify his height so that he appeared immeasurably tall, a stretched shadow-person, dark against the pale mud and cloudless sky. He stopped at the edge of the pan and shaded his eyes with one hand. Two figures he saw, one trapped in the mud, the other huddled on the ground but he mistook Tark for the second hunter. Perspective and scale were lost in that glaring, rippling light.

Tani was too pragmatic to attempt rescuing the trapped man. He leant on his staff and peered across the flat, trying to make sense of what he saw. For both figures were motionless.

'Hoy!' he shouted, and the cry, thin and shrill, yet carried clearly through the trembling air. 'Get up, you coward, and help him!'

Hearing that hated voice, Tark shuddered, but it roused his mind from the stupor of horror and dread. Gradually, as Tani began to yell threats and imprecations, he realized the thin man's mistake and it occurred to him also that while he stayed where he was, he was safe from capture. For he doubted his enemy would dare set foot in the hollow when the danger was so manifestly before him.

To the trapped hunter, Tani's presence meant the renewal of hope. He raised his head with infinite care, saw the elongated, wavering figure far away on the rim of the sink, and lifted one hand, as if to draw the thin man's attention. But even this slight movement altered the precarious balance by which his position had been maintained: he felt the edge of the surface layer give beneath his belly and shrieked for help as his body slid into the liquefying mass.

Tark shrank within himself as the man's cries turned to wordless screams; he heard the suck and splash of mud as, panicking at last, the hunter tried to claw his way out, then there was the sound of choking and a slow, thick bubbling. It ceased abruptly.

From where he stood watching, safe on solid ground, Tani was consumed by rage. He stamped his feet and waved his staff, raving at the figure he could see before him, naming him coward, traitor to his people, a thing of no account, unworthy to be called a man. And slowly, as his fury subsided, it dawned on him that the huddled form was too small for a hunter: he looked across the sink and saw that the dark blot on the surface, which was all that marked the drama that had just been enacted, was repeated. Then, at last, the truth struck him.

Crouched with his face low to the ground, eyes stinging from the salt, his mouth parched, Tark had no choice but to listen as Tani's curses changed to threats. Whatever distance the boy managed to put between them, the thin man promised, it would never be enough: he would always be following. For what had begun as a wild idea, formulated as much to gain power over his clan as to bring rain, had become an obsession: he could not rest until he had the boy in his clutches, could release that young, pulsing blood, and thus deprive Mingar, his rival, of his only son.

Some understanding of this Tark was able to glean from the nature of the thin man's invective. The words were vicious, menacing, intended to hurt and intimidate and though he tried not to listen, it was hard to ignore when the only other sounds were his own quick breaths and occasional cracking noises from the ground. For the clay was drying rapidly now; the heat seemed to press upon the boy like an unrelenting, heavy hand. And while he tried to comfort himself that here he was safe from Tani, he knew he could not stay much longer. Already he felt sick and dizzy. He licked his lips and his tongue seemed thick and swollen: if he did not drink and cool himself soon, he would die.

Since threats were having no effect, Tani changed tactic. Now, instead of cursing, his voice became gentle and persuasive: it was as if someone else were using his mouth to speak. With soft words he tried to entice the boy, promising water, food, shelter; professing regret for what had happened by the lakeside and grief for the unnecessary suffering Tark had endured.

'Come boy,' he called. 'Do you think I wish to harm you? I desire only to take you back, home to the loving arms of your foster-mother and father. Would you let Mingar kill himself with grief? The deaths of your mother and sisters you lay unfairly upon me: it was the others, Tark, a madness overtook them and they were deaf to reason. I could not prevent it, believe me. Come back and you will see: there is water in the lake again and the land will turn green and our people be content once more.'

After all he had experienced, it should have been easy for Tark to dismiss this speech. But so subtle was Tani's tone (and the weakness of his voice increased its pathos), that the boy found himself considering these words and re-evaluating all that had happened since the firestorm. For the first time he realized it was possible that the spear had been thrown deliberately wide that morning and that Tani really meant to capture rather than kill him (and the more he thought about it, the more likely this seemed since the hunters had had ample opportunity to slay him). Almost he was persuaded to accept the thin man's argument and submit. But as he shifted carefully to one knee as a preliminary to rising, he touched the talisman Draa had given him, the little shell that had belonged to his mother, and saw again, clearly as if it were being played out on the shimmering air before him, Tani mocking and berating Eeli, then urging the crowd to bloodshed; again he heard her screams which shrilled like those of a trapped animal, then failed beneath the tumult of the mob.

'No, no.' He did not know if he spoke the words aloud but as the vision dissipated, he found himself clutching the shell as if it alone could protect him from Tani's cunning. 'It's all lies.' And he pressed his hands against his ears to shut out the thin man's voice.

Realizing his efforts were in vain, Tani at last fell silent. He stood leaning on his staff, weighing his chances of catching the boy alone. A simple choice lay before him: to return to the lakeside, a journey which, with the subsiding floodwaters would be comparatively easy, or to continue his pursuit though only luck could now deliver Tark into his hands. And though Tani was tenacious by nature and almost fanatical in his desire to crush Mingar, he was not stupid. He did not deny that the hunt had not gone as planned, nor that with each day he spent away from his people, his hold over them might weaken, even that someone might set himself in his, Tani's, rightful place (though not in his direst imaginings did he consider this could be Mingar). And he had the deaths of his companions to explain to their kin and friends, something that would not be easy.

As he wrestled with these problems, Tani's eyes remained fixed on the boy huddled in the centre of the pan and all at once an answer presented himself. Tark himself could be blamed, having wilfully led his pursuers onto the treacherous ground in the hope they would be trapped. The first to venture into the pan had become stuck and the others had perished in their attempts to rescue him despite Tani's efforts to dissuade them from the hopeless task. And all the while Tark had taunted them, dancing in mockery on the thin surface which supported him, a mere child, but had given way under the weight of the hunters, swallowing them so completely that no trace remained.

This solution pleased Tani for it made a good story that would surely turn the last of his supporters away from Mingar: who could trust the father of so malicious and recalcitrant a son? And best of all, there were no witnesses to the truth except, of course, the boy himself.

The boy . . . The thin man's eyes narrowed into a glare of such ferocity, his skull-like face appeared almost demonic. For the boy would have to be silenced, otherwise Tani's beautiful story would forever be in doubt. And if Tark escaped, he, Tani, would always be looking over his shoulder lest the truth somehow become known to the people of the lake, either through the boy or someone he had met on his wandering.

There was, then, no choice. For peace of mind, the boy must be killed, else Tani's life would become intolerable. And rather than the triumphant sacrifice he had envisaged by the lakeside, it would have to be done somewhere out here. Then there would be no-one to hold him, Tani, accountable for this or his other crimes.

Exactly how this was to be achieved, Tani neither knew nor cared. For now, it was enough that the decision had been made. Like any hunter, he knew patience would be rewarded: he had only to track the boy, watch and wait long enough, and the chance would come.

The sun was high now, the heat merciless, and the shadows of the two shrank to tiny bluish pools. For Tark, thirst had become a torment. With every moment the blood seemed to thicken in his veins and his heartbeat pounded in his head. His thoughts, slow and laboured, were all of water: the lake as he remembered it when he was very young, fringed with reeds; the rivers that had flowed into it. Even the floodwaters he had struggled through were now desirable for that world of water seemed impossible here where the crackle of desiccating mud filled his ears.

In an effort to protect himself from the burning rays, he tried to make himself even smaller, curling into a tight foetal ball around his talisman, knowing that if he did not move soon, he would die. But he lacked willpower and strength to stand.

High above, a kite circled, sensing that the creature stranded below would soon be carrion, an easy meal. It gave a shrill scream that seemed to pierce Tark's brain, rousing the fading tendrils of his consciousness as no human utterance could have done.

With a huge effort, the boy raised his head. His eyelids were gummed with mucus, his nostrils crusted with it: he rubbed it away and forced his eyes open, bleared, stinging, flinching at the brutal light for the light and heat were the same. They pinned him on the bare salt flat and there was no escape.

The kite called again and its mate answered: soon there would be a flock of carrion birds circling, waiting for him to die. He clambered unsteadily to his feet, clutching the shell talisman as if, somehow, it could lead him to safety. Black spots whirled before his eyes and waves of nausea heaved through him. He staggered and felt the ground quiver beneath his feet and then fear of sharing the hunters' doom overcame all else, for any fate seemed preferable to that slow, inexorable sinking.

From his position on the edge of the pan, Tani watched the boy's progress with a kind of cruel satisfaction. The thin man had half-expected Tark to die huddled there under the sun for he had been motionless for so long, it had seemed impossible any creature could remained thus exposed and survive. But though such an outcome would have suited his plans admirably, it would have lacked a certain completeness to have pursued the boy so far and then have no hand in his death. Therefore as Tark stumbled across the sink, Tani also began to move, skirting the wide hollow in the knowledge that while he might not intercept the boy, he would not be far behind when, at last, the lad stepped onto solid ground.

Tark was completely unaware of Tani's presence. All his powers of concentration, every frisson of energy in his muscles, were focused on moving, putting one foot in front of the other, testing the ground at every step before shifting his weight. There was no room for anything else in his mind, even the need to drink, until he reached the slight slope that marked the edge of the hollow.

Tark felt a momentary relief at having escaped the salt pan. Then raging thirst overwhelmed him. He stood still, shading his eyes with one hand, and turned slowly, searching for water.

For two days and nights, the lake folk paid homage to Mingar and also Draa who had, in their eyes, assumed almost supernatural status: her strength of will and monumental calm served to comfort all. They brought such food as they could find, themselves going hungry to expiate their crimes. The pair ate gladly, the woman feeding her husband with tender care because he was so weak, he could hardly lift his head unaided. On the second day, Draa called for a shelter of skins to be erected to protect him from the sun and once this was done, he regained strength swiftly. Of water there was no lack for floodwaters streamed into the lake from all directions although the volume of the flow was diminishing steadily so that islets made by the flood joined into long ribbons of mud which cracked and dried quickly under the burning sun.

But though he thanked his benefactors, Mingar did not engage them and while this had more to do with a natural reticence than aloofness, it increased their awe. They whispered among themselves and told their children that no doubt he was conversing with the ancestors and that soon he would awaken and be like the Mingar of old, before misfortune had twisted his body and embittered his mind, a man both bold and resolute. And this was a measure of their desperation because few truly remembered Mingar as he had been in those far-off days: he was as much a myth as the lake before the Great Dry, something the young folk of the clan had never imagined, far less seen with their own eyes.

Draa was keenly aware of what was going on. She noted the furtive, almost fearful glances directed at her husband, heard the hushed whispering and whilst grateful for the shade and food, she knew how swiftly the adulation of the people could turn to contempt if their expectations were not met. And so, with great subtlety, she reminded Mingar of those who had left long ago and never returned – because they had perished in some terrible desert he had always maintained – but maybe, she now urged, because they had discovered the land of plenty they had dreamt of since the start of the Dry.

'Look around you,' she said, 'the lake is dying despite the rain, the mud drying to salt even as we sit here: we cannot wait in the hope more rain will come. And Tark is far away: do you not wish to see your son again?'

Mingar understood well enough what she was attempting: he also was mindful of the people's fickleness. But deep in his heart he resented the responsibility they were forcing upon him, the unfairness of being singled out. With daylight and food, the vision that had rejuvenated him in the night had faded and he recognized it for what it was: a dream. And with this realization he was gnawed by doubt for how could he, with his broken body, truly be the man to lead them to the fabled land? It seemed laughable, even pitiable, that in their extremity they should look to him for guidance and he almost pushed away the handful of grubs that was being offered by a skinny child in disgust, not at the gift but the desperate hope it represented.

Draa watched his features settle into the hard uncompromising lines she had learned to dread. Once Mingar's mind was set, she knew only death would break his resolve. And remembering his stubbornness in the past, the obstinacy that had led them to this pass, she reached out and popped some of the grubs into her mouth, saying with deceptive softness, 'Come, my love, we must eat to gain strength for the journey. It will avail our people nothing if we scorn their generosity only to fail them on the way.'

He stared at her, astonished at her audacity (it was the custom for the men to eat first, then the women and children), and in wonder at how confidently she had seized the initiative. For it was as if an oppressive weight had been lifted from him, the burden of choice. The decision had been made: they would leave the lake, and seek the rest of their kin while the bounty of the flood still blessed the land. For Mingar was old enough to remember the last true rains and though he guessed that even the lake shores, barren and desolate as they were, might bloom after the storm, he knew also how swiftly that season of abundance passed and that after so many years of failure it would be madness to expect the rains to return soon. And so he resolved that even if the land turned green and bright with grass and flowers, they should still leave in the knowledge that once that blooming was over, they would be trapped once more beside a dying lake.

Therefore, once his first astonishment had passed, Mingar bent his head in acknowledgement of Draa's wisdom and said, 'No, we must not fail,' and their eyes met and they smiled in a moment of perfect understanding.

At dawn on the third day the clan gathered at the shelter where the two were sleeping. No meeting had been arranged: it happened inevitably as the rising of the sun, as if pre-ordained. No word was spoken: one man saw a couple walking towards the canopy, roused his family and followed and, in turn, was seen by another. So it went on until everyone was there, waiting. They knew intuitively that this was the moment of reckoning. They had given all they had to their chosen ones, now a leader would arise, must arise, to command and inspire them. Otherwise they saw only despair and death ahead.

When Draa and Mingar woke, clasped in each others arms, to find themselves surrounded by a silent yet expectant crowd, they were not surprised. The evening before, under blazing stars, Mingar had opened his heart to her, exposing all the bitterness and guilt that had festered within him since his maiming, which had been exacerbated by grief for Eeli and their children. And Draa, while secretly amazed by his honesty and the trust he was laying upon her, took his hands and told him that the past cannot be changed but past wrongs can be righted or atoned, as long as there is the will to act. Then he was long silent, sitting with his head bowed and his hands loose yet warm in hers while she, who had learned by experience the wisdom of patience, waited in silence. At length he raised his head and his eyes gleamed in the starlight but all he said was, 'Tomorrow.' And when they lay down to sleep, Draa's heart sang within her because she knew she had succeeded in her plan and his pride and courage had been restored.

Thus it was that waking to find the waiting people was but a fulfilment of their own hope. In the eastern sky, darkness had already fled before a pearly twilight which grew steadily paler, more lucent. It spread an opalescent hue across the landscape against which the people appeared like shadows, featureless yet significant in their singularity. And the tension of the people was mirrored in the rippling of water all around.

United in resolve, Draa and Mingar looked deeply into one another's eyes then sat up, yawned and stretched out their arms as if unaware of the circle of watching eyes, the expectancy that held the gathering in an agony of silence. And then, since the people could no longer be ignored, they bent their heads in welcome and acknowledgement and Mingar, with an imperious wave, motioned them to sit.

Rarely had Draa felt such pride in her husband for the once-reviled cripple now held such authority over the remnant of the clan that they obeyed without a murmur, sitting or squatting in silence. Only an infant, sucking futilely at its mother's flaccid breast, made a sound: a persistent mewling, the voice of hunger to which all had become inured. In the tense quiet that utterance seemed magnified and to many it was as if they heard it for the first time. The layers of indifference, which had grown through necessity, suddenly dissolved and each woman felt a pang of grief for her own lost or starving children while the men were assailed by shame at their passivity. And they looked upon Mingar, remembering how his obstinacy and empty promises had kept them there and doubt flared in them like a wild flame.

Mingar sensed their changing mood but he was no longer afraid of these people who had trampled his wives and children to death on the word of a madman and now looked to him for help. He kept them in suspense until the rim of the sun appeared over the horizon, thin as a fingernail paring. Light spilled across the landscape, revealing its starkness: bare cracked mud; turbid pools and churning river channels; the lake, already fringed by glistening rings of salt where its waters had begun to evaporate. Over this land he looked and the people followed his gaze, craning their necks to see past or over their companions, and when at last he looked into the sky, which was cloudless as far as the eye could compass, a collective sigh arose, so heavy it sounded like a groan.

'Ah my friends,' Mingar said (and his voice was quiet yet clear so that even those sitting furthest away could hear), 'though rain came, has our suffering ended? The time has come to leave, to follow those who left us long ago. Eh, and Tani and his companions and my son, Tark, for they also went away and have not returned. Perhaps, even now, they are all together in some green forest or grassland where food and clean water are plentiful and this place of death seems like a dreadful dream.' He paused and took a deep breath, then continued: 'It may be though that none has returned because all have perished and beyond this dying lake and ruined forest lie lands even more terrible. That was what kept me here: it was easier to deny our suffering than face the uncertainty of the path into the unknown. But my son has shown me the way and the rain has given us a chance to escape this place which has held us for so long. For now even the burned lands will bloom, if only for a brief time. Therefore I say to you, let us wait a little longer, until the green comes, then leave. And our journey will be all the easier though I do not know where it will end.'

With these words, he bent his head and spread his hands in an age-old gesture of submission to indicate that he had finished.

The gathering considered his speech in silence, then a murmur arose like the soughing of the wind. A woman asked, 'Should we not wait for Tani?' and a few added their voices though most were still uncomfortable at their part in the killings instigated by the thin man.

'I do not claim to command any of you,' Mingar answered.

'Even Draa, my wife. But she and I will leave when we deem the time is right and those who wish to join us will be welcome. For we do not know what dangers lie ahead and there is safety and counsel to be found in numbers. Beasts that have not been seen here for many years, which prey on man, may still live in distant lands and there may be people who do not welcome strangers to their hearths.'

This time the murmur that greeted his words was louder and more agitated: the noisy child began to cry and the mother despairingly put it to her other breast; a young man let out a mirthless laugh and said scornfully, 'Is this what we've fed and sheltered this cripple for?' and the murmurers fell silent, cowed by the speaker's aggression and embarrassed by it. But Mingar was undaunted. He rose to face the challenger and all looked upon him amazed for while he was still painfully thin and his body twisted, his very stance exhibited a vitality and strength of purpose that had been missing since the day of his accident.

'What did you expect, Nyangah?' he asked, looking the young man in the eye with a steady, penetrating gaze. 'We are each responsible for our own decisions: the burden I have to bear is that I chose wrongly in the past. Therefore I do not presume to tell anyone what they should do: I know no more than you what lies ahead. But I believe with all my heart that to stay here is to submit to death.'

The young man opened his mouth as if to argue but the silence of the crowd made him suddenly self-conscious and he said nothing. And then the woman with the fretful child lifted her face, filthy like the rest, with red swollen eyes all crusted with mucus. 'I will follow Mingar and Draa,' she said, 'there is nothing for us here. And Tani, who made it rain, has deserted us.' She lifted her child, stick-limbed and pot-bellied, for all to see. 'How many more must we bury here?' she cried. 'As many as I have fingers on one hand I've lost since the Dry began: the last slipped from my womb and never breathed. This rain, paid for with the blood of our kin, will not save us. We must leave while we still have strength to walk.'

Better than any argument of Mingar's, these words moved the crowd. Looking at the ring of faces, Draa saw doubt and uncertainty change to acceptance and knew they had been persuaded.

'Then, if you are coming with us, do as we shall do,' Mingar said and his tone was humble rather than triumphant for he felt the responsibility of leadership press upon him. 'Rest and gather your strength as best you can. And make ready for the journey with such things you still possess, for when the first flowers bloom we shall leave.'

Slowly the gathering dispersed, many of the people pausing to touch the two as if to draw hope and strength from them. When at last they were alone, Draa and Mingar looked at each other with a kind of wonder and no little trepidation. And seeing weariness creep over her husband's face now that the tension was all gone, Draa held out a hand to draw him into the shade saying, 'Come, love, and rest, for the hardest step is always the first and that is now behind us.'

Chapter 4.

Heat haze formed a rippling, semi-transparent ring around Tark, distorting the horizon and amplifying mirages of cliffs, trees, pools, even a distant mountain range of blood-red stone. It was impossible to tell what was real. He stared, trying to make sense of the wavering lines of red, silver, fawn and grey which melded into the glaring whiteness of the sky, his senses bemused by thirst. And then something else appeared. A shadow thrown onto the liquid mirror of hot air and vapour, it was tall and insubstantial as a ghost. As it came closer, it shrank and took on the solidity and shape of a human being, a man with a spear or staff.

Such relief overcame the boy, he had taken a few faltering steps towards the approaching figure before a presentiment of danger checked him. He stopped to rub his dry and stinging eyes then, as his vision cleared, recognized his enemy.

But whereas at one time the sight of Tani would have frightened Tark into flight, so depleted were his reserves of willpower and strength, he felt only dismay. Without any exclamation of terror or surprise, he simply turned and began to walk away. Indeed, his pursuer's presence intensified the illusion that he was living in a dream. Even the ground seemed fluid, as if it were rolling beneath his feet which moved but did not advance. Behind him Tani toiled to catch up yet remained always at the same distance while the landscape of mud and water, rock and salt flowed all around.

Thus, with infinitesimal slowness, the two advanced across the great plain, heads bowed, feet dragging, each impelled by a dogged determination, in Tark's case to escape his tormentor, in Tani's to catch and slay the boy whose very refusal to lie down and die strengthened his need to kill. Gradually their shadows lengthened for though, to them, this day seemed endless, the earth turned and the sun moved across the sky at the same rate as on any other. As it sank, the haze dissipated and solid shapes replaced the shimmering walls that had trapped the two in a kind of trance. But the flatness of the terrain gave rise to new illusions for there was no tree or hut to bring the landscape to a human scale: a boulder was as a smooth, rounded hill; a bone lying in the dirt might have been the wind-scoured trunk of a great tree; a massive dome of rock in the far distance seemed no more significant than an anthill. Red mud and white salt stretched as far as the eye could see and that, too, was illusion because the floodwaters had incised deep into the soft earth underlying the baked crust and so were invisible until one stood on the very brink of the channels they had eroded.

Whenever he came to such a channel, Tark climbed down to drink, splashed his body in an effort to cool himself and then set off again.

The sun set and twilight spread across the sky and still the two trudged on. Stars blazed overhead and their shadows formed little pools beneath their feet and now the land was silver and the air chill: they shivered as they walked. And when Tark could no longer put one foot in front of the other, he simply sank to the ground and slept.

In the vastness of that starlit landscape, the huddled form of the boy was so diminutive, so insignificant as to be indistinguishable from the many boulders which littered the plain and Tani was forced to stop and wait for daylight for it was as if his quarry had suddenly disappeared.

Tark woke just before dawn. Painfully, he clambered to his feet for all his muscles had seized in the night. Hunger griped his belly and he stumbled towards a sunken river that ran close by in the hope of finding something to eat though he had no spear or throwing stick with which to catch an animal come to drink. No living creature was there but a carcass, seething with maggots, lay on the bank so he feasted on these then drank deeply and set off again as a faint bar of light appeared on the eastern horizon. When, after a while, he looked back, he saw the thin man in the distance, following.

This pattern was repeated for several days for the plain seemed endless and the resolve of hunter and hunted was set. Yet though they were unconscious of it, the landscape slowly changed. The watercourses became sparser, the terrain more undulating and the lump of red rock which had at first seemed insignificant as an anthill, was revealed as part of a mountain range, sculpted by aeons of erosion into smooth domes which were intersected by deep gullies and ravines. Most significant of all, the streams and rivers they now encountered flowed in the opposite direction to those they had known all their lives for they had left the basin of the great lake.

Of all this, the two remained unaware save that water became scarcer as they travelled. Otherwise they walked in a kind of reverie, eating and drinking whenever the opportunity arose, resting only when their feet would carry them no further. And yet despite the distance they had travelled from the clay sink, Tani was no closer to his intended victim than when they had set out.

As the sun reached its zenith on the fifth day, thirst became an added torment for neither Tank nor Tani had drunk since the evening before. To the boy, as he stumbled on, past and future no longer existed: there was only this hateful, interminable present which he lacked willpower to change. It seemed to him that all his short life had been spent trudging across this barren plain with his enemy a little behind and the sun beating down. Now there was only one choice: to continue his journey or to stop and allow his enemy to take him. Yet he trudged on. He did not question why this should be so: the simple fact of it was enough.

He was at the very limit of his strength when a muffled roar came to his ears. At first he barely acknowledged it, assuming it to be a manifestation of the darkness which lurked at the edge of his sight and crept into his brain, an inexorable fading of sensation and thought he was powerless to counter. But the noise increased, forcing itself into his consciousness.

He reached the brink so unexpectedly, it was as if the earth had opened at his feet. Within a single step a steep clay cliff, many times his own height, formed one side of a deep river channel. The confined waters were turbulent - this was the source of the roaring – and it seemed impossible to the boy that while he struggled across the desert, this churning watercourse should have been here all along though he had only to glance behind to see that this was so.

Tark stared into the gorge and the smell of water, the coolness of the rising air tormented him. The cliff was sheer and smooth: there were no paths where animals went to drink, nor any possibility of climbing down. The flow stretched from side to side, cutting at the clay even as he watched. Every-so-often, pieces of the cliff collapsed and were washed away, the clay disaggregating so that the water ran red-brown and turbid between ochre-stained walls

The boy licked cracked lips with a tongue that felt thick and dry and the faint taste of moisture maddened him. He crouched and looked over the edge but there was no way to reach the water save by jumping into it. And that he was loth to do until it came to a stark choice between making the leap or dying of thirst.

As Tark hesitated on the brink, Tani drew ever closer. His eyes were fixed on his intended victim like those of a hungry predator. At first he had been nonplussed by the boy's immobility until he guessed the source of the muted roaring that seemed to reverberate beneath his feet then, when he saw the river, the steepness and depth of the gorge it had gouged through the earth, it came to him that this was the answer to his prayers. He imagined himself explaining the mishap to Mingar and Draa: how he had seen Tark fall into the raging torrent; how there had been nothing he could do as the boy was swept away and, at last disappeared, nothing save bring news of his fate home so those that loved him could mourn as was proper.

As these thoughts passed through his mind, Tani's eyes narrowed and his skull-like face contracted into an expression of such malice, it appeared more hewn mask than human visage, an illusion heightened by the layers of dried sweat and dust caking his skin. Only the protruding, bloodshot eyes and the tongue, which flicked snake-like between his lips as if to test the air, looked alive.

Closer and closer he crept: two spearthrows, one, and still the boy was unaware of him, his hands clutching something at his chest, staring into the chasm as if entranced. And then the distance between them could be measures in spearlengths: Tani could see the knobs of the boy's spine, the movement clf his ribs as he breathed, pieces of twig and leaf that had tangled in his hair during his long flight. There was a string around his neck Tani longed to jerk tight but, with an effort, he quelled this urge. Tark's exhausted state meant the river would be enough and Tani, unlike the boy, had been acute enough to realize which way the water flowed: no corpse would ever reach the lake to accuse him.

Five spearlengths, three and still the boy was oblivious to his danger for the roar of the torrent drowned all other sounds and Tani's bare feet were almost soundless on the baked dirt. And then, at last, the thin man stood poised, staff raised, to prod the boy into the fatal step. After his long pursuit, such a climax could not be contained and he yelled in triumph as he thrust, sending Tark straight into the gorge.

Then, his eyes bulging horribly with glee, Tani dropped to his hands and knees, crawled to the brink and looked over. At first he saw only brown, churning water and, despite his joy, he could not quite quell a pang of disappointment that his enemy should have been destroyed so easily. But looking further downstream, he glimpsed the black dot of a head and a wildly flailing arm. Only for an instant was Tark visible, then he was swallowed by the torrent.

When he was certain that the boy had gone, his body swept far away, Tani sat back on his heels feeling curiously empty. His purpose had been achieved: all that remained was to bear the sad tidings to the clan and resume his position as leader. And yet the journey, the privations he had suffered, had left their mark: he was in desperate need of water and then food if he were to survive the long walk home.

The sun was westering when he began to make his way back. But he did not set out at once into the desert. Now that the problem of the boy had been solved, his priority was to regain his strength. Having come across so great a river, he was loth to leave it and so followed it upstream, searching for a place where he could drink.

The day had come to leave the dying lake. Three nights had passed since Mingar made his decision and in that time periods of almost frantic activity had been interspersed with long hours of quietude in which the people of the lake rested. At Draa's instigation they made water-bags from animal skins for while water would be plentiful while the floods were still draining from the land, none knew how long the journey would last or when such an opportunity to craft the things they might need would come again.

So the women worked while the men hunted, then they rested and the children ate and slept mostly as they were told. Even those too young to understand the full significance of the preparations were affected by the sense of urgency pervading the whole settlement and all, young and old, were struck by awe whenever they looked upon Draa or Mingar, for in these two all their hopes resided.

A time came when the preparations were finished and the anticipation became excitement, a restlessness that could barely be contained. Quarrels broke out within and between families and Draa, mindful of the tension, said quietly to Mingar: 'They are as ready as they will ever be: we must leave soon or there will be trouble.' And word went out swiftly that the journey would begin next day.

Few slept that night and long before the first light appeared in the east, the clan gathered around the shelter where Draa and Mingar lay in each other's arms. They were not asleep but savouring the last precious moments before beginning the journey on which not only their own but the lives of all their people depended. Thus they lay still, eyes shut in an effort to delay the knowledge that the night was over and the time had come to leave.

A soft pink light appeared in the east and spread across the sky. It strengthened to flame as the salt reflected it, then the rim of the sun breached the flat line of the horizon and they could deny it no longer.

Slowly, first Draa, then Mingar stirred and stretched and opened their eyes and when they saw the waiting people they embraced, a quick hard gesture of mutual understanding and affection, before rising to their feet. Then, without pausing to eat or drink, Draa picked up two bundles, one a waterskin, the other a cape in which their scant possessions were wrapped: a couple of flat grinding stones, tools for making fire, a sharp flake of stone to use as a knife, a length of rope woven from grass, a short digging stick. Mingar carried only a long staff. A gift from the men of the clan, it was stout and strong yet smooth to the touch and light.

The pinkish hue faded as the sun rose and already the heat rising from the flats smote the eyes and skin like the touch of flame. Mingar did not pause to make any speech to commemorate their leaving: it seemed to him that the time for talk was over. And this was a measure of his wisdom for in truth each of the clan had already made their farewells to the place in which they had dwelt for generations. In their minds and memories, this was not the desolation of mud, stagnant water and salt the lake had become but the clear, glittering waters which had been before the Great Dry, the reedbeds and fringing forest, a land and water-scape of ever-changing greens and blues, thronged with life, resonant with birdsong and the voices of children. To kin they had known and loved who had died there, to these also they bade farewell and that was hardest of all for a people who had forgotten their nomadic roots for it seemed to them that their very blood and bones belonged to this earth, these waters. It was this that had held them when the lake began to die: to leave seemed like a betrayal of their ancestors, an uprooting that wrenched them deep within themselves. And so they had lingered too long.

Now, having bade farewell in the way that seemed best to each of them, there was no more to say. In spirit they had already made the break: now they wanted only to be gone before there was time to reconsider. So as Draa and Mingar began to walk along one of the ridges that splayed like a bird's foot between the mud-pools and waterways (which were now flowing so sluggishly as to appear more like long lakes than rivers), the people followed in silence. No-one looked back to where the partially replenished waters of the lake shore silver in the sunlight.

As to direction, this was something the two leaders had agonized over. North was, by tradition, considered ill-fated since it was from there, according to legend, that the Night-Stalkers had come. All the land to the east had been devastated by the firestorm: no comfort was to be found that way. This left the south and west and since there was nothing to commend one over the other, Draa suggested that to follow the sun might be the simplest course: then they would always be sure of their path.

This then was the direction in which they walked and the rising sun flung their shadows before them so that they seemed to point the way and those that were dismayed by this (for some considered that to walk in your own shadow was ill-omened), were comforted by Draa's assertion that no evil could come of it since, at day's end, their shadows would be behind, unless anyone was foolish enough to try and follow their shadow all day, in which case they would end up where they had started.

Soon they had left the former lake bed and climbed the shallow rim and still Mingar kept his face set towards the west. Heartened by his steadfastness, the clan followed, walking in little family groups, men and women carrying the smallest and weakest, old or very young. And none paused to look back.

Gradually their shadows shrank and the two leaders took care to check that all who had set out were still with them. For they had passed into the region of stumps and the floodwaters had contracted into intricate mazes of meandering channels which made the way hazardous and forced long detours where the water proved too deep or the current too strong to wade.

Being so young, Tark had few memories of this place as it had been before the Great Dry but Mingar and his peers looked upon the ravaged forest with sorrow, recalling hunting expeditions into its cool, green depths where rivers ran through shallow fern-lined valleys and the trees grew tall and strong, their trunks so wide as to take the outstretched hands of a large family to span. To Mingar it hardly seemed possible that the transformation of living forest to this desolation of blackened stumps and brown, stinking water could have happened within a man's lifetime, let alone in the space of a single day. Though green shoots had begun to break through the sodden earth, few birds and animals were visible and there was more evidence of death than life for piles of debris were heaped upon the mudbanks, tangles of burnt branches and decaying carcases whose stench tainted the air.

The sun was past its zenith when they stopped to rest on a muddy eyot between two wide but shallow watercourses. Many of the children who were too big to carry were tired and fretful for the journey was already proving harder than most had anticipated. The families squatted together to drink and eat and the few who, through lack of foresight or laziness, had failed to bring provisions, were grudgingly offered a share for this custom was so deeply ingrained, none dared break it.

Draa and Mingar did not sit with the rest. They walked together to the furthest end of the eyot to spy out the best way ahead. In the far distance the ground rose into a line of low hills but even Mingar, with his hunter's experience, could not tell how long it would take to reach them, the land had changed so drastically since he had last trodden it. And for a moment he was overwhelmed by despair because the same desolation stretched in all directions, as far as the eye could see, and the vestiges of green amongst the red-brown mud and grey ash seemed but a mockery of what had been before, the many-layered forest with its myriad forms of life all of which depended on the others for their very existence.

Draa viewed the landscape differently. She was appraising it with a purely pragmatic eye for by nightfall they would need a place with clean water to drink and enough dry ground for all to sleep comfortably, somewhere that could be defended against prowling animals. And fuel was another consideration. Many families were carrying fire with them in the form of embers but dry wood had become a rare resource since the deluge and fuel of any kind took time to collect. Yet without fires to cook upon and sit around, she knew the morale of the people would deteriorate swiftly. Moreover, whilst the gathering of fuel might slow the journey, this might not be a bad thing, especially for the weakest.

Having spotted a raised area perhaps two hour's walk away, Draa turned to Mingar, intending to point it out as a good place to spend the night. But at the sight of his stricken face, her heart went cold. She feared his old sickness had returned and all her efforts had been in vain.

'Mingar!' She laid a hand on his arm. 'What's wrong?'

He turned and regarded her with tear-blinded eyes. 'It is all gone,' he said wonderingly. 'What possessed us, Draa? Where is there to go? Maybe we should return to the lakeside: it is not too late.'

'Quiet!' Draa looked round to make sure no-one was within hearing. 'We cannot falter now. The people have put their faith in us: we must not fail them. Where is the courage that set us on this path?'

Mingar saw the fire in her eyes and was ashamed. Yet still his heart wavered for it seemed to him that he alone could see far into the future and the hope that had driven him to leave the dying lake now seemed futile, a delusion.

'Maybe I was mistaken,' he mumbled. 'It was just a dream: what made me believe I could lead the clan? There is nothing out here but hunger and death.'

There was such misery in his voice and mien that beneath her exasperation, Draa pitied him. But she turned and swept her arm to indicate the little groups sharing food or talking or simply taking rest and some waved back cheerfully.

'Will you tell them that?' she spat. 'Or would you rather slink away, leaving them to their fate? Mingar, we shall all die one day but for our children and our children's children's sake we should at least make the attempt.'

'Our children are dead,' he replied, 'and I am still a cripple. Why should I deserve their faith?'

Draa was silent. She thought back to her parting with Tark, how she had given him the shell talisman that had been Eeli's, and was filled with such conviction that he was alive, joy coursed through her. She grasped Mingar's arm and he was astonished by her fervour.

'Tark lives!' she said forcefully, 'but he would die of shame or strike you down if he could hear you now. How dare you talk of failure, whose cowardice drove him away? If you are afraid to lead, then keep silent and I will do so in your stead. But breathe a word of doubt and see how quickly the people turn against you. For do you not see that you are their last hope?'

He stared at her and raised a hand to his brow as if in pain. 'How do you know Tark is alive?' he stammered. 'How could he be after the storm and the flood?'

Draa's lips closed in a mysterious smile. 'Do not ask,' she said simply. 'Yet I am sure of it as I am that you stand here.'

In former times Mingar would have dismissed such a statement but he found he had no recourse against her utter conviction. And it occurred to him that as wise-men and healers claimed to communicate with spirits, perhaps his wife could somehow sense the boy's presence in the world. Thus, instead of arguing, he said nothing but his eyes strayed to the groups of families upon the eyot and the look upon his face wrenched the woman's heart.

'Mingar,' she said quietly, 'you cannot turn back. If you break your promise, our people will tear us apart and no blame to them. There is still hope: there is always hope so long as we have strength to draw breath. Otherwise why did you not lie down and die long ago?'

Again he was silent but the struggle going on within was evident from his expression and the convulsive clenching of his hands, hands which even after food and rest still seemed overlarge, the wrists and knuckles knobby lumps of bone at the end of pitifully thin arms whose every sinew and muscle was visible. And his frailty frightened Draa for it seemed to her that if he so willed, his spirit could fly away, shedding this fragile shell of skin and bone like a husk, leaving her bereft and their people lost.

'Mingar!' she said, scared that by the very thought she might make what she feared come true. 'Please talk to me. We are strong, you and I: together we can lead our people to another place, a new life. But you must believe it! Otherwise the journey will have failed before it has even started. Listen to me, for Tark's sake if not the others.'

'Aue.' Mingar's utterance was more groan than sigh: his fists unclenched and he looked away, across the stumpy flats to the distant hills. 'I am weary already. What if, after everything, we find only desolation? I do not share your faith, Draa.'

'Then trust me,' she replied, 'if you cannot trust yourself. And do not think too far ahead. In the end, all journeys move step by step however distant the destination or hard the purpose. Look forward to day's end: a camp on dry ground, with shelter and water to drink, and as one day follows another we shall be closer to journey's end though we do not see it. For when our ancestors set out long ago to escape the Night-Stalkers they were guided by the same faith: they also had no idea how far they would travel or what hardships they would encounter along the way and they did not falter.'

In the silence that followed, the two became sharply aware of children's voices: revived by food and rest they had begun a noisy game of chase. And at last the grimness left Mingar's face, he sighed and pulled Draa close, holding her with rare tenderness.

'I have been wrong so often in the past,' he murmured, 'how can I know that what I do now is right? Stay with me and together we shall lead our people to journey's end, wherever that may be.'

Overwhelmed by relief, Draa pressed herself against him for a moment, then pulled away. 'Come then,' she said, 'before they start thinking something is amiss.' And remembering the potential camping ground she had spotted, she pointed. 'There: that might be a good place to spend the night.'

Chapter 5.

Tark woke. His mind was slow and his body ached as if he had been beaten. Long before he had strength to open his eyes, hearing returned to him. The thunderous roar of water had been replaced by birdsong, the soft susurration of leaves, the quiet murmur of human voices.

So far were these sensations from his memory of drowning, his desperate efforts to fight the river, Tark could make no sense of them. And when something (someone?), stroked his brow, he tried to jerk away only his body did not obey his will.

Panic overwhelmed him: terror of being a cripple forced his eyes open. And so unexpected was what he saw, he closed them immediately and opened them again, in case it was a dream.

He was lying on a thick bed of leaves and grasses covered with animal skins. Overhead was a roof of interlaced branches through which soft green light filtered. The air was moist and heavy with the scents of fresh water and lush vegetation, a damp earthiness that reminded him sharply of the ancient forest still surrounding the lake when he had been a very young child. Then the dark shape of a woman's head and shoulders blocked out the living greens and bluish shadow of the roof and in his confusion he was jerked back to those lost childhood days and thought it was his mother, Eeli, who bent over to caress him and it was her name that came involuntarily to his lips.

Faint though his utterance was, the woman heard. She withdrew her hand and called out and he heard the chatter of many women's voices, voluble and excited. He tried to focus on their speech but it was as if his long ordeal had dislocated something in his mind: his thoughts broke into chaos whenever they reached the edge of coherency until, exhausted, he gave up and lay passive. And it was as if his carer understood for he heard her hush the others, then she slid one hand behind his head to raise it slightly. Something hard pressed against his lips and he recognized the edge of a shallow wooden bowl such as his own mother had possessed. There was water in this one, cool and pure, tasting of nothing, and he drank greedily. Though he had not been aware of thirst, his journey had so depleted his body's resources, his tissues still craved liquid for he had struggled not to swallow any of the turbid, foul-smelling river in which he had so nearly drowned.

When he had drained the dish it was taken away and replenished: he drank again. And this time his mind stirred to true awareness. He realized the woman could not be his mother because Eeli was dead, yet her actions were still those of someone who cared, who meant him no harm. Most wondrous of all, the voices he heard were speaking a tongue little different to his own. And though they were talking quietly now, as if fearful of disturbing him, the familiarity of their speech reassured him and he relaxed and slept again.

When he woke next the light had changed. It was golden, slanting through gaps in the woven walls and Tark realized he had slept most of the day without stirring. There was no-one else inside but he could hear people talking close by, men's voices and children's mixed with those of the women. A tantalizing smell of woodsmoke and cooking fish made his nostrils quiver: he was suddenly racked by hunger. So much had happened in so short a space of time, he could not recall when he had last eaten, knew only that he was ravenous. He lay still, waiting and listening, willing someone to bring food but no-one did, most likely they thought him still asleep.

He was drawing breath to call out when a shadow fell across him. So light-footed was the woman who had entered, he had not heard her yet she was not young. She squatted beside him with a wooden bowl and the smell of broiled fish made his mouth water. He tried to sit up but his head swam and he sank back, shaken by his weakness.

'Eh, there is no hurry,' the woman said and her voice was low and gentle. 'My name is Manalah. I'll hold you while you eat. When you are strong again we will hear your story, until then you must rest.'

Laying the bowl aside, she sat on the bed and pulled him up so that he was propped against her. He was surprised by the ease with which she moved him: the truth was, he was so thin he weighed less than a healthy child half his age. She lifted the bowl and fed him succulent pieces of fish which he wolfed down, hardly chewing the morsels before swallowing. It seemed to him that he had never tasted anything so good though his shrunken stomach soon felt uncomfortably tight and full.

'I'll bring more when you are hungry,' Manalah said. 'Now you should sleep,' and she eased away and rose to her feet. He sighed in contentment and closed his eyes while she stood looking down upon him, her face expressionless. Then, once certain he was settled, she padded outside with the empty bowl while he sank into a deep and healing slumber.

Rest, clean water and food did their work: when he woke again all Tark's senses quickened and his stomach griped with hunger. He stretched out his limbs, fingers and toes until they tingled. The exhaustion and weakness of only a few hours before already seemed a distant nightmare.

Darkness had fallen while he slept and the only light came from a fire outside. The ruddy glow illuminated the square doorway of the hut but the blaze was offset and he could see nothing distinct beyond except the dark humps of what he assumed to be other buildings. The sound of voices came from the direction of the fire, someone telling a tale while their audience laughed and clapped and the boy felt a sudden pang for all he had lost though it was long since there had been any cause for joy beside the dying lake.

Manalah had promised to return but for all he knew, she might have done so while he slept. He thought of calling out but pride restrained him: to do so would be the act of a helpless child. Yet his hunger would not be stayed: he was frantic for food. He rolled onto his side and levered himself into a sitting position, waited for the pounding in his head to subside then, carefully, stood upright.

It was at that moment he realized his true state. His legs buckled when he tried to walk and it was only by staggering forward and clinging to the doorframe that he managed to stay upright. He leant there, gasping, his legs trembling uncontrollably, and longed for someone to notice him before he collapsed.

Luckily the flickering firelight picked him out. The folk of the village were sitting in a circle around a central hearth, men, women and children all together. A woman saw him, exclaimed aloud and pointed and two rose and hurried to his aid. One was Manalah.

'Did you think we'd forgotten you?' she scolded as they helped him back to his pallet. 'Twice I came and you were asleep. Wait a little and I'll bring food.'

She left but her companion, an old woman bent and shrivelled with age, remained behind. She said nothing but waited beside the door. A delicious lassitude stole though Tark's body as he lay there. No longer the oblivion of exhaustion, the body's desperate need for rest, it was a deliberate languor to be savoured and enjoyed, a rare luxury in his world. But suddenly he was aware of the old woman's gaze.

The hut was not large, a couple of steps was enough to bring her within arm's reach. He could smell the sourness of her skin and breath and when at last she crouched to touch him it was like being prodded with sharp bones, as if the flesh of her fingers had withered away. He recoiled instinctively and she chuckled deep in her throat. He could not help thinking of a carrion bird settling beside a corpse.

'What do you want?' he gasped.

'Why are you here?' Her voice was crow-like, harsh and low. 'Where are your kin?'

'I was lost.' All Tark's sense of well-being had been replaced by dread before this terrible old woman. 'I fell into the river. I don't know how I came here.'

'Ah, Myenah, let the boy rest.' To Tark's relief Manalah returned at that moment bearing a wooden bowl. While her voice was low and gentle as before, Tark now sensed an extraordinary strength behind it, a kind of calm self-assurance such as his foster-mother, Draa, possessed. She knelt beside him while the old woman levered herself to her feet and shuffled out, muttering under her breath.

'My mother has a rough tongue but a good heart,' Manalah said. 'She thinks only of our safety. Yet she sees deeply: do not try to deceive her.'

She eased him against her shoulder and fed him as before, pieces of cold fish and fruit that was new and strange to him. When the bowl was empty, she moved away. 'Sleep now,' she said tenderly. 'There will be time enough for questions and answers when you are strong again. Do not let Myenah worry you.'

Tark thanked her and closed his eyes though he was not sleepy, mindful that by the glow of firelight outside she could probably see his face though he had not seen hers, silhouetted as she was against the doorway. 'Sleep well,' she murmured and he felt the air stir as she rose and left, moving with a quiet grace that reminded him sharply of his mother.

When he was sure he was alone, Tark opened his eyes. This time he did not feel like sleeping at all: he was more awake and alert than he had been for days when hunger and exhaustion had numbed his senses. Indeed his perception had been blighted to such a degree that much of what he had experienced now seemed unreal as a dream. And so, lying there in the semi-darkness, staring up at the roof of branches though which the glitter of stars could be discerned, he tried to remember all that had happened since Tani's hunters had caught up with him.

At first the pictures that filled his mind were fragmented: men screaming for help as the ground swallowed them; a long plodding across endless flats; a sickening plunge into a chasm; incandescent heat and roaring water. It took an immense effort to make sense of these, to order them, and he was left with a nagging question: how had he come to fall into the river at all? Then, for the first time, he recalled a hard shove, something prodding the centre of his back. Carefully, he explored the place with his fingers and winced. Though he could not see it, there was a dark purple bruise there, no bigger than the circle of his thumb and forefinger: the mark of Tani's staff.

This discovery was profoundly disturbing to the boy. It meant that his plunge into the torrent had been no accident but a deliberate attempt on his life. And there was only one possible suspect: his enemy, the thin man Tani who must have approached with a hunter's stealth while he stood exhausted and despairing at the cliff edge.

This realization was more shocking to Tark than the fact he had nearly drowned. That his enemy could have come so close without being discovered struck to the very centre of his being: he might have been speared instead, his body shoved over the cliff and no-one would ever have known the truth. In that moment (for he had forgotten how the journey had weakened both him and his pursuer), he was overwhelmed by shame: he sat up, drawing his knees to his chest, and ground his teeth bitterly. And recalling the gentle kindness with which the women of this place had treated him it seemed to him that they also regarded him as no more than a sick child.

As his thoughts seethed he began to rock, the force of his anger requiring some outlet in movement and the little shell, his talisman, tapped against the bony ridges of his chest. At first he was hardly aware of it: if anything, it served to exaggerate his sense of dislocation, as if his body were but a husk while his thoughts soared far away. But as his rocking grew more violent, the tapping grew harder, more insistent as if something were demanding entry and he stopped, his hands closed upon the talisman and his memories finally resolved. And now that they made sense, his anger was replaced by self-pity. More than ever he felt himself alone. For while he had been saved from the river, he had no knowledge of where he was, nor of the people who had rescued him. If Tani was still following, he would have to flee again.

The fire outside had sunk to a heap of glowing embers and the people had gone to their huts to sleep. There was no sound but the snores and grunts of the sleepers, the distant calling of a night-owl, an occasional rustle of leaves where some small animal was foraging. Tark rubbed his eyes, which were stinging with unshed tears, and listened hard. If his enemy was close, now would be the time for him to strike, while the whole camp was asleep.

There came another rustle of leaves, louder this time, as if something large were approaching, an animal or person either unfamiliar with the territory or else lacking the need for stealth. Tark froze, holding his breath and his hands clenched involuntarily. There was nothing in the hut he could use as a weapon if this was Tani yet he could scarcely believe that the thin man could have found him so swiftly. He waited, his heartbeat pounding in his ears.

A faint scuff of a foot against packed earth, then a figure appeared, silhouetted against the glow from the campfire. The breath hissed between Tark's teeth for this person was small and slight, a mop of hair falling to the shoulders. Whether a girl or boy he could not tell but one thing was certain: it was not his enemy. He lay back staring, unaware that the ruddy light falling though the doorway reflected in his eyes, making him appear like the Night-Stalkers of legend whose eyeballs were said to bulge red as they drank their victim's blood.

The figure stood utterly still and Tark began to wonder if it were witless or an outcast to be wandering about at night. To his eyes it was a child (though he was only slightly taller and even thinner), and when it raised a fist to its mouth and began to bite savagely at the knuckles, his rising impatience turned to pity.

'Are you lost?' he asked.

Although his tone was gentle, the intruder started wildly as if speech was the last thing it had expected from him. Then it took a couple of paces into the hut, and stood still, hands planted on narrow hips in an attitude of belligerence.

'Of course I'm not lost!' came the reply. 'I live here. Is it true you crossed the Death Flats alone? How did you know where to come? The elders were talking about you.'

Although it was impossible to tell from the pitch whether this was the voice of a girl or boy, its scornful tone and the barrage of questions were enough to identify the speaker as female and Tark's sympathy evaporated. He felt annoyed, both with himself for his naivety and with her for the intrusion.

'Shouldn't you be asleep?' he asked. 'What do you want? Go away!'

'My mother's been looking after you,' she said importantly. 'I wanted to see what you were like. I often walk round the village when I can't sleep. I'm not afraid.'

Tark shut his mouth, determined to say no more in the hope she would be discouraged and leave. But she tilted her head slightly and though he could not see her face, he could somehow feel her gaze upon him and sense her wary hostility.

'So you're the one who's lost,' she continued. 'When they found you they couldn't tell if you'd fallen in the river or tried to swim across deliberately. That's why they're waiting. If you were older, they'd have killed you.'

'Killed?' Tark sat bolt upright, his mouth suddenly dry. 'Why?'

For the first time the girl seemed ill-at-ease. She half-turned to look outside and her profile was sharp against the dim glow, her forehead less rounded and the nose straighter and longer than was common among the Lake People. Only when she was satisfied no-one could see, did she move closer, just beyond Tark's reach. He could smell the warm, faintly acrid scent of her skin and it made him acutely self-conscious.

'Not long ago a group of people came down the river,' she said, her voice barely more than a whisper. 'They said they belonged to the Lake Clan but the lake had dried up and they were forced to leave their homes. Here it is always green and there is plenty of water, not just the river. But the lands all around have become drier and drier and so the Council decreed that the strangers should be put to death, to protect the Valley and everything in it. Otherwise more will come and everything will be destroyed.'

Tark frowned, profoundly shaken by these words. 'But how can that be?' he asked, outraged by the cool manner in which she spoke. 'Do you mean those Lake people were killed?' And when, in the same level tone, she replied, 'Of course,' he forgot the need for caution and exclaimed 'But they meant no harm!' so loudly that the girl hurried to the doorway to make sure no-one was abroad.

'Shh!' she hissed on her return. 'Do you want the elders to hear? That's what happened. This valley is our place: we found it and the elders want to keep it for our children and our children's children. I bet it was the same beside the lake.'

'It wasn't!' he said hotly. 'There were many camps there but we shared water and the fish and birds we caught there and until the Great Dry there was plenty for all. Strangers were welcomed and many stayed. Then, when the lake began to shrink, some left in hope of finding somewhere better but no-one forced them to go. And no man said to another: 'This is my water, not yours' – how could that be possible? Even on the worst day . . .'

His voice trailed into silence as memories of the cataclysm, the fire and smoke, the desperate struggle to reach water, the mob closing on his mother crowded his mind and the girl, sensing his distress, crouched beside him though she did not touch him or speak. He breathed deeply and blinked hard in an effort to push the images away, then said slowly, 'We were all thirsty and hungry but even then no-one fought: the lucky ones lived and the rest died.'

The girl said nothing but he felt her gaze upon his face acutely as if she were touching him. And the silence between them became agonizing. A light sweat broke out over Tark's body and words thronged his mind but none of them made sense. It was as if someone had laid a spell on him, to confuse and embarrass.

'I must go.' It seemed his visitor had been overtaken by the same awkwardness. She rose smoothly to her feet and left as quietly as she had come.

Alone again, Tark felt bone-weary yet his mind raced. He wondered which of his people had managed to reach this place, whether they had been his kin or friends and grief pierced him as he imagined how joyful they must have been to discover this green land only to be murdered by the inhabitants. And he struggled with the very idea of the killing, wondering what had so corrupted the hearts of the girl's people that they were unwilling to share the bounty of the land in which they dwelt. Indeed, so abhorrent was this to him, so alien to his own traditions, he had difficulty comprehending it. For his people believed that food and water belonged to all. Then if one hunter was successful and another failed, the families of both partook of the kill: next day their fortunes might be reversed yet the weakest, the old and the very young, would still eat. And water, the most precious resource of all, was likewise for sharing: no man or woman, whatever their status, could claim precedence over a child when they came to a spring or creek, simply because an infant perishes from thirst more swiftly than an adult. This law, ingrained in his culture, was so fundamental, Tark had never questioned it or imagined it could be broken, least of all scorned as this girl described.

Then a more insidious thought crept into his brain. If it was the custom here that adult strangers were slain on sight, then at least he was safe from Tani. And the irony of this acted like a poison. He clenched his fists and grinned: had the girl seen his expression, she would have been afraid. A moment later the shadows swirled and melded behind his eyelids, weakness overwhelmed him and he sank half-fainting into a morass of lurid dreams.

For three days Tark was left largely to himself. During that time it was the crone, Myenah, who tended him and she hardly spoke. When he tried to engage her in conversation (for he was desperate to know more of this place and its people), she stared at him from under heavy brows and said 'Not now, boy' so forbiddingly, he dared not speak again for fear of furthering her displeasure.

But the enforced rest and isolation (after the girl's warnings he was loth to leave the shelter uninvited), were not without effect. His strength returned, he gained weight and his skin was no longer cracked and desiccated but smooth though to anyone that had not seen him before, he still appeared painfully thin. His eyes were no longer sunken and bloodshot, they had regained their old lively glance but the bruised-looking hollows in which they were set attested to the suffering he had endured.

On the fourth day, he was taken before the elders.

This was the first time he had been outside the shelter (a clay bowl had been provided for his toilet which his carers had taken away and brought back clean each day), and as he walked with Manalah through the settlement, he began to understand why the inhabitants were so fiercely protective of this place for it was unlike anything he had seen or imagined before.

The village consisted of a double ring of huts made of stakes and woven leaves, all set around a central space. Some were square, some rectangular, others dome-shaped but all were neat and well-constructed and their doors faced into the circular courtyard for those in the inner circle were offset from those in the outer. Each dwelling had its own hearth for cooking and behind each was a little patch of cultivated earth where plants taken from the forest were tended with loving care. There was no litter of bones and excrement such as he had known in many of the lakeside camps, but several paths led away into the forest which loomed like a green wall all around.

In the distance, just visible through gaps in the leaves, Tark glimpsed towering cliffs of red sandstone. These were capped by a layer of some dark volcanic rock which, being more resistant, had protected the underlying strata save where a fault-line clove them, a weakness that water had, over aeons, exploited, eroding a deep river gorge and the basin in which the forest had taken root. The river, the very means by which Tark had entered the valley, had become shallower during the Great Dry and, each year, more of its rocky bed was exposed, something the inhabitants noted with dread. Yet it was not the only source of water in the valley.

Manalah stood patiently as Tark surveyed the village and its surroundings, then she touched his arm. 'Come, they are waiting.'

She led him between the huts to one of the paths which ran into the forest. The trees were tall and cast cool green shadows so that at first Tark did not notice the figures sitting in a small glade just off the path. Indeed, so diminutive did they appear beneath the lofty vegetation that at first he mistook them for boulders and when the woman gestured him forward, he hesitated. 'Where -?'

'Hush.' There was a look almost of pity in her eyes as she took his arm and led him into the clearing. Then dread overtook him for the elders were silent, their eyes fixed upon him in an uncompromising, judgmental stare.

'Do not be afraid,' Manalah whispered and then she let go his arm and walked away between the trees.

Never had Tark felt so alone or self-conscious as under the piercing scrutiny of these elders. There were eight of them, four ancient men and four aged women and they regarded him as they might have looked upon some creature wholly new and strange. The crone, Myenah, was there but he could discern no more recognition or sympathy in her gaze than any of the others.

'What is your name and who are your people?' The man that spoke was older than anyone the boy had ever seen before (so hard were their lives, few of the Lake Clan attained the age of forty-five, especially since the start of the Great Dry). The skin of this elder's face and body was furrowed and wrinkled so finely as to appear like tree-bark; his hair and beard were white, his eyes milky with age. He leant forward to peer at the boy with the intensity of the partially-sighted and a thread of spittle drooled from the corner of his mouth.

Tark tried to stay calm and focused but he was intimidated by the formality of the proceedings and the stern dignity of the meeting. Also, at the back of his mind was the fate of those other Lake people, who had died by decree of this Council. When he spoke, his voice trembled and was little more than a whisper.

'My name is Tark,' he began, 'and I belong to the Lake Clan. Mingar is my father and my mother was called Eeli. I was lost after the firestorm. I wandered for days and then I fell in the river. That's all. I don't know where I am. I was drowning, then I woke up here.'

These words fell into a well of silence. The scrutiny of the elders did not waver nor did they exhibit the slightest sign of pity. Then, unexpectedly, the ancient who had spoken pounded his thigh with a bony fist.

'How long?' he barked and his eyes narrowed to slits. 'Are they far behind? How long before they arrive?'

'And how many?' interjected his neighbour, a younger man (though still ancient to Tark's eyes), whose lean body was scarred as if a huge beast had raked him with its claws. 'Speak!'

Tark quailed before their hostility and his tongue clove to the roof of his mouth. He swallowed desperately.

'I was alone,' he stammered. 'Maybe they all died. I ran away when the rain came. It was many days ago. I don't know what happened to them or where they are.'

The elders turned their heads and looked deeply into one another's eyes as if they could communicate by thought alone. Then Myenah spoke and her voice was cold and shrill, her eyes bright and inhuman as a crow's.

'He admits he is one of the Lake folk,' she said. 'How then can we believe that he came in ignorance, since he is not the first of his kind to trespass here? Most likely he's a spy. When he's strong again, just wait: one day he'll disappear and when he returns it will be at the head of his clan, coming to take the valley from us!'

'That's not true!' Resentment overcame Tark's fear for he had been ready to trust this old woman. 'If I knew where they were, don't you think I'd be with them? We' - he hesitated as a vivid picture of Draa urging him to leave filled his mind — 'we were separated in the storm and then the floods came. Everything was changed: I couldn't find my way back. And then, after days of wandering, I fell in the river.'

'Lucky for you,' the crone remarked dryly and many of the elders exchanged glances and chuckled with the envy of the aged for the passion of the young. 'Yes — yes, very lucky to fall in the very river that flows through the Valley!'

She rocked with glee while Tark stood trembling. Then the scarred man held up his hand for silence and looked at Tark with so penetrating a gaze it seemed to the boy that the very core of his being was being scrutinized, his thoughts exposed, even his spirit, the secret element of his self, laid bare.

'Please!' he begged. 'It's true! I knew nothing of this place. I was lost in the desert, dying of thirst, then I fell in the river. It wasn't my fault someone found and brought me here!'

The silence following this speech was, if anything, more profound than before and certainly more intimidating because the elders all stared as if to force the truth from him by sheer willpower.

'Part of your story may be true,' the scarred man said slowly, 'but you are not telling all. You were separated from your kin you say but you also say you fled. What were you running from, boy? In times of danger most folk flock together. What are you trying to hide?'

All at once Tark realized he would have to tell the whole truth: these ancient men and women could sense the slightest deception. And so, falteringly, he began again, starting with Eeli's quarrel with Mingar, and, with the telling, he soon forgot to whom he spoke, that he was, effectively on trial for his life. His voice grew strong as he relived the terrors and small triumphs of his journey: how he had escaped Tani's spearmen; been brought to the very brink of death from hunger and exhaustion, then nearly drowned after being pushed into the gorge. And he found that as the tale took hold, he remembered many details forgotten in the blankness to which he had awoken in the village so the telling took on a new vitality and urgency which bound the listeners to him like a spell.

But as with all tales, the time came when he had no more to say. He thanked the elders for the care he had received and Myenah's eyes crinkled and she smiled, not her usual smile which was more a grimace but one of acknowledgement and sympathy. Then she and the scarred man exchanged glances and nodded as if, in their opinion, Tark had passed the test. But there was another man, grizzled with age, lacking two fingers on his right hand, who seemed unaffected by the pathos of the tale. He scowled and chewed at the stubs of his fingers, then leant forward to stare at Tark.

'He has a pretty tongue in his head,' he said in a voice harsh as granite. 'But however he came here and for whatever reason, he is not one of us. Even if he is not a spy, are we sure we want him in the Valley?'

At this many of the elders looked askance at each other and some whispered together. Tark's heart sank for he could tell by their reaction that this man's words carried weight. He wondered if he had been responsible for the decision to slaughter those other Lake People and a chill crept though his blood.

'Ach, are you blind?' To Tark's astonishment, Myenah clambered to her feet and came to stand beside him. 'This is a boy you are talking about. He is young and lost and if he is a spy, that is of no account for there is no way back up the river unless he sprouts wings to fly. All we have to decide is whether to welcome him into our ways and customs until he becomes one of us. For he has suffered, that much is certain, and most likely his folk are already dead. Do not forget, long ago we were all one people: that we understand his speech proves it!'

A murmur of approbation arose at this and the six-fingered man grunted and shrugged. Then the ancient who had spoken first hawked and spat and held up one hand for silence.

'Myenah speaks wisely,' he said, and his voice was strong and clear as if his decrepit appearance was but a façade. 'By his actions we shall judge this boy rather than condemn him because he is a stranger. He shall live with us and grow into our ways. One day he will marry and his children will belong here as much as the children of our sons and daughters. And he will defend the Valley as one of us and when he dies, his bones will mix with the earth and water which have sustained him through his life and his children and their children will honour him for the fate that brought him here.'

Tark heard this speech without fully comprehending it beyond the first sentence: relief and the unexpected cessation of suspense made him light-headed. He felt himself stagger, a roaring arose in his ears and his vision blurred as if he were on the verge of fainting. Myenah and the scarred man guided him back to his shelter and he was deaf to the hubbub as the folk waiting in the courtyard learned the outcome of the trial.

Chapter 6.

It took Tani many days to return to the lakeside and all the time he refined his tale. When at last he reached the line of sandhills and looked out over the stump-forest he felt a sense of homecoming though the landscape had changed from when he had last seen it. The floodwaters had retreated to deep, winding channels but thick red-brown sludge blanketed the ground and there were still heaps of debris piled like walls marking where the flood had reached its height. But in the far distance the thin man glimpsed a pale line on the horizon, sunlight reflecting on a large body of water or salt, and then his heart leapt because he knew he was seeing the lake and that, against all the odds, he had retraced his steps.

Yet the remainder of his journey seemed the most arduous, in part because he was so close to achieving his purpose. The new waterways forced him into long detours and down on the plain there was no landmark to guide him: more than once he found he had wasted time walking in circles. And so it was that when he reached the lakeside, he found it deserted.

At first, seeing the empty flats spread before him, Tani refused to believe his eyes. Indeed, he wondered if instinct had failed him and he had come to the wrong place. But between the stagnant pools and sluggish watercourses were crude piles of sticks and ragged skins, the remains of shelters, and when he turned to look around, the lie of the land was unmistakeable for the edge of the basin was sharp still, marking the rim of the lake as it had been before the Great Dry. And yet as far as the eye could see there was not even a thin spiral of smoke from a cooking fire to betray the presence of a single family.

That those who had done murder by his command could have left without him was something so unexpected it left Tani stunned. He wondered what new disaster could have compelled them to go instead of waiting, then the thought came to him that perhaps they had not fled their homes but were all dead. And since this prospect was more palatable than the idea that they had abandoned him, Tani decided to search for clues guessing that even if scavengers had devoured the corpses, some scrap of hair, skin or bone would remain.

Walking across the mud, the thin man saw that it was criss-crossed with the marks of many feet but he was too distracted to pay them much attention. He hurried to the first pile of sticks, found a heap of ashes before it, the remains of a cooking fire, and held his free hand over. There was the faintest trace of warmth: he dug his fingers in deep and then snatched his hand back for the embers were still hot enough to burn. Cursing, he sucked his fingertips while his mind seethed with the possible implications.

And it was now, realizing that the seemingly empty land was perhaps not as deserted as it appeared, that Tani felt strangely discomfited. The skin between his shoulder-blades prickled as if some multi-legged insect were crawling up his back and he rose and looked intently all about, thinking he was being watched. Yet as before, there was no sign of any living creature in all that vastness of water and clay: even the sky was empty.

Tani walked deliberately to the furthest shelter, a flimsy structure of skins suspended from four sticks to make a canopy. Beneath it was a flattened pile of grass and the ground around it was strewn with the detritus common around any hut: bones, pieces of root and stem too hard to eat, scraps of hide, excrement. But there was nothing to tell who had dwelt there or why they should have left so abruptly and this increased the thin man's uneasiness. He felt exposed, vulnerable, lonely. He turned to stand with his back to the lake but though there was still nothing to see, he could not rid himself of the sense that hostile eyes were watching.

Muttering curses under his breath in an effort to ward off ill-fortune and to bolster his courage, Tani grasped his staff firmly in his right hand and went to drink at the nearest rivulet. The water was turbid and foul-tasting but he had encountered worse in his travels.

A crow flew overhead as he got unsteadily to his feet. It cawed once as it passed and was gone, a diminishing speck, then a dot in the vastness of the sky, then nothing. And the thin man's disappointment and loneliness combined in a spasm of rage: he flung down his staff and stamped a wide circle, screaming imprecations, then threw himself upon the mud, beating the ground with his fists and biting at it frenziedly, his cries turning to anguished sobs.

Exhaustion at last brought calm. He rolled onto his back and lay alternately gasping for air and spitting out the foul-tasting sludge that filled his mouth. Now that his frenzy had passed he was left with a corroding bitterness. He thought of the effort and suffering he had undergone to pursue Tark and ground his teeth in frustration and self-recrimination: instead of following the boy he should, he saw now, have stayed here to tighten his grip upon the clan while he had the chance. For he had nothing to show for his long journey except what his own cunning could conjure into being.

As he contemplated this it occurred to him that in reality his situation had not changed: unless, by some miracle, Tark had escaped, there was no-one to bear witness against him. And there was encouragement also to be found in the warmth of the ashes: the rest of the clan could not be much more than a day ahead.

Wearily Tani sat up, spat out the last of the dirt and wiped his mouth with a forearm. To be sure of catching up with the others he knew he should set out at once but realization was one thing, the will and strength to act another. Every muscle in his body cried out for rest for he had pushed himself to the limit of his endurance to reach the lakeside and disappointment had sapped the last of his resilience. It took all his willpower to lever himself to his feet with his staff and limp the short distance to the shelter with its bed and ragged canopy, then to crawl inside and lie down.

Stretched out on the mattress of matted leaves, Tani breathed deeply and, after a last careful scrutiny of the empty flats, closed his eyes and allowed his body to relax at last. Within moments he was asleep.

The Lake Clan journeyed on until they reached the place Draa had spotted from afar. It was a long hummock surrounded by shallow pools and although biting flies swarmed over the water, it otherwise made an ideal camping ground for the ground on the top was sandy and dry while the pools formed a natural moat.

Here, Mingar declared, they would spend the night and the people flung down their bundles with relief, weary not so much from walking as the pain of leaving. In the desolation of this stump-forest the barren shores and salt flats of the lakeside seemed familiar and safe: already they felt the longing that characterizes exile.

Since the most prudent of the families had brought fire with them, it was not long before smoke from little cooking fires spiralled into the air and the homely smells of woodsmoke and food pervaded the camp. Mingar and Draa, instead of tending their own needs, went round the camp, pausing to talk with each group and such was the esteem in which these two were held, the people were comforted by their presence. Even the tired children ceased squabbling and sat quietly to hear what the great ones had to say and whenever Draa or Mingar looked upon or spoke directly to them, all but the boldest became tongue-tied.

Darkness had fallen by the time the pair returned to the place they had picked for themselves in the lee of a massive, fire-scarred stump. Here Draa quickly kindled a small fire to see them through the night but they had already eaten since every family had insisted they join their meals and, in courtesy, they had accepted a morsel from each. Once the fire was burning steadily therefore, Draa spread out her cape and sat upon it. Mingar was already seated and the flames reflected in his eyes and picked out the deep wrinkles and folds of his skin, making him appeared far older than he really was.

Watching him surreptitiously, Draa shivered. In that wavering light with the looming bulk of the dead stump behind there was something terrible in Mingar's appearance. When she could no longer bear his stillness and silence, she whispered, 'Mingar, speak to me beloved. What is wrong?'

He did not respond at once and she wondered if he had heard. But then he sighed and passed a hand over his face as if to brush away clinging cobwebs.

'I do not know,' he said distractedly. 'It is not the journey or the people here but there is something. A weight upon my heart, as if some powerful spirit ill-wishes me. Yet who can it be and why?'

Draa thought unhappily of Tani's contempt for her husband, an enmity which had transferred to Tark when Mingar refused to rise to it. Such hate, she knew, would not easily be appeased without bloodshed yet she could not believe the thin man was the author of Mingar's disquiet. Since she was certain Tark was alive, she was sure Tani would still be pursuing him. Above all, the thin man was tenacious: otherwise he would have succumbed to his sickness long ago and died.

Thus Draa reasoned for she had known Tani well in the days before Mingar's accident yet some deep prescience countered the logic of her thoughts and her unease grew. For no other enemy came to mind unless someone in the clan harboured a secret ambition for the leadership. And that made no sense given the hospitality they had experienced in the camp that very evening.

'Perhaps you are just tired, love,' she answered carefully. 'For I am sure you have no enemy here. And unless Tani is close, who else could there be?'

'Tani?' Mingar muttered. He looked around, peering into the soft darkness beyond the fires as if he expected to glimpse the thin man lurking there. 'But surely if he were still alive he would have returned already, with or without my son's blood on his hands?'

His bitterness smote Draa's heart: she prayed silently that the thin man's bones lay scattered on some far plain or had been swept away in the flood for above all, she dreaded an encounter between the two. And so, because she, like all her people, believed that ill-fortune could be enticed or repelled by the power of thought alone, she answered deliberately, 'That is what I think also. But if you are still troubled come the dawn, let us travel more swiftly. Then, if he is following, he will be hard-pressed to find us and if there is no-one behind, still we shall come to our destination sooner and that will all be good.'

Then Mingar reached out to take her hand in a gesture of acknowledgement and affection. 'You ease my heart,' he said, 'we will do as you say. And I shall keep watch behind. In a land so bare as this even one skilled as Tani will find it hard to follow us unseen. And if he catches up at last, I do not fear him.'

As he spoke she felt his hand tremble slightly and her

foreboding deepened. But with an effort she forced it aside and smiled. 'Come then and sleep,' she said. 'It will be a long day and a hard journey tomorrow.'

'No-one, not even you, can tell what the new day will bring before it has begun,' he replied.

With his presence in the valley endorsed by the elders, Tark became the subject of great curiosity and interest. People were constantly visiting, the women to fuss, the men to interrogate though their questions were often concealed within tortuous circumlocutions. The boy saw through their subterfuge yet he was patient and answered politely, knowing himself still a stranger. Many families invited him to their hearths and he was showered with gifts: a fine cloak of animal skins; a necklace of hard seeds strung on thread; a soft leather bag containing lumps of red and yellow ochre. This last was bestowed by the scarred elder, Nygeli, and it came with a condition: 'Learn the customs and stories of the Valley for soon you will be a man, if you pass the test.'

All this socializing after his long journey and convalescence wearied Tark and he was glad when night came and he was left alone to lie on his bed and watch the stars though gaps in the thatch while the camp grew quiet all around. Then at last he could relax his guard instead of being constantly on the alert for a question or slip of the tongue that might arouse suspicion. Though the Council had found in his favour, he was not yet at ease among these people for he sensed that they could alter their opinion, and thereby their decision, as swiftly as they had accepted him.

Part of his disquiet was due to the fact that despite the attention lavished upon him and the pleasure he took in his rare periods of solitude, deep in his heart Tark was lonely. Among the families he had visited there had, of course, been folk of his age but they seemed aloof and diffident in his presence, as if he came not only from a different clan but another order of beings entirely. Being proud by nature, he was unable to understand that their apparent disdain stemmed from shyness (rather than believing themselves superior, they were in awe of one who had experienced and endured so much). And so it seemed to him that an insurmountable barrier existed between him and his peers.

The girl that had visited in the night, Manalah's daughter, was the only one he could have talked to without the crippling self-consciousness that assailed him whenever he came into contact with others of his age. Children they seemed to him despite their seeming arrogance, soft in body and naive having never suffered hardship in this lush valley. But though Myenah and Manalah were his most frequent visitors, she did not come with them, nor did he glimpse her when he explored the settlement.

He could, of course, simply have asked her mother or grandmother where she was, but to do so would betray the secret of her first visit. And so he said nothing, partly because he did not wish to get her into trouble but also because he was loth to betray his interest. For the simplest explanation for her absence was that she disliked him.

Thus while he was fêted and cosseted until he longed for the wide open expanse of the lakeside, even the awful emptiness of the desert he had crossed, Tark was constantly on watch for the girl though he had no idea of what he would say to her if they met.

He had almost given up hope of seeing her again (impossible though it seemed in so small a community), when he saw her as he went to Nygeli's dwelling. She darted behind a hut as soon as she realized she'd been seen and he continued on his way (the scarred elder was not a man to be kept waiting). Yet he was oddly comforted by her presence, and the fact she had been watching him proved that she was interested in him though he could not tell whether this was from curiosity or liking.

That morning, for the first time, Tark found his session with Nygeli tedious. The elder was teaching him the things that a boy born in the valley would have learnt from his father and uncles as he grew up: the great stories from the very beginning of time; the laws and customs of the clan; even the lineages of each family, for in their isolated existence the ancient codes of marriage which among Tark's people forbade the union of close kin had, by necessity, been changed though it was still taboo for brother and sister, parent and child to join together.

As Nygeli explained the intricacies of the marriage laws in the

Valley, Tark listened with only half his mind though ordinarily he would have been shocked. Many legends of his people told of the dire consequences of such close relationships, the children of which were often possessed by evil spirits and wrought havoc within their clan. But the sight of the girl had distracted him and he made no comment, unaware that the old man was looking at him forbearingly.

'Tark!' Nygeli said at last, sharply. 'What's on your mind, boy? Has some sorcerer put a spell on you or did a night-prowler steal your tongue?'

Tark did not reply. For days a kind of sullen resentment had been festering in him against the assumed superiority of these people who sought to assimilate him into their culture without any consideration for his own. And this, combined with his confused feelings towards the girl, made him reckless.

'Leave me alone!' He jumped to his feet and stood looking down upon the old man with wild eyes. 'Your stories aren't mine. Why do I have to learn your ways? I never meant to come here!'

Tark instantly regretted these words but by then it was too late. Yet Nygeli was slow to anger and had, in any case, expected an outburst at sometime for he was accustomed to deal with the young men of the clan and knew that passion, even if misdirected, was preferable to indifference. Therefore, instead of reacting with anger, he merely fixed the boy with his dark, penetrating gaze and said gravely, 'However you came, you are here for the rest of your days, Tark. Do you not then think it right that you should understand our laws and customs, and respect them? Would you not expect it from a stranger who came to live beside your lake?'

Held those eyes which seemed to pierce deeper than he wanted, Tark flushed, squirming inwardly with embarrassment and shame. In his heart he knew Nygeli was right, that even a passing traveller would be expected to comply with the traditions of his host from courtesy alone. And yet something within him balked at submitting so easily to the old man's reasoning, a profound dissatisfaction with himself and his situation that he had not yet recognized as unhappiness.

'But our laws are better,' he said defiantly. 'We share everything and welcome strangers to our hearths. We don't kill them.'

For the first time since the Council, Nygeli seemed discomfited. His eyes narrowed and his frown deepened. 'Where did you hear that?'

From the elder's sternness, Tark realized he had gone too far.

'I didn't –' he stammered. 'I mean, I don't know. Maybe I overheard it.'

Even to his ears this explanation sounded lame. Nygeli shook his head and his countenance hardened.

'Sit down: you will have to do better than that,' he said grimly. 'We do not tolerate liars. Yet what you have heard is true: those who come uninvited are put to death.' He paused and Tark quailed before his steady gaze. 'You should be grateful for our mercy, son of Mingar.'

Tark obeyed but fidgeted where he sat, longing to be anywhere but here, under the scrutiny of this fierce old man. Yet his respect for Nygeli was too deep to allow him to leave.

'Also,' the elder continued relentlessly, 'you should not forget that despite all you have endured, you are not grown to manhood. Arrogance ill-befits one who is here on sufferance yet it has come to my notice that you disdain others of your own age. That is unwise when they will be your companions all your life, on the hunting trail and maybe on the war trail also: one day your life may depend on their friendship. And from the girls will come your wife: scorn them now and be sure they will never forget it.'

Although his tone was still grim, there was a glint of humour in Nygeli's eyes as he spoke the last words and Tark knew he had been forgiven. And he relaxed his guard and bowed his head saying 'Thank you Nygeli, I meant no offence. But it's hard, being alone in a strange place.'

It was difficult for Tark to make this admission and he kept his head bent, afraid what his face might reveal. But to his amazement Nygeli seemed to understand for he said nothing to press the boy only, after a moment's silence, putting out a thin, sinewy hand to grasp Tark's wrist in a brief gesture of sympathy. Then he let go, saying 'Go along then and heed what I have said, for of all you may learn in future, today's lesson may be the most important.'

Far away, under the shelter erected for his enemies, Tani slept through not one night but two. So deep was his slumber, he was unaware of the day's heat or the night chill or the fleeting visits of animals and birds which, seeking food, water or shade, wandered towards the shelter then, finding it occupied, veered away. Even the carrion-eaters disdained to touch him for though he was weak and emaciated to look upon, there was no smell of blood or sickness to excite them. They had long since learned that men were dangerous and, unless incapacitated, best left alone.

At dawn on the second day a crow landed on one of the sticks that supported the canopy. It cocked its head and listened to Tani's soft, steady breathing. Then, judging that a sleeping man posed no threat, it swooped down, landing with a little puff of dust an arm's length from Tani's face.

The thin man stirred as if sensing the presence of another living being but he did not waken. Under the thin membranes of their lids, his eyeballs twitched and rolled. Drawn by the movement, the bird hopped closer. A single peck away was, it knew, a tasty morsel. It took another step, bringing it within easy reach of Tani's face but as it draw back for the stabbing thrust that would pluck an eyeball, a trio of brightly coloured butterflies fluttered between. And the slight fanning of the cool, still air by their wings disturbed Tani: he groaned and rolled over, his hands moving instinctively to shield his face, and the bird leapt back. It snapped up one of the butterflies then took to the air and this time it did not circle but headed westwards for the presence of the insects signified a momentous change in the heart of the great flat land.

Where floodwaters had flowed and sunk into the parched soil a broad carpet of flowers spread, turning what had been a waste of wind-scoured earth and glistening salt pans into a melange of colour, scent and movement. For the flowers, fragile and ephemeral, bobbed and swayed under the wind's caress and the weight of insects swarming to take advantage of their bounty; butterflies fluttered to sip the nectar, and birds flocked and swooped to feed upon both nectar and insects. Where pools or lakes had formed, larger birds congregated as, from deep within the mud, creatures held dormant by drought woke to life. Frogs, shrimps, even fish joined the frenzy of growth and procreation, needing to reproduce before the dry returned and the plants turned to dust, leaving only the anlage of life, the seeds, eggs and capsules, to wait buried in the dust until the rains returned.

Into this vibrant landscape Draa and Mingar led their clan and it seemed to most that this must be the place they had long dreamt of. The flowering was at its peak and many animals had trekked to the plain: seed and plant-eating grazers and croppers, followed by feasters-upon-flesh some of which lived there all year round, eking out the fat stored in their bodies from the last time of plenty.

Most of the carnivores were, by nature, wary of men, so the lakeside folk walked largely unaware of the fierce, cold eyes that watched their every move. Beguiled by the abundance of game, plants, flowers and even insects that could be eaten, the pools of clear water and running streams, the apparent lack of danger, the heads of families begged Mingar to stop so that they could make a new home on this Flowering Plain as they named it.

The only paucity in this land was wood for fuel since there were few trees. But this lack, the elders argued, could be overcome by using dry dung and such dead and dry vegetation as could be found.

Even Draa implored her husband to at least break the journey with a sojourn on the plain when she saw how the rest grumbled before setting out each morning. Dissension was her greatest fear, that the group would split and a new leader emerge to contest Mingar's authority. At yet, none had but every day, as the discontent deepened, her anxiety increased.

Mingar, however, was deaf to all these voices, even the most beloved. Whilst he had professed indifference towards his rival, Tani, dread of an encounter haunted him though it was not injury or death he feared but humiliation. It was this, in part, that compelled him to go on, driving his people at such a pace that ere half the day's journey was over, the youngest had to be carried and the eldest raised their voices in complaint and protest. (Striding at the back as had become his habit, Mingar wondered that some of these ancients possessed breath enough for walking and railing but he schooled himself to take no offence because, after all, they had kept faith).

But the possibility of pursuit was not the only reason for Mingar's determination. He alone among the Lake people was unaffected by the beauty and plenty of the Flowering Plain for it seemed strange to him that no other people lived there and that the only trees grew along the line of the deepest watercourses. And the frantic activity all around (even the snakes they happened across were entwined in mating), made him uneasy for it seemed unnatural to one accustomed to the rhythms of the lakeside. It was as if a kind of madness had overtaken the world and everything in it, save him alone.

One evening, he tried to explain these feelings to Draa. The sun had just set and the western sky glowed a pale translucent pink while in the east a crescent moon rose as if to balance the sinking sun. Mingar sat a little apart from the main camp, his hands resting loosely on his knees, his eyes on the horizon which, as the sky darkened, became a black line unbroken by any hill or tree, seemingly infinite in remoteness: there was nothing relating to a human scale at all.

So wrapt was he in thought, when Draa came looking for him she almost passed by: still he was and silent as a boulder or stump. But some instinct alerted her to his presence and she sat quietly beside him. She knew his moods of old and was loth to disturb him.

This time, however, Mingar was glad to see her for the vastness of the land had begun to frighten him. He reached out and touched her shoulder tenderly, taking comfort from her warmth and the simple fact of her being there.

Sensing his disquiet, Draa began to talk of little events in camp: how a child had found a giant egg, enough to feed a whole family; how another had a swollen foot after treading on a thorn, how a woman had discovered a nest of swarming insects which, when squeezed, exuded a clear liquid sweet as honey. Mingar listened patiently until she had finished, then asked quietly, 'Do you think we should settle here?'

By now the last flush of pink had faded in the west and a greenish hue, translucent as deep water, spread across the sky save where a silvery radiance haloed the moon. Only for a brief while did the green last, then it faded into the blackness of night and stars appeared

Draa considered his question long and carefully and the radiance of moon and stars picked out the sharp planes of her cheekbones and reflected glossily in her eyes.

'This place has everything we need,' she said at last. 'Why should we not stay? That no-one else is here means we are the first to discover it. And if others come, there is plenty for all. Do you not see it?'

'Eh, I see the flowers and animals, the pools of water and the rivers that run between,' Mingar admitted, grudgingly. 'But there is something about this place I distrust. Maybe all is not as it seems.'

She stared at him in dismay, then smiled. 'Ah Mingar,' she said kindly, 'not everything is set to trick you. This place is different from the lakeside but that doesn't make it bad. We shall learn to live here as our ancestors learned to live beside the lake, for to them also the land was strange and new yet it became their home.'

He was silent, staring broodingly out across the plain where the flowers and grasses bent under the night breeze. 'Maybe,' he muttered, 'but my heart tells me it would be better to journey on until we know what lies beyond. Should we not at least follow one of the rivers in the hope it leads us somewhere we understand?'

Her hand tightened on the lean muscle of his thigh. 'Ah my love,' she whispered, 'you who sees so much: are you blind to the feelings of those around you? They are weary and some are sick. All around they see such bounty as we dreamt of when the lake began to shrink yet you would have them pass it by, or so they believe. Some are beginning to say that you refuse to stop from fear that Tani may be following. If you wish to keep their loyalty, you must listen and allow some respite from this journey at least.'

He was silent for a while but she felt the tension grow within him. Then he sighed and turned his eyes to hers.

'Very well,' he said heavily. 'We will stay on the Flowering Plain in the hope that it will sustain us. But understand this: it is not my wish that we do so, nor have I changed my mind. Yet I too have felt the mood of the others. I would rather risk being proved wrong than be the cause of unrest within the clan.'

Mindful of Mingar's stubbornness, Draa was at first astounded by his capitulation, then proud, knowing how hard and yet how necessary it had been. In token of her love and respect, she took his right hand (which was clenched into a fist), and gently straightened the fingers before pressing it against her brow.

'You are a true leader,' she murmured, 'And should you prove right after all, I shall take the blame upon myself, for urging you to this course.'

'There is no need,' he said. 'I will call a Council and abide by the will of the elders. And then we'll discover if this is truly the land of plenty that it appears.'

Soon after dawn, Mingar called all the heads of families together. Some of these were barely grown to adulthood, their parents and grandparents having perished in the cataclysm, yet all had an equal say. There was little debate for everyone wanted to stay on the Flowering Plain and when Mingar consented, a wild celebration began. Even those that had complained of exhaustion or sickness joined in and though the central fire, which formed the focus for the dancing and singing, was smaller than usual due to the paucity of fuel, the festivities lasted all day and long into the night.

When it was dark, Mingar forsook the celebrations. Only Draa saw him leave and pity wrenched her heart. But though she longed to follow and comfort him, she remained behind, guessing he would rather be alone. And also, the mood of the clan had infected her: she too was glad that the journey was over, the search ended. For, deep down, she believed Mingar's doubts unjustified, symptomatic of the pessimism that had grafted onto his nature after his accident. When she woke next morning, he was curled up beside her, the grim lines of his face softened in slumber so that he looked trusting and peaceful as a sleeping child and she rejoiced, thinking him reconciled.

Once they had recovered from the excesses of the night, the people wasted no time in setting up camp. Since there was little material close by to make shelters, the men trekked to the straggling lines of trees which bordered the main watercourses. Sometimes waist-deep in water, they tore down branches and bore them triumphantly to their families. Before long, bitter rivalry broke out over who had the biggest pile and so the destruction of the trees became a kind of frenzy. Soon of those closest to the camp nothing remained but the trunks and thickest branches, those too thick to break. And when the men were exhausted, they sat and watched as the women constructed dome-shaped shelters by bending and weaving the branches together.

Mingar alone among the men did not take part in the despoliation of the trees. In part his status as leader and his infirmity excused him; for the rest, while he understood the necessity that drove them, he was appalled by the savagery they displayed as if the trees were some enemy at last brought to bay and torn to pieces. And while he and Draa accepted the branches they were offered since they also required shelter, he was uneasy for trees were sparse enough in this land and the mutilated trunks (whose wounds wept sap thick and red as blood), seemed almost to accuse him though in his former life, before the Great Dry, he would have collected green branches from the forest edge without a thought.

Of course, he could not admit these feelings: even Draa would have laughed at such foolishness as to pity a tree. And deep within himself he was ashamed, yet the feeling would not go away. Even when Draa and some of the other women proudly showed him the shelter that would be his home, he had to force words of gratitude and acknowledgement from his throat and they looked at him askance. And that evening, when after the meal men and women re-enacted the day's labour in their dancing, Mingar watched with a sense of alienation and bitterness he had not known since waking long ago to find himself a cripple.

Days passed and alone in all the clan Mingar became gaunt and ill-looking. His eyes were sunken, his mood restless and foul. For his sleep was disturbed by dreams of violence and by forcing himself to stay awake in order to avoid them, he only grew more tired despite Draa's efforts to calm and comfort him. Everyone noticed his decline for most felt the lash of his tongue at some time during the day and rumours spread that he was sulking because they had thwarted his will. Indeed, it seemed to them that the Mingar they had known beside the dying lake, stubborn to the point of unreason, had returned, and they could expect nothing more from him than dark moods and bitter glances until he had come to terms with his defeat and learned to live in this new place.

Meanwhile, with the demand for firewood, the despoliation of the trees continued, the people travelling further each day as the nearest sources of fuel were depleted. The flowers for which they had named the Plain slowly faded and dropped their petals and seed-heads of diverse and cunning forms developed while the leaves and stems hardened and withered, turning brown then bleaching to straw under the sun which beat down mercilessly day after day. Slowly, almost imperceptibly, the waters receded, exposing bare mud which dried and cracked but at first the people were glad of this because they could reach the trees more easily.

Chapter 7.

After the lecture from Nygeli, Tark put more effort into making friends, especially with his peers. But it was difficult to break down the barriers of shyness and reticence that had grown up in their first encounters and the person he most wanted to speak with, Manalah's daughter, Myalah, still seemed to be avoiding him. Though he often made elaborate detours to pass by where she lived, he never caught more than a fleeting glimpse before she dodged out of sight. And it was unfortunate that most of the girls and boys tended to go around in exclusive groups rather than mixing: when forced together, a huge amount of baiting and teasing ensued. Thus on the rare occasions he encountered the girl face to face, conversations took the form of boasting on his part and barbed retort or coyness on hers.

But when Manalah invited Tark home, the two could no longer avoid one another. The invitation came as a great surprise to the boy, for while Manalah and Myenah still tended him at mealtimes, they had never taken him to their dwelling though he had visited many others in the village, a circumstance which had made him wonder if, in some way, he had displeased them. Now that the invitation had been given, he felt nervous because he knew that the whole family, including the girl, would be there.

Nor was she the only cause for apprehension on Tark's part. Manalah's husband, Gullilli, was a revered elder. Though he had taken no part in Tark's trial (for what reason the boy did not know), from the awe and respect in which was held by all the Valley people, Tark had realized early on that this man was one of the great ones of the clan, a skilled hunter who was also a renowned storyteller and healer. For one with such a reputation however, he was unusually reserved, a quality that reminded Tark of his father, although Gullilli's self-containment came from natural dignity rather than bitterness.

Tark had, of course, met and spoken with Gullilli before: he was a tall man in his prime with a steady, penetrating gaze. But it seemed to the boy that there was always a flicker of doubt in those eyes when they looked upon him, a circumstance which, real or imagined, made him inordinately self-conscious in Gullilli's presence. Now, therefore, he was filled with dread, for it seemed to him that his whole future in the Valley might depend upon this evening.

To Tark the day seemed to fly past. He and the other boys practised spear-throwing at targets, then, when they grew tired of this, they played a game of dare, taking turns to dodge while the others cast their weapons. None of the spears was really aimed to cause injury (they knew well enough that if harm came to any of them, retribution would be swift), nevertheless when Nygeli caught them at it he promised a sound beating to the first boy he caught at which they scattered though none took the threat too seriously.

After that, Tark was in no mood for games. He went to his shelter and lay down, fingering the necklace he had been given as if the answer to his perplexities lay within the smooth, polished seedcases. He wondered if he would ever feel truly at ease in this Valley, become so much assimilated into the culture of its people that he no longer remembered or cared about his own. And as he mused, his mind wandered into reminiscence of the days before he found salt until, at last, he drifted into sleep.

He was woken by the sound of a soft footfall and sat up abruptly, astonished and angry with himself for having slept, expecting to see Manalah. Instead, a slight, slender figure was silhouetted in the doorway, one that affected him in ways that as yet made little sense to him: a kind of dread and a hot melting in his loins. Yet it seemed she felt none of these complex, inchoate longings: she stood looking down on him, hands planted on hips barely noticeable in the youthful straightness of her body, and asked scornfully, 'Do all your people sleep so much?'

'I wasn't asleep, I was thinking!' he retorted, aware even as he spoke of the stupidity of such an answer when she could have been watching him for some time. 'What do you want?'

'You were asleep: I heard you snoring,' she said and then, as if tired of arguing, shrugged. 'Anyway, my mother sent me: it's close on sunset.'

Looking past her, Tark saw that this was true: the pathways just outside, the other shelters, the distant ramparts of rock, even the vegetation, were tinged with a fiery glow while what little could be seen of the sky was all red and gold. This was the time of day when families gathered to eat and the boy realized suddenly that Myalah had been sent because he was already late. Hurriedly, he scrambled to his feet and flung his cape around his shoulders, not for warmth but because it acted as a kind of shield against the feelings of isolation and strangeness that were growing upon him under the girl's cool stare.

'Come on then,' was all she said when he was ready. He followed her though the settlement and many of the folk sitting around their fires waved or called out, inquiring where the two of them were creeping off to, he with his cape to keep them warm? The girl responded with a disdainful toss of her head but Tark, cringing inwardly with embarrassment, felt the blood rush to his face and pulled the cape closer as if it could somehow make him invisible.

Gullilli's hut was unique in the Valley. It was twice the normal length for two buildings had been joined together. It had two doors on the outside and an internal partition with an open archway but a single fire burned outside because it was shared by one family. As Tark and Myalah approached, the women were already busy, roasting meat and cooking the flat cakes of pounded seeds and fruit which were prepared to mark special events such as a birth or marriage.

As the smells of baking food reaching his nostrils, Tark found his mouth watering despite his nervousness for he was hungry, having only picked at his meal earlier in the day. And when Manalah, hearing the two, looked round and smiled, the boy's trepidation all but disappeared and he felt ashamed of having made so much of the occasion.

She gestured him to sit and he shrugged off the cape, feeling a little ridiculous at having worn it on so warm an evening, while the girl went inside. The crone, Myenah, who sat by the fire to help with the cooking, cast the boy a swift, appraising glance, then turned back, the women working together in the comfortable silence of old companions, having no need for speech. Their quiet absorption in their task calmed the boy and as he relaxed, a feeling close to contentment stole over him until he fell into a reverie. The sky darkened and the flames burned brightly, sending showers of sparks flying up when the crone moved branches to ensure the meat cooked evenly. Stars glimmered then glittered white as twilight turned to night: from far away in the forest an owl-call sounded, echoing eerily against the encircling cliffs.

Tark was jerked abruptly from his peaceful contemplation by the arrival of Gullilli, accompanied by Nygeli. They sat down on the opposite side of the fire to the boy (as a minor, Tark was confined to the women's side), and with a bare nod of acknowledgement in his direction, continued what appeared to be an intense though good-natured argument audible only to themselves.

Only when the girl came outside again did the men cease their conversation and the two women stood and exhaled softly at the sight of her. She had decorated her hair with bright feathers; around her neck were strings of shells and polished seeds (Tark's hand wandered to his own shell talisman at the sight), while her body was adorned with carefully painted patterns of white clay, red ochre and charcoal, all designed to accentuate the promise and beauty of her imminent womanhood.

Meeting her gaze, which was somehow both shy and provocative, Tark realized the true significance of the occasion and all his apprehension returned at once, overwhelming him like a wave so that his mouth dried and his palms became sticky with sweat.

She sat down next to him but was careful not to make contact even with the cape he had so casually discarded. Nor would she look at him though he stole more than one secret glance at her under cover of one hand as he pretended to brush flies from his face. And then the elders, well aware of his subterfuge, exchanged swift, meaningful glances of their own.

Yet though the atmosphere was charged with expectation, the talk was all of the small, seemingly insignificant events of the day while the meal was served and eaten. Apprehension had overtaken

Tark's hunger. Every mouthful of the dry, sweet cake had to be forced down: it took all his willpower to chew and swallow it and his nervousness, despite his efforts to conceal it, was obvious to all. The women nudged each other and winked when they thought he wasn't looking and even the grim-faced Nygeli smiled though there was no malice in his amusement, it stemmed rather from reminiscence.

At last the eating was done, the bones and gristle thrown into the flames. A tense silence fell in which the crackle of green wood on the fire and the noise from other families seemed inordinately loud. Tark was so acutely conscious of the girl sitting beside him, his skin prickled; the warm scent of her made him restless and the sweat that dampened his hands broke out over his whole body: he felt at once embarrassed and exalted.

Gullilli broke the tension by rising to his feet and stamping hard, twice. At this a low wail arose from Manalah and Myenah, as if some great grief had overtaken them yet their eyes were wide and bright so Tark guessed their ululation was ritualistic rather than spontaneous. Then the elder asked 'Who speaks for this boy?' and his eyes were bent upon Tark in a steady, daunting gaze.

Unsure whether he was meant to answer the question himself, the boy licked his lips nervously: this was, in a way, more terrible than his trial. But to his surprise and heartfelt gratitude, Nygeli, after looking around as if half-expecting someone else to step forward, raised his right hand and replied simply: 'I do.'

Tark was sure the crone shook her head slightly, as if in secret disapproval, but if so, her actions were belied by what followed.

'He is not of the Valley but that is, perhaps, a good thing,' she said. 'Long ago, before we came here, it was the custom to marry outside the clan for though tongues and customs may differ, in truth we are all one people, sprung from those who came from across the sea in terror of the Night-Stalkers. And it is long past the time when Myalah should be betrothed.'

At this confirmation of his deepest hope (and fear), Tark's nervousness turned to something else, a heady mixture of apprehension and joy, though the old woman's tone was grim. But Gullilli, whose gaze had never wavered from the boy's face, said slowly, 'Time indeed, for my daughter is almost grown to womanhood. Thus it is for Tark to prove himself: when he becomes a man, she will be his and he hers, so long as the choice is pleasing to them both, that is.'

When Tani woke, the pale dawn-light, the chill of the morning air, the pangs of hunger in his belly were all hateful to him. He lay staring at the sky through lens-shaped holes in the tattered canopy of hides and it was featureless, the colour of ash. A cool wind was blowing across the flats, bearing the taint of rotting slime from the drying clay: when he licked his lips, he tasted salt. Sky, mud and water were all grey-hued; he lifted one hand and even that had taken on the same pallor, the skin dry and dead-looking as bark, the fingers thin and splayed like a lizard's.

Wearily, Tani let the hand fall to the ground. He was close to giving up his idea of finding the rest of the clan and reasserting his leadership: in the cold light of a new day, such aspirations seemed futile. Yet without them he was left with nothing save the prospect of a lonely wandering until, by chance, he came across people or perished from want or sickness. And this, after all the killing, the deaths of his companions in the mud-holes, his long journeying, was too much to bear: to have gone to so much effort, to have endured such suffering, for nothing.

It was this, which amounted to a kind of bitter resentment of the world and all that was in it, including himself, that in the end compelled him to move. The sun had risen over the horizon, flooding the land with a crystalline brilliance that seemed to strike directly into Tani's brain, making him flinch and turn away. His shadow stretched before him, undulating where it intersected footprints in the mud and with a hunter's instinct he realized that the means of tracing the others had been at his feet the whole time for the clay, which had been damp at their setting off, had dried to a rock-like hardness, marking a trail clear as a path for those with the skill to see it.

This discovery effaced his maudlin self-pity. With a renewed sense of purpose he searched for the trail, disregarding tracks with the slightest overprint. An observer might have thought he had lost his wits for he ranged back and forth on a long, zig-zagging transect of the ruined village but though his movements appeared random, in fact he was covering the ground in the most efficient pattern possible, one in which he could determine both the relative timing and the direction of the clan's exodus. When he became certain that they had left all together not more than three days before, his old malice stirred within him, lending him a vicious strength and the tenacity of a scavenger.

At last he came to a place where all the tracks converged. It was on the low terrace that marked the ancient rim of the lake and the trail led into the fire-blackened waste beyond. It was so clear, a child could have followed it. Then a feeling he barely recognized swelled within Tani, a kind of joyous relief, in part because his persistence was justified but also because this proved he was not alone. And in the security of this knowledge he allowed hunger to impinge on his senses (for he could not remember when he had last eaten), and set off to find food.

Upon the Flowering Plain each day brought change, almost imperceptible yet inexorable. The drooping grasses and flower stalks released their seeds upon the wind or let them fall to earth and then they bent and broke or were trampled into dust. At times the air was silvered by the density of seeds, each with their filaments to catch the passing breeze or to hook in the fur or feathers of animals and birds. The latter flocked to eat them for they knew this was the last bounty the Plains had to offer, the final benison of the rains, and that once this glut of fruit and seeds was over, they would fly away in the wake of the herds of plant-eaters which had already begun to leave as the grass died.

But to the Lake Clan, this was still the land of their dreams, a place of everlasting plenty: their minds denied the evidence of their senses. They gathered the dry vegetation to fuel their fires, harvested the seeds and ignored the flocking birds, the sting of dust in their eyes and nostrils, the scarcity of animals to hunt. Where getting meat had been a simple task on their arrival, game being so abundant a lone man with a spear was certain of a kill within a short distance from camp, now it was too dangerous for anyone to go out alone for fear of predators; hunting parties could be away two days and return empty-handed. Yet though the truth was plain before them, in the crying of hungry children and the gripe in their own bellies, the people refused to acknowledge the gradual withdrawal of life all around.

Mingar watched this denial of the obvious with a sardonic eye but he maintained a silence stubborn as the people's intransigence. Only to Draa did he reveal his thoughts and she was shaken by the depth of his bitterness as he railed against what seemed to him wilful stupidity. And the others, frightened by the look of grim amusement on his face, avoided him save at meal-times for the custom of sharing was ingrained in their very being though now the gifts of food to the couple were given more in fear than reverence.

Sensitive as ever to the mood of the clan, Draa tried to warn her husband that there was danger in his isolation, which was being interpreted as a kind of overweening arrogance. For at last it was dawning upon the people that this Flowering Plain might not be the place they sought after all, that its bounty was fleeting as a mirage and they had been mistaken: this land was dying as the lake had died. And their disappointment was as visceral as his bitterness. A rumour began that Mingar had brought about the change by sorcery, his will having been set against staying from the first: they had forgotten how he had led them from certain death and how they had revered him as their saviour. Some even begrudged the scant food he accepted from them for, as the dry continued, the hunters and foragers struggled to find enough and while everyone ate a little, none was satisfied.

'If you do not relent, they will turn against you,' Draa warned. 'Why not call a Council and prove your leadership as before? For they are beginning to understand that this is not the land of plenty they thought it and they blame you.'

Mingar stared at her and his eyes glowed with the light of the setting sun. 'What?' he said, and laughed. 'They have only themselves to blame. It was against my wishes they chose to stay: now that the choice proves ill, what has it to do with me? They would not listen when first we came here.'

Draa was silent. It seemed to her that he was, in his own way, as blind as the rest save that while their denial stemmed from a profound need to find a good place to live, his intransigence was due to wilful pride. And his lack of compassion frightened her for it was as if he had reverted to the taciturn, embittered man of the past who had blamed the world for the misfortune that had maimed him, allowing an accident to twist not only his body but his mind also.

'Well, woman, have you nothing more to say?' he snapped, for her misgivings were written clearly upon her face. 'Why not speak to them yourself since you understand them so well?'

Tears filled her eyes, not from his harshness but sorrow, remembering how, at the very start of the journey, he had listened to and taken comfort from her, how strong they had been together.

'Ah Mingar,' she said softly, 'have a little pity, for yourself if not me and the rest. For whatever else happens, this much is certain: if you do not help them soon, even in contempt, our people will revenge themselves upon us for all they have lost and are about to lose again.'

These words were spoken with such grave tenderness, Mingar was at once astonished and ashamed, realizing how clear-sighted she was and how tolerant: while many woman would have renounced so difficult a husband she remained steadfast, unwavering in devotion yet neither slavish nor overbearing. And seeing all at once how his stubbornness might again lead to disaster, not only for him and Draa but for all the clan, he struck his thigh in self-recrimination and said, 'You are right, I have watched the land wither around us and done nothing: no wonder they are angry. I shall call a Council tomorrow.'

By morning, everyone in the village knew of Tark's betrothal to Myalah. Many of the women teased him as he walked past and although the humour was good-natured, he lacked experience to respond in a manner that would not send them into fresh paroxysms of laughter. But others, especially those who had sons of a similar age and had hoped to match them with Gullilli's daughter, looked upon him with envy or turned their backs. And when he joined his peers it was even worse: the boys who deemed themselves slighted by Gullilli's choice were openly hostile while others he had counted as friends were strangely awkward in his presence, as if his betrothal somehow set him apart.

'What did you expect?' Nygeli asked when Tark complained of these changes. 'Her father is powerful within the clan: many hoped he would honour their family by his choice. Instead he has chosen an outsider, one moreover who is young and untried. This is against our custom though, if old tales be true, it was how things were done in the past. And yet, by choosing thus, he has perhaps avoided greater trouble. Had he chosen from within the clan, it might have caused much strife between families with eligible sons who are eager for power.' He paused, seeing incredulity in the boy's face, then continued in a tone of wry amusement, 'Of course, this means there will be sharp eyes watching for you to make mistakes, perhaps even jealous minds weaving spells to make you fail when it comes to the test of manhood. But I shall be watching too and there is no more powerful sorcerer in the Valley. Though in the end, when it comes to your trial, you will be on your own as we all were.'

Tark knew better than to ask what form the ordeal would take or when he would have to undergo it; the look in the elder's eyes precluded such inquiry. But Nygeli unexpectedly leaned forward and touched him on the shoulder saying, 'Do not worry: to me and Gullilli you have already proved yourself. For unless you possessed a man's strength of will, you could never have reached here alive.' He paused and his rather grim features softened. 'Get along with you,' he said, 'and use these last days of your boyhood as seems best. There is nothing more I can teach you.'

The boy walked away from this meeting feeling strangely downcast. Among his people the ceremonies marking the transition from boy to man were occasions for celebration: while the mysteries of the actual initiation were a closely guarded secret, there was none of the dread that seemed to characterise the custom in the Valley. For amid the teasing and baiting related to his betrothal, he noticed that people looked at him with a kind of diffidence, as if he was still a stranger: it was as if a barrier had descended between them and often they refused to meet his eyes.

This was especially true of Myenah and Manalah, his grandmother and mother-in-law to be. Whenever he encountered them, most often at meal-times (for he now ate as one of the family), he was aware that while they pretended all was the same as before, they avoided his gaze however trivial the conversation and when he tried to speak of the future, the crone would say sharply, 'It will come in its own time boy, why hasten towards it?' And if Gullilli was within hearing, he would shake his head and point two fingers stiffly at the ground, a gesture meant to avert misfortune.

Without his daily tutorials with Nygeli, despised by some of the boys and teased mercilessly by the others, Tark took to wandering alone down some of the many paths that led away from the settlement. By now he knew most of these intimately as if he had been Valley-born but there was one he had never explored because it led over a series of rock outcrops and scree slopes to the closest of the massive cliffs which encircled the valley. No-one, to his knowledge, ever hunted in this direction, game being so abundant in the green glades to be found deep within the forest yet the path, though narrow, was well worn and clear even over bare stone.

It was on the morning of the third day after his betrothal that Tark set out upon this path. He was in a foul temper having come close to blows with a boy called Matah who had resented him from the start and considered himself Myalah's rightful suitor. Tark had not even attempted to defend himself against the tirade of insults and insinuations that came from this boy and his cronies: as Nygeli had taught him, he simply shrugged and walked away with his head held high but though he had the satisfaction of knowing that this response infuriated his rival even more, inwardly he seethed with anger. His frustration was exacerbated by the fact that had he reacted with violence, the whole gang would likely have set upon him and he would have been soundly beaten for he had no friends of his own age to come to his aid.

Thus distracted, Tark had wandered far beyond sight or sound of the settlement before he realized he was on the path to the cliffs and this mistake (for he had made no conscious decision to go that way), turned his anger inward. He increased his pace without paying much attention to his surroundings, so focused was he upon his own concerns.

It was only when he came to a great expanse of bare rock criss-crossed by deep fissures that he was forced to stop and take heed of where he was. And the silence, which up till then he had been unaware of because of the turmoil in his mind, descended like a pall, muffling and oppressive. In the wastes of saltpan and desert the quiet seemed part of the landscape, crystalline in its purity; here the looming rock walls, which half-enclosed the rock pavement like an amphitheatre, made it seem unnatural.

Skin crawling with suspense, Tark crouched and looked around. Heat-haze made the air shimmer and he licked his lips feeling suddenly thirsty. Here there was no water nor, upon the expanse of stone, any shade, and he wondered why anyone should want to come here. It was bare and desolate compared with the living forest, yet the path was well trodden as if the place was visited regularly.

Uneasily, he rose to his feet. There seemed no reason to stay longer yet something held him. He stood still, listening but nothing disturbed the menacing silence and stillness except that high above the blood-red cliff, several kites wheeled and cried.

An indefinable sense of horror overcame him then and, at the same time, the air stirred, bringing a foul waft, the stench of decaying flesh. No doubt it originated from some hapless creature that had fallen down one of the gaping cracks yet it was enough for Tark. He turned and walked swiftly back down the path, trying not to betray his discomfiture by hurrying though, as far as he could tell, there was no-one to see.

Chapter 8.

The trail left by Mingar and his followers was so clear a child could have followed it unaided and Tani did not hurry. He needed time to recover from his journey and to formulate a new plan. While they would only have his word to go on, he knew he must be careful for he had no intention of revealing the truth even to the kin of those that had perished in the mud.

And, in any case, as he followed the trail, his journey became easier every day. The blooming upon the plains had spread even into the stump-forest. From the waste of mud and ash, fronds and seedlings sprouted and even some of the blackened stubs put forth tentative green shoots which gradually strengthened and spread where all had seemed burned and dead. And as the clan had found on the Flowering Plain, the abundance of food and water drew animals of all kinds, thus there was no shortage for the thin man also.

An opportunist like all his people, Tani took full advantage of this bounty which exceeded his wildest dreams of plenty. Gorging himself every day, he grew indolent, rising long after dawn, lighting a firestick from the embers of his cooking fire, walking a little until he felt hungry (which as he ate more, seemed to happen with greater frequency than before), then setting up another camp. Once a little fire was going, he would munch upon some juicy leaves or fern roots, then go hunting.

Yet even moving at this leisurely pace, at last he reached the edge of the stump-forest and the beginning of the Flowering Plain. The trail had become harder to follow because of the vegetation springing everywhere but always there was something to keep him on his way for he was keen-eyed and tenacious. And by now he had a tale prepared to make the hardest man weep, one that would mark him among the great in the mythology of the clan whilst making the boy a coward and weakling, a shame to his kin, most especially

Mingar, his father. As he walked or sat by his fire at night, Tani rehearsed and perfected his story and it seemed to him as his voice rang out upon the still air that the rocks, the sprouting trees, were listening, that the animals and birds, even owls which flew so close he could hear the sough of air through their wings, all paused to hear his tale for there was a hushed expectancy in the stillness and quiet that he, in his arrogance, attributed to himself.

In truth it was impending change that invested the landscape and all that inhabited it with tension, a kind of vibrancy akin to the charging of the atmosphere before a storm breaks. All the creatures of the night were sensitive to it except the man. And after he had fallen asleep, curled between two fires for warmth and safety, the animals crept closer, drawn to see what kind of creature this was and their muzzles wrinkled at the unfamiliar scent and the reek of smoke but they did not attack for none was hungry. And when dawn came, spreading a pale translucency from the east, they crept away to sleep, curiosity satisfied though their tension remained. For a little wind stirred the grasses as the light increased and it was dry and warm though the sun had not yet risen.

When Tani woke, the sun spread a golden light across the plain yet already there was a hard quality to it, a harsh glare which made the thin man frown and shade his eyes as he got slowly to his feet. For in addition to the painful brilliance of the sun, there was an aridity to the air that made his eyes sting and his lips go dry; an acrid taste that reminded him of the first days of the Great Dry when the lake receded and dust veiled the dying forest.

'No, it cannot be,' he muttered for as far as he could see, the plain stretched golden with waving grasses and, in the far distance, he made out a dark line of trees or bushes. Then, as he stared, he thought to glimpse a pale spiral of smoke and his heart beat faster. There had been no storm, no lightning-strike to generate fire, therefore there must be people close by.

Picking up his spear, Tani began to walk purposefully in the direction of the tell-tale plume.

Despite the best efforts of Draa and Mingar, the Council was, for their purposes, a failure. For the people refused to listen, even though they were hungry and their children thin and fractious. Here on the grassy plains the gradual desiccation of the land was more subtle than beside the lake where the falling water level was clear for all to see and they were loth to leave, preferring to blame Mingar for their misfortune than forsake the belief that their journey was ended.

In vain Mingar argued, pleaded and at last threatened them, promising a return to the want and misery they had been forced to flee but they remained unmoved, staring as at a madman or else taking pains to avoid his gaze as if they feared his passion. And when, despairing, he flung down his staff and decreed that if they were determined to sit here and starve, he would go on alone, no-one remonstrated or tried to prevent him. In the end, he walked away in disgust and Draa, her heart torn between pity and anger, followed.

'Enough!' he shouted when they reached their shelter. 'Let them stay! But I will not wait here for death. We shall go on, you and I. We have done all we could.'

Draa stood watching and tears ran down her face as he crouched in the entrance and began pulling out their few possessions. Rage and frustration were evident in his every movement, his muscles stood taut against his skin and though blameless, she was frightened to speak lest he turn his wrath on her.

'This time I will not change my mind,' he muttered, 'and we shall travel faster without those fools,' and having dragged out the grass bag, the skins they used as rugs, the grinding stones, he jerked his head to indicate that she should do the rest for so wild were his movements, his hands fumbled when he tried to tie the things together.

'Let me do it then,' Draa said quietly and he shuffled aside while she knelt in his place. Soon she rose, moving with the grace of a young woman though by the measure of her people she was already old.

While they were thus occupied, the elders sat like stones but the rest of the clan, who had watched proceedings without participating, waited for them to act. Gradually their whispering grew to a clamour for they were confused and frightened, shaken by Mingar's vehemence and his denial of their dream which they longed to cling to but, deep in their hearts, had begun to doubt.

Draa heard the noise and reached out to touch her husband's arm for he seemed oblivious to it. But when he turned towards her, she recoiled. The muscles of his face were so tense, it had taken on the appearance of rough-hewn wood, hard and inflexible, while his eyes glittered as if he were feverish.

'What is it, woman?'

His voice was harsh yet it was then that Draa realized the depth of his anguish. She looked at the noisy, seething crowd and it seemed to her that she and Mingar could do no more for no-one even glanced in their direction. His declaration had sundered them irrevocably.

Draa turned her back on the people and picked up the bundle. Mingar was still watching her but now his face was full of perplexity and his eyes had lost their febrile stare. Looking upon him, Draa was overwhelmed by love and pity but, with an effort, she restrained herself from embracing him, knowing his pride. Instead, she pulled a long strip of bark from their shelter and, with practised skill, folded it to make a fire-stick.

'Here.' She passed it to Mingar. 'Light this, then we will fetch your staff. It is time to leave.'

By now squabbling had broken out within the crowd, some of whom blamed Mingar for their misfortunes, others the Council. And the elders, who despite their fervent denials were affected by the same doubts as the rest, responded with harsh words and accusations, clinging still to their faith in the Flowering Plain because they were loth to admit their mistake. Frightened by the noise and latent atmosphere of violence, children began to scream and cry and many ran and hid, unnoticed by their parents who were too intent upon the argument to care.

When Mingar and Draa appeared, walking steadily through the crowd, the quarrelling subsided, then ceased altogether. So grim was Mingar's visage, so contained Draa's calm, they struck awe into all that beheld them. And when the people saw that he carried a fire-stick, she a bundle, their confusion and fear increased for none had taken Mingar's threat seriously, deeming the onward journey too perilous for two to attempt alone.

Mingar's staff lay where he had thrown it: he picked it up and wiped the dust off with one hand, ignoring the crowd and the elders who watched in silence. Draa stood beside him with her head held high but her eyes stared straight ahead and she did not acknowledge the frightened glances of the clan. At last Mingar settled the staff in his right hand.

'Come,' was all he said and he walked on, heading towards the line of broken trees for it was his intention to follow the river wherever it might lead.

Then at last the people realized the truth: that their leader was forsaking them and a new outcry arose in which only the elders remained silent. Some caught hold the couple's arms in an effort to stay them but these were unceremoniously shoved aside for Mingar was in no mood to compromise and Draa was focused upon him, deaf to the entreaties of those for whom she had formerly risked everything. Desperate now, the crowd followed them and the boldest walked alongside but none attempted to block their way because all could see that if they did so, Mingar would strike them down and they feared his wrath. As the two strode on, looking neither to the right nor left, so the fear and dread of the people grew, seeing they would not be dissuaded.

By the time the couple reached the ravaged trees that lined the river bank, some of the crowd had given up. But there were many left to watch as the two clambered down the ramp of trampled red earth that marked the main watering place used by the clan and wild animals alike.

When they first came to the Flowering Plain, this river had flowed high and swift between steep mud banks and the trees had been tall and green, their leaves providing precious shade for the myriad birds and animals that went to drink there. No nothing remained of those trees but torn stubs and the river had shrunk to a sluggish trickle, thick with sediment, which linked shallow pools in which trapped fish thrashed and gasped while birds and lizards preyed upon them.

Mingar walked across the cracked mud of the river bed and squatted to drink. The water was foul-tasting but he drank anyway, having no choice, then stood and faced the crowd who were strung out along the bank, watching him intently.

'Do you see this?' he cried. 'What happens when the river dries up completely?' And as they continued to stare, as if incapable of comprehending his words, he gestured violently at the ruined trees. 'What will you do for fuel and shade? Are you all blind?'

His eyes were wild and white foam bubbled in the corners of his mouth: fearing what he might do next, Draa put a hand firmly on his arm.

'Quiet, love,' she said. 'They have made their choice; we have made ours. Let us leave.'

He hesitated then, grasping his staff with such force the knuckles of his hand stood out white, turned and splashed through the water. Draa followed close behind, appalled. They clambered up the steep opposite bank and the red dirt stained their hands and feet like blood.

The crowd watched numbly as the couple walked away. Heat haze shimmered all around them, distorting and stretching their figures until they seemed insubstantial as ghosts. In silence, the people waited until the two had disappeared from view and then many of the women sighed while the men bowed their heads to hide their faces. Without Mingar they were leaderless; bereft of Draa it was as if they had lost a mother. The sun beat down relentlessly and their shadows slowly shrank but the pair did not reappear. At length the crowd trailed back to the camp, the children subdued and frightened; the men and women quiet and full of uncertainty.

The spiral of smoke rose high into the candescent sky, drawing Tani like a moth to flame. His heart beat faster at the thought of coming face to face with Mingar: the long awaited climax to all his endeavours. It was inconceivable to him that his enemy could be dead or that these might be different people to his own yet when he reached the wide area of bare earth that surrounded the huddle of shelters, he stopped. To walk across that expanse of naked ground (for it had been stripped of every blade of grass in the clan's search for food and fuel), would leave him horribly exposed.

As he stood there, a thin wailing reached his ears, a poignant keening that made him shiver despite the heat. It was the sound of grief, of mourning, and as he listened, more voices joined in until the air seemed to shudder with their ululations.

Obsessed as he was, Tani's mind was now seized with fear that he had missed his chance and this wailing was for his rival. Irrational though this was, he found himself striding towards the camp, compelled by the need to know the truth. But when he reached the huddle of shelters, there was no-one there. He stood still, listening, then followed the sound to the riverbank. Only when he drew close did he realize that many of what he had taken to be spindly tree-trunks were the figures of men, paralysed by grief.

It was the women who were wailing. Once begun, it had become compulsive, an outpouring of woe. The children began to cry also but the men stood or squatted a little apart, watching helplessly as their wives and daughters worked themselves into a frenzy. Thus it was that no-one noticed the thin man approach until he was among them and then the shock was so great, their jaws dropped and they stared, amazed. The wailing ceased abruptly and even the children fell quiet, sensing that something momentous was happening.

As for Tani, his eyes ranged over the crowd seeking one face and it was not there. Once, twice, he scanned them and, missing both Mingar and Draa, rage overtook him for in that moment, seeing how stricken the people were, he was convinced the couple must be dead. He bent and grasped the nearest man, an elder named Myall, by the throat. The ancient did not resist as he was pulled forward but there was terror in his eyes when the thin man thrust his face almost into his.

'What's happened?' Tani demanded, loth to name his enemies lest their spirits be disturbed.

A murmur arose within the crowd and many looked at one another askance for the coming of Tani so soon after the departure of Draa and Mingar seemed uncanny, like a dream or the unravelling of a tale over which they had no control. Yet the good living he had enjoyed on his journey from the lake to the Flowering Plain had changed him to their eyes: although he was still thin, his skin was smoother than before and his tremor less violent, and this too seemed strange.

'Aie, they have left us,' Myall moaned, writhing under Tani's grip. 'And now we are lost . . .' His voice trailed into a pathetic whine. 'What shall we do?'

Revolted, Tani was about to let go when the old man suddenly froze. A strange look of doubt and dismay came into his yellowed, bloodshot eyes.

'Who are you?' he cried shrilly and then, taking Tani wholly by surprise, began to flail wildly with his hands.

Astonished by this reaction, Tani let go and stepped swiftly beyond reach. That any of his clan should fail to recognize him he refused to believe: the ancient must have lost his wits. He took another step backwards, gripping his spear with both hands, and in all the faces surrounding him he saw the same doubt and a growing anger. Then he remembered those he had killed, all of whom had living kin, Myall not least for he was the father of one of those that had perished in the mud.

And for an instant, Tani was close to panic. The figures of the riteless dead seemed to appear before him. He thrust the spear forward to ward them off and although he did not know it, his eyes took on the wide, fixed stare of madness; his face was rigid so that the shape of the underlying skull was stark; the mouth drawn-down like that of a grieving child: spittle drooled from one corner.

Then those that had doubted this could really be Tani knew him at last. And yet they sensed also that he had undergone some profound experience that had altered him not only physically but to the very depths of his soul. The fit that had fallen upon him they interpreted as the trance of a wise-man preparing to converse with the ancestors and suspicion was far from their minds for it seemed miraculous that he should have returned at this moment: they were sure now that he would save them. As his breathing steadied and his eyes lost their fixed stare, the murmurs of awe and doubt changed to shouts and laughter as they began to celebrate.

It had taken the thin man an immense effort of will to gain control of himself, to push away the crowding ghosts and the guilt that threatened to overwhelm him like a mighty wave. But the acclamation of the crowd aided him and when recognition dawned at last in Myall's eyes and the old man stepped forward, took Tani's left hand and pressed it against his brow in a gesture of supplication, he knew he was safe and then he smiled.

'Tani, it is you!' the ancient exclaimed in a feeble, trembling voice. 'Have you returned from the dead? Where is my son?'

Keenly aware of the attention focused upon him, Tani's stopped smiling and gently took the old man's hand. 'Ah, Myall, my friend,' he said, speaking quietly but clearly so that all ears could hear, 'Your eyes see truly: it is I. But it has been a hard journey and a bitter one: my companions are dead and I have no tidings to comfort you in your loss.'

He paused to let these words sink in and when the inevitable wailing resumed, a feeling of evil satisfaction writhed beneath his ribs. The old man had staggered and nearly fallen with the impact of the news, now Tani detached his clinging hands and gestured the women to lead him away.

Yet while he was unaffected by the tide of grief that swept through the crowd, the thin man was careful to conceal it. As the keening rose, heart-rending, piercing, he let his spear fall and sank to his knees, bowing over so that none could see his face. From his lips came a series of groans that seemed to be dragged from the very depths of his being and he spread his hands over the back of his head to hide how his eyes watched the people in their throes, appraising and calculating when to make his move.

By its very nature, the wailing could not be long sustained. Gradually its intensity subsided, leaving the mourners spent. The women lay in the dirt, and the red dust stained their skin while the men crouched or knelt with hanging heads and arms dangling loosely at their sides. And the children, confused and frightened, sat crying quietly among them.

Tani waited until the only sound was the soft grizzling of the infants, then, cautiously, he lowered his hands and raised his head. What he saw exceeded his wildest expectations. The whole clan was prostrated by grief: he knew he would never have a better chance to impose his will upon them. And so, before they stirred, he got to his feet and picked up his spear, then descended into the river bed so that all would have a good view of him, lined as they were upon one bank.

So cleverly did he pitch his tone that all who heard were at once spell-bound: emerging from the trance-like state induced by their grief, his voice acted as a life-line, something to cling onto amid the uncertainty and emptiness which had overwhelmed them. And having practised and refined his tale so often during his journey, it came smoothly from Tani's tongue so that he was forced to hesitate or falter at times to give the impression of spontaneity.

Yet inwardly, even as he spoke with such assurance, the thin man seethed with a mixture of anger and disappointment because Mingar, the person for whom the whole tale had been devised, was not there to hear it. He looked at the crowd, sitting or lying on the crumbling bank and was filled with contempt for their weakness. Each face was rapt, the eyes blank and unseeing as the story unreeled in their minds, and a vicious edge crept into his tone because with his rival gone it seemed to him that all the suffering he had endured, the effort he had put into his fabrication, had been needless: he could have told these people anything and they would have believed him.

What Tani had failed to consider however, was the love these people still bore Mingar even though they had refused to listen to him. As the thin man described how Tark had ambushed one of his companions, spearing him in the back before fleeing, then led the rest into a clay sink, counting on his slightness to save him while they floundered and sank to their deaths, incredulity crept across their faces and some muttered doubtfully. Yet in his arrogance, the thin man was heedless of the unease growing and spreading through his audience. He told how he had pursued Tark into the desert, how the boy had mocked and taunted him until at last they came to a great cliff at the base of which a mighty river flowed though all around was barren rock and dust. There, he said, Tark sprang upon him and tried to fling him into the water churning far below but had himself fallen despite Tani's efforts to save him.

'Aie, I lay on my belly at the brink,' Tani said, 'and called his name until my voice was spent; I watched the river until my eyes blurred and it seemed I looked down upon a great writhing snake, but no sign was there that the boy was still alive. The river had taken him and there was nothing left for me to do but return to his kin bearing the sad tidings. Deserved though his death was for the shedding of so much blood, it would have been fitting to have him face the judgement of the clan. But that cannot be and maybe it is better so: were his father alive to witness and share his shame (for the crimes of the son must be partly laid upon the parent), it might have been too much.'

So engrossed was Tani in the telling and embellishment of his tale, he did not notice that with these last words the crowd's mood shifted from grief to anger. As soon as he finished speaking, an outcry arose for the whole clan was still distraught from the departure of Mingar and Draa and this speech seemed like a curse upon their memory. Like figures from nightmare, dirt-smeared, their faces marked with the tracks of tears, the women rose from the ground and rushed forward, hands clawing as if fighting an invisible web. As one they poured down the bank and the men leapt after, their eyes, like those of the women, wild and staring as if some malignant spirit had hold on them.

Tani realized his mistake at once. He had seen such eyes before, when he had urged these same men and women to kill Eeli and her children. He turned, dropping his spear in his haste, and fled along the river bed, certain that if he tried to climb out they would catch and tear him to shreds. He dared not look behind as he ran but he could hear the onrush of bare feet and terror lent him strength. Then his foot twisted under him and he fell heavily and they were upon him.

The dust rose in choking clouds as they closed in. They cried aloud their grief and anger and their high unearthly voices drowned Tani's shrieks, though these did not last long.

With every step he took away from the camp, Mingar felt a kind of joyous relief as the burden of leadership fell away. At last he was free: he and Draa could wander as they willed with only themselves to please and if they encountered other people, there would be less likelihood of trouble than there might have been with the whole clan behind them.

That first night they camped beside the river. The light from their fire glowed like a red star in the darkness of the plain, illuminating their faces so that their eyes shone like polished stones. A lizard was roasting on the coals and the smell of it rose tantalizingly into the still air. Draa reached out with a piece of stick to make sure it cooked evenly and, having moved it slightly, leaned back sighing with contentment. She did not think of the future but revelled in the moment and was glad.

Mingar, however, whilst outwardly serene, was troubled in his heart. During the afternoon he thought he had heard screams, faint with distance, from the direction of the camp. By then they had travelled far beyond sight of the place and Draa had been dismissive when he brought it to her attention, attributing it to some trapped or dying animal. As if to confirm her view, the cries had ceased abruptly and the quiet of the plain had descended again. Yet there had been something in the sound, some piercing agony, Mingar could not dismiss so easily: whatever the cause it seemed ill-omened, though he did not regret his decision to leave.

When the meat was ready, they ate in the companionable silence of soul-mates, having no need for petty speech, and threw the bones and skin into the fire. Then Draa, looking at her husband, sensed his disquiet and her contentment dissipated as she recalled his earlier passion when he had seemed on the very brink of madness. She rose and went to sit beside him, thinking he mourned his fall from leader to outcast, knowing his inner pride.

'Be at peace, beloved,' she murmured. 'They have chosen their own way: they no longer have any claim on you. We are free until such time as we meet other folk and then we can choose whether to join them or wander alone.'

'It is not that,' he said, and turned his head to stare back the way they had come. And though Draa waited long, he did not elaborate.

Once their anger and bloodlust were appeased, the people were exhausted. They lay in their shelters and slept and when they woke it was dark and the night-chill made them shiver. Then they dragged themselves to their fires for warmth but even the bright flames could not cheer them. They sat in silence, benumbed by the events of the afternoon. Only the children were active and they wandered from shelter to shelter grizzling with hunger but no-one heeded them and eventually they huddled miserably by their own fire, roasting insects on sticks for sustenance.

As the night deepened, a sense of menace oppressed everyone in camp. The adults called the children to them and gradually they congregated round a single fire, the biggest and brightest, in the hope that warmth and light would chase away the night-terror. Long past the time when they would normally have gone to their beds, they stayed there, each taking solace from the presence of others for there was something dreadful in the quiet stillness they could not name.

And then, on the very edge of hearing, the sharp-eared among them heard a shrill keening, faint with distance and tremulous, like the shriek of a mouse caught by a snake. As they listened, it grew louder and they looked at one another in terror and confusion for the sound pierced to the very depths of their being: it was the voice of death. Husbands and wives clutched at one another for reassurance; children pressed against them for comfort but there was no escape. The crying continued until it seemed to fill the night: it wrapped round the unwilling listeners like mist and they could no longer tell whence it came.

'Soon it will be over,' the women whispered while the men tried to guess what kind of creature could be responsible and how long it would last, for it was clearly in agony. And yet, beyond expectation, the cries continued until the boldest of the men suggested that they should take their spears and go to finish it off.

Yet the terror that had hold on the rest was too great to allow this. An instant outcry arose to dissuade the hunters from leaving and so they sat down again, hoping in their hearts that death would come swiftly to the wounded creature and thus restore their peace.

At last, eerily, the voice trailed into silence. The people waited, all their senses straining for the slightest sound and now the very silence of the night, the surrounding darkness, seemed full of fear, as if the cries had emanated from the substance of night itself, to haunt and intimidate the guilty. But when the stillness and silence continued, measured by the rapid beating of their hearts, the people began to relax. The children stirred and yawned, wanting sleep and the women hummed lullabies to soothe them. Only the men remained alert, staring tensely into the distance though there was nothing to see, and their skins crawled as if with fever because they could not shake off their unease.

And then, just as the women were about to carry the dozing children to bed, the noise arose again. Previously the cries had been wordless, the utterance of a mindless beast they had thought, but now it called names: -Tark, Eeli, Myee – a litany of the dead, in a voice that itself sounded like the utterance of a lost spirit, an unquiet soul wandering the night in a torment of loneliness, calling on those it had known in life.

After the traumas of the day, this was too much. Men and women leapt to their feet in panic, dragging their children with them, and ran for their shelters. They believed that to name the dead was to disturb them, wrenching their spirits back into the world of the living, therefore this calling of those that had died by their hands terrified them. Fumbling in the darkness, they grabbed whatever possessions they could find, and then they fled, wanting only to be beyond hearing of that voice crying endlessly into the emptiness of sky and plain.

Even when the stone pavement was far behind, Tark could not shake off the sense of horror that had descended upon him. The forest with its myriad scents and colours, soothing greens and browns scattered with flowers of delicate or dazzling hues, calmed him a little for by now he was at ease there as if he had been born to it. Yet it was not until he came close to the village and could smell woodsmoke and the reek from the middens, that he felt safe. Then his footsteps slowed for he did not want anyone to know where he had been, nor how it had affected him.

When he saw the settlement before him, the circles of huts with their little gardens, smoke rising from the central fire, he paused to catch his breath. Before him, the life of the Valley people unfolded as it had done for generations: a group of men, Nygeli among them, sat honing and straightening spears and no doubt talking as they worked; a band of children ran past, laughing and shouting in a game of chase while the women waved and called to them in mock chastisement from where they sat preparing food or nursing infants; others tended their patches of vegetables. It was a peaceful scene, and the boy was glad as he entered it: for the first time it seemed to him that he had come home

Occupied as they were, none of the villagers noticed the boy's arrival until he reached the central court. Then Nygeli looked round and saw him. A smile spread upon his usually grim features and he raised a hand to draw the attention of his companions. Inevitably, their eyes also went to Tark and so obvious was his discomfiture under their gaze, Nygeli clambered to his feet saying, 'Come with me, boy, for you look as if you have some tale to tell,' and led the way to his hut.

So disingenuous was the invitation, Tark found himself following automatically though he dreaded this encounter for he had never tried to deceive his mentor before. By now he had realized that the stone pavement must hold some special significance: a place so often visited that the path through the forest was kept clear, yet one he had never heard of, could only be taboo.

Therefore, when they sat down inside the cool darkness of Nygeli's home and the elder invited him to speak, Tark admitted only that he had wandered in the forest and described a path he had explored some days previously but he was uncomfortable with the deception and, worse, sensed that Nygeli sensed and guessed the reason for it. The elder was too wise to accuse or argue: when Tark came to the end of his account, he merely nodded, but knowledge of the lie acted as constraint on both of them. As soon as he could, the boy took his leave and when night came he felt his loneliness more keenly than ever because he had estranged himself from his friend and mentor and his horror of the stone pavement lingered.

Chapter 9.

Mingar remained awake long into the night, Draa cradled in his arms. It was cold and though they had spread their capes to make a bed, he shivered now and then as a slight breeze stroked his face. Yet though the chill was discomfiting, it was not the cause of his restlessness. He thought he could hear distant crying in the night but he was uncertain whether it was real or existed only in his imagination.

Thin and shrill, faint as the hiss of a dying wind through dry grass, there was a haunting quality to the sound Mingar could not ignore. Carefully, so as not to disturb the sleeping woman, he eased himself away and tucked the cover around to keep her warm. Draa moaned softly then settled back to sleep while Mingar rose to his feet.

The stars wheeled overhead as he stood listening, his twisted body as erect as he could manage, tense with concentration. And when the wailing ceased, the silence seemed to roar in his ears for the sudden quiet exacerbated the utter stillness that had descended on the plain. He could hear Draa's breathing, slow and steady as she slept and his own, more ragged simply because he was trying to keep quiet; from somewhere close by, the dry grass rustled as a rat scuttled through it. He listened and the thud of his heartbeat resounded through his ribcage and skull but the sound he sought had gone.

Mingar sighed and shifted his weight from one foot to the other, wondering at the foolishness that had urged him from his bed to listen to the cries of an animal dying far away. He turned to look the other way (though the flatness of the plain made this also seem futile, there being no more to see in one direction than another), then sighed again and crouched to worm his way back under the cover, wanting to nestle close and share Draa's warmth without waking her.

Then, just as he had dismissed it, the voice sounded again, Mingar froze for this time the cries were focused, more like words than mindless wails of fear or pain. Slowly, he rose to his feet, to listen and make sense of what he was hearing which, he now realized, must be the utterance of a human being, a man like himself, a woman or a child.

This knowledge pierced Mingar's heart, pity and compassion swelled within him yet he remained perfectly still, intent on listening. And then, incredibly, he heard his son's name, followed closely by those of his murdered wives. His heartbeat thundered in his ears, muffling the voice and he banged his fists against his head in an effort to clear it.

The sudden movement disturbed Draa's slumber. She muttered and groped sleepily for her husband, then, finding the space beside her empty, woke abruptly. Seeing him standing close by, silhouetted sharply against the sky of stars, she sat up, pulling the covers close against the chill air.

'What is it?'

He was concentrating so hard on the failing voice that the question, loud and sharp in the stillness, startled him. He swung round to face her, one hand lifted in threat. 'Silence woman. And listen!'

Draa stared then, recognizing the nature of his passion, obeyed. But though she listened hard she could hear nothing but her own breathing and the immeasurable silence of the space around them, the limitless sky and the vast plain.

Having turned back to face the direction of the camp, Mingar tried to focus as before but it was in vain: the voice had fallen silent or else was so weak as to be inaudible across so great a distance. And such was Mingar's sense of loss and disappointment, he stood as if stunned, hands clenched at his sides while the breath escaped his lungs in a deep groan.

Accustomed to his moods as she was, Draa waited patiently then, as he remained motionless, she rose and went to him. He did not move or in any way acknowledge her until she put a hand gently against his face. Then he quivered all over and, so as not to upset her, held himself still though he longed to step away and listen lest the cries sound again.

'What did you hear?' Draa said at last and though she spoke quietly it seemed to Mingar that the din made the air shudder. 'I heard nothing but a rustle in the grass.'

'There was a voice,' he answered sadly. 'It cried the names of the dead and lost into the night: my wives and the thin man's companions and Tark. But Tani it did not name, as if he or his ghost had returned. Only . . .'

His voice trailed into silence for he was reluctant to speak aloud his thoughts, a terrible possibility forming in his mind even as he spoke.

'I don't understand.' Draa withdrew her hand and looked intently into her husband's face. In the starlight the sharp angles of the underlying bones and the weathered texture of his skin lent his visage the impassive appearance of wind-sculpted stone, his eyes glossed and unreadable as pebbles, his mouth a shadow-filled crack. And yet behind this façade, his mind was in turmoil.

'We must go back.' He turned abruptly and, crouching, gathered their scant possessions, stuffing them into her grass bag with frantic haste while she looked on appalled. There was such ferocity in his every movement she was afraid to intervene and when he thrust the things into her arms, she did not resist. Only when he settled his spears on his shoulder and strode away without pausing to light a fire-stick or any word of explanation did she move, springing after with a wordless cry of protest and clinging to his arm in an effort to stay him.

'Get off!' He knocked her aside and she stared, sprawled on the ground where she had fallen, as he hurried away without a backward glance. Then, realizing he would not wait, she scrambled to her feet, snatched up the bundle and ran after, little spurts of dust rising at each footfall. When she reached him, she put out a hand, tentatively, to restrain him then, remembering, withdrew it and fell into step beside him. At length she said deliberately, 'Mingar, talk to me: I am your wife, not your enemy. Are you sure what you heard was real?'

He did not answer at one nor turn his head to look at her but she sensed his resentment from the heat that emanated from his body. It took all her courage to speak again. 'Mingar, please!'

Then at last he stopped. His face was stern and she quailed under his gaze but her own did not waver. And he sighed, relenting, and reached out to touch her with an unexpected tenderness that filled her with fear, not for herself but him.

'It was Tani,' he said quietly. 'He alone knows what has happened to my son. I must find and speak with him before he dies.'

She stepped away from him aghast, he hands going involuntarily to her mouth to hide her distress. 'Tani, how? This makes no sense, my love. Surely you were dreaming?'

'No!' His voice was suddenly terrible; his eyes glittered like those of a madman. 'It was him! Who knows what those fools have done?'

With that he turned on his heel and strode away even faster than before, as if it was his desire to leave her and her doubts far behind. She stared for a moment, then hurried after, terrified not so much by what he might find (for she did not believe the thin man could be close), but of what he might do.

The people had scattered over the plain, each family thinking only of themselves. Some, glimpsing Mingar and Draa in the distance, hid as best they could or ran away. In the moonlight, the two seemed insubstantial as ghosts and that they were striding towards the voice the rest were fleeing exacerbated the people's terror.

So intent was Mingar upon his purpose, he was oblivious to the furtive scurrying in the dark but Draa saw and recognized her kinsfolk and was greatly perplexed. She was tempted to call out to them but the oppressive silence and strangeness of the night constrained her. When she realized that the people were trying to conceal themselves from her eyes, that they were afraid, her trepidation increased and she forced herself on though the breath sobbed in her throat and her legs shook with the effort, so swiftly did Mingar make his way.

They were close to the deserted camp when Mingar veered towards the river. In the starlight the pools were dark and flat while the mud was a pale, glimmering grey in which cracks formed sharp black lines. The ruined trees cast maimed shadows across the river-bed and Mingar paused on the bank, staring down. It was the place where he had last spoken to the clan and when Draa joined him she was too wise to speak or otherwise disturb him. They stood together on the brink, the dry earth crumbling beneath their toes and the interplay of light and shadow confused their eyes.

Then, from almost directly below, they heard a faint noise, a scuff of movement. Had the silence been less profound, no human would have heard it: as it was, Draa and Mingar looked at each other askance, to confirm that what one had heard, the other had too. Then Mingar leapt down into the channel for he had seen something solid entangled in the shadows. He approached it cautiously, staff held before him, then dropped to his knees with a groan. A rat scurried away along the river bed but Mingar took no notice of it. A foul stench of blood and entrails hung in the air.

Draa climbed carefully into the gully and knelt beside her husband. 'What is it?'

Mingar did not answer but leant forward to examine what he had found more closely, Then he sat back on his heels with a sigh. 'They have killed him.'

His tone was heavy with defeat: Draa did not need to ask of whom he spoke. She too leant forward and then she saw that what she had taken for a twisted root sticking out of the bank was a foot, bent at an impossible angle from the stick-like limb to which it was attached. The rest of the body was trampled and torn almost beyond recognition and she looked away quickly for the sight brought memories of Eeli and Myee's deaths crowding in. But Mingar sat as if stricken, head bowed: he reached out tentatively to touch the corpse and snatched it back instantly. 'He's still warm!'

Draa shivered: the oppressiveness of the night was compounded by the closeness of death. With an effort she rose to her feet. 'You were right: it was his voice then,' she said and her words seemed to come from far away, cold and remote: she was hardly aware of having spoken. And then, realizing what this death meant to Mingar, who had lived in hope that Tani knew of Tark's fate, pity overwhelmed her.

'It is finished, my love,' she said and now her voice was full of compassion. 'You can do no more. Let us leave.'

For a moment, it seemed he had not heard her. Then he raised his head and his eyes were blinded by tears. 'Why did they have to kill him?' he asked. 'It was my fault for deserting them. Now we shall never know what happened to my son.'

'Come away.' Draa spoke with great urgency for all around there were rustlings in the grass, the pad of stealthy feet as scavengers drawn by the stench of death closed in. She caught hold Mingar's shoulder and shook it to rouse him from his reverie. Her fear was infectious: he clambered heavily to his feet, using his staff as a prop and looked all around and it seemed he had shed his grief for his face was stern and resolute.

'Maybe the others know,' was all he said and he climbed swiftly out onto the bank, Draa close on his heels. Far in the east, a faint lightening of the sky heralded the dawn and as they walked back to camp, the carrion eaters swarmed to feed.

Whether it had to do with his last conversation with Nygeli, Tark never knew but next day he was summoned by the Council. This time Myenah was absent and a feeling of foreboding assailed the boy as he stood before the elders for their faces were grim. He wondered if they knew of his visit to the stone pavement and what his punishment would be. But their purpose was otherwise.

For what seemed long while, no-one spoke. Tark stood motionless, head erect, his eyes focused on a leaf hanging maybe a hand's breadth from the top of Gullilli's head for his prospective father-in-law sat in the place of honour at the centre of the semi-circle. He could feel the collective gaze of the elders upon him, unwavering and penetrating, and realized suddenly that this was some kind of test. He waited, determined not to move or speak until prompted. Despite all Nygeli's teaching, he had no idea what was expected of him.

The silence became excruciating fand Tark, at first daunted, grew resentful. Surreptitiously he eased his weight from one foot to the other. Gullilli's eyes narrowed and he said flatly: 'Maybe this boy is not yet ready. Is not patience the first sign of wisdom?'

Tark stiffened, realizing that his foreboding was justified: this was the day of his initiation. Therefore, even as a protest rose to his lips, he bit it back, guessing that the rites among these people would be a test of maturity rather than mere physical strength and endurance. Whatever happened, he must control himself or fail.

Indeed, it seemed that Gullilli's question was but part of a proscribed ritual. One by one the elders spoke and each denigrated Tark, questioning his abilities, his integrity, his loyalty to the clan. All the time their eyes were bent upon him, watching for the slightest reaction, anything that could be interpreted as weakness.

To keep his countenance, to appear indifferent as insinuation turned to studied insult, was harder for Tark than any physical ordeal they could have devised. Pain he could endure to some degree; hunger and thirst he had already experienced on his journey, nor, after the cataclysm and long pursuit, was he easily frightened. But this deliberate and cruel provocation assaulted the very centre of his being, the core of pride that had kept him from despair so often in his short life and it took all his willpower to restrain himself, to remain outwardly calm while inside he seethed with rage. Despite his best efforts his hands clenched until he felt the nails dig into the palms and he tried to think of something else: the way Myalah had looked at him on the night of their betrothal; the spear he was halfway through making and how the patterns in the grain changed as he honed it, anything to divert his mind from the hateful, haranguing voices.

The sun broke out as the early morning mist dissipated and then Tark realized how carefully this encounter had been planned. For while he was in the direct glare of the sun, the elders sat in shade. As the sun rose, physical discomfort exacerbated his woes: since entering the Valley, he had rarely been exposed to its full force and now the heat seemed to press upon him, shrinking and burning skin grown soft and supple in the dappled shade of the village.

And now the nature of the ordeal changed. Gullilli stretched out his right hand, palm downwards, and the haranguing ceased. The silence that followed was so tense it seemed worse in a way than the provocation because the elders stared at Tark as if to probe to the very heart of him. He felt sweat break out all over his body, making him itch as it evaporated but still he did not move though he longed for the test to end.

As time dragged on, measured by the thudding of his heartbeat in his ears, Tark began to tremble with restrained passion and his teeth clenched until the cords of muscle in his jaws and cheeks stood out, hardening the planes of his face so that the underlying shape of the skull was delineated. It was the visage of a young man, not a boy and the elders noted and approved, Nygeli especially because this justified all his efforts.

But while to some degree the Council had achieved its purpose, the trial was not over. Gullilli rose, picked up a spear that had lain beside him and led the way into the trees, the elders rising and following without a word. Tark stood watching until they were swallowed by the cool darkness of the forest then, feeling acutely self-conscious, went after simply because he could not think what else to do. In fact this was a test of courage and boldness: had he waited for their return or gone back to the village, he would have failed, to the derision of all. But he did not feel brave as he followed them, he felt humiliated, hating their power over him.

All such resentment vanished however when he realized where Gullilli was going. The elder had taken a narrow, winding path at first, little more than an animal track overhung by low branches and trailing lianas so the walkers were often forced to stoop. Deep into the forest it led and soon, despite his bushcraft, Tark lost all sense of direction for the sun stood almost directly overhead and the canopy was so dense, only stray shafts of light penetrated it. But then the path joined another, broad and well trodden and the forest was lighter, the trees taller, affording glimpses of the encircling cliffs between clumps of foliage. And with a sick lurching in his chest, Tark realized they were heading towards the stone pavement he had visited the previous day.

There was, of course, nothing to prevent him turning and going back to the village. But this was his home now and he could not countenance failure. He tried to reassure himself with the thought that the elders would not have embarked upon the test unless they considered him worthy, and forced himself on.

All too soon from Tark's point of view, the forest lightened, indicating the treeless space beyond. Gullilli's pace slackened a little and the boy was thus able to catch up without any of the elders realizing how he had lagged behind.

But though the procession slowed, it did not stop and Gullilli paced steadily from the cover of the trees onto the bare rock. It was so hot in the stone amphitheatre Tark found it painful to walk there but the elders seemed indifferent to the blazing sun. The red cliffs wavered in the heat and the figure of Gullilli became stretched and oddly insubstantial as he strode into the very centre of the stone pavement, leaping over the cracks as though they were of no account though many were wide enough for a man to fall into and so deep the sun's rays could not plumb their depth.

The elders stopped at last and formed a semi-circle as before with Gullilli in the centre and Tark standing directly opposite, between the arms. There was utter silence and the faces of the old men were stern and unreadable. The boy's heart quailed as he wondered what new ordeal they had devised for him yet though sweat dripped into his eyes, he kept his hands clenched at his sides. From far away, the piercing call of an eagle broke the silence but nothing moved within the candescent ring of rock.

Then, as at an invisible signal, all the elders except Gullilli sat down on the baking stone. He stood straight and tall, his shadow pooled at his feet and his eyes looked keenly into the boy's as if he were pleased with what he saw.

'Thus far you have conducted yourself as well as any boy born in the Valley,' he said. 'But one thing remains to test: your loyalty to us, your adopted clan. For as no-one can foretell what is to come, so none may say 'this will never happen'. One day you may have to choose between us and the ones you come from, the people of the Lake. And we must be certain of your choice ere we welcome you as our own.'

So measured and reasonable was the delivery of this speech, Tark did not fully understand its implications. Frowning, he took a step forward, hands clasped before him, and said in an aggrieved tone, 'But I've already made that choice: this is my home now and my people are far away!'

From the disapproving expressions of the others it was clear he had breached some code of propriety by speaking but Gullilli raised one hand as if to quell any outcry and said calmly, 'Words are easy:

action will be the proof of it. Are you ready, boy?'

There was challenge in his tone and like a fish to a baited hook, Tark rose to it. Eyes narrowed, he nodded and lest this be insufficient, said firmly, 'Yes, of course.'

It was only then, as Gullilli bent his head in acknowledgement, that the boy's gaze fell on Nygeli, who sat next to the leader and there was such compassion in the ancient's scarred visage that Tark was assailed by a sudden, deep misgiving. But Gullilli turned abruptly, saying, 'Come, then,' and Tark followed him further across the stone pavement, the others rising and coming after at their own pace.

The cracks intersecting the rock grew wider as they progressed but those too broad to step across were bridged by slabs of stone. The elders walked over without pause but Tark paused often to look down though there was nothing to see but smooth rock dropping vertically into darkness. A foul waft of decay came from some of the clefts where, he assumed, animals had fallen to their deaths.

They were but a spearthrow from the towering cliff when they came to a crack greater than all the rest. It was spanned by a single tree trunk. This was no wider in girth than Tark's waist and bowed alarmingly in the middle. The branches had been trimmed but otherwise it was unfashioned in any way and from the smoothness of the bark, Tark guessed it had been put there very recently. A few paces on the other side of the chasm lay a flat boulder upon which a wooden dish had been set.

Seeing this, Tark's foreboding deepened. Up till then it had seemed to him that this ritual had been embarked on almost impulsively, now he realized this was not the case: it had been planned to the minutest detail. But there was no time for regret. Gullilli strode across the log without hesitation, apparently unfazed as it bounced beneath his feet. Once he was on solid rock again, he called in a commanding voice: 'Tark, son of Mingar, come!' and then the boy had no choice but to set foot on the flimsy bridge though all his instincts warned him to go back.

The cleft yawned, a foul reek emanating from the darkness below, the putridness of decay mingled with the smell of cold, damp places the sun never reached. Tark edged cautiously along the trunk and it shuddered alarmingly; he stopped and waited for it to be still again and then he began to tremble for with every heartbeat he felt the precariousness of his situation increase and his resolve falter. He thought he could feel the eyes of the elders bore into his back and in his imagination their laughter mocked him and he was crushed by the ignominy of failure.

Then the deep-seated pride that had aided him in the past came to his rescue, compelling him to step forward in the belief that it would be better to die in the attempt than live ever after as a known coward.

The tree trunk slipped beneath his feet, threatening to roll and the boy realized that safety lay in swiftness. Emulating Gullilli, he hurried across the remaining span, the supple wood bouncing at every step: as he leapt for solid rock, the log rolled twice then came to a stop, quivering along its length like a live thing.

Gullilli had been busy at the stone table but on hearing the boy's light tread behind he turned, the shallow dish in his hands. His face was impassive as he held it out. 'Drink.'

The dish held a dark opaque liquid, the sight of which made Tark aware of thirst. He almost snatched it from the elder's hands and gulped it down. It was bitter to the taste but he drank to the lees without hesitation. Only as he handed back the dish did his relief turn to misgiving for his stomach heaved suddenly and a strange dizziness overtook him. Gullilli's face seemed to swell and shrink alarmingly.

'Good.' The elder's voice was oddly distant and Tark found he had to concentrate hard for his mind reeled as if he were fever-struck. 'Listen well, boy, and obey, and it will soon be over. But first you must be blindfold.'

He bent behind the boulder and when he straightened there was no dish but a long strip of supple hide in his hands. Tark did not resist as this was tied firmly over his eyes. For one thing, it was taking all his willpower to stay upright, for another the shutting out of the blazing sunlight was welcome. But as the draught took effect, dazzling multi-hued lights seemed to whirl and coruscate around him and it made no difference that a tiny part of his brain knew these must be inside his head because he was unable to control them and they made it even harder to concentrate on Gullilli's voice.

'Listen!' Gullilli commanded, and then Tark heard (or thought he heard), the desperate whimpering of some person or creature brought to an extremity of pain or fear. It seemed to come from directly in front and he swallowed hard to keep from vomiting for it reminded him of how his mother and sisters had died. As it increased slightly in volume and intensity, he took an involuntary step backwards, forgetting the yawning chasm in his distress.

'Listen!' Gullilli repeated and his tone now was harsh and pitiless. 'You hear an unwelcome stranger, one who came uninvited. He, like you, claimed ignorance of the Valley, but he is a grown man and will pay for his folly. Indeed, his misfortune is your chance to prove yourself beyond doubt. He lies before you on the stone, tied and helpless. Take his life and you become one of us, bound by blood. Refuse and we shall throw you into the cleft and your name will be forgotten.'

Even through Tark's nausea, these words were stark and he shuddered. Then his wrists were taken in a firm, cool grasp and he was pulled forward until his toes touched the stone table.

'Here he is.' Gullilli guided the boy's hands down until they encountered something warm and soft. It shrank under his touch and he tried to pull away but the elder's grip was relentless. Feeling a quick pulsating beneath his palms, Tark realized with horror that his hands were being pressed against a man's torso, just below the sternum. It was the prisoner's heartbeat he could feel and then such revulsion coursed through him, he gasped 'No - I can't do it – let me go!'

'That is your choice.' Gullilli's voice was heavy with disappointment. 'But think well before you decide. Once made, the decision cannot be revoked: there is no going back.'

This speech seemed to reverberate strangely in Tark's head and for an instant he thought it was his father, Mingar, speaking and that he was back by the lakeside before the cataclysm, arguing over the best time to leave. And because of this, it was a while before he realized that the dreadful whimpering had ceased. Beneath his hands the beating heart had steadied a little and the flesh no longer recoiled from his touch, as if the man had lost all hope or else was simply resigned to his fate.

'Choose!' Gullilli released Tark's wrists yet rather than snatch them away from the body as he would have done only moments before, Tark did not move. He felt a curious affinity with this unknown man, lost and alone as he had been and, through the horror of it all, a righteous anger began to seethe within him though he knew himself to be as helpless as the victim trussed on the slab.

He sensed movement beside him, then his right wrist was taken in a talon-like grip, his hand lifted and something hard pressed into it. His fingers closed upon it automatically and he lifted his other hand to help define and identify it. It was a polished wooden stake, no longer than a woman's digging-stick. One end was sharpened like a javelin and realizing its significance, he froze.

'To make a clean kill you must hold it in both hands.' Gullilli's lips were so close to the boy's ear, the elder's breath stirred his hair. 'Choose the spot between the wings of the ribcage and strike hard.' He paused then added deliberately, 'One blow will be sufficient if your heart is resolved.'

Tark heard him step away, leaving the boy alone with the captive. He reached down tentatively with his right hand, keeping the weapon, which he had no intention of using, in his left.

When his fingers met warm skin and flesh that no longer cringed, Tark knew that this killing was beyond him. He traced the man's sternum to the hollow at the base of the throat, then bent close to where he judged the head to be. Though not aware of it, he was trembling from the effects of the draught and nervous strain but his voice was steady as he murmured, 'Whoever you are, don't be afraid. I won't hurt you. I also was a stranger here but I was only a boy so they spared me. This is not the way of my people.'

The body beneath his hands went rigid for a moment then a voice hissed furiously, 'Fool! Use your head, boy, and strike! But be sure to use both hands upon the slaying-stick!'

Tark had spoken from the heart without anticipating a reply. He snatched his hand away, shocked beyond speech by this response and his mind reeled for the voice was somehow familiar. He recalled his father saying 'When a man's body fails him, he learns to use his head' and was tempted to whisper Mingar's name save that the possibility that he could be bound upon the stone was unthinkable.

'Did you hear me?' The voice was barely audible yet compelling. 'If you hesitate longer, they will cast you into the crack. Do it for me if not yourself!'

In his confusion, it did not seem strange to Tark that a stranger could know so much of Valley customs. Instead he wondered what Gullilli and the others had done to bring the man to such a state he longed for death and pity wrenched the boy's heart.

'Do you wish to die?' His whisper was so faint it is doubtful whether the stranger heard for he hissed suddenly 'Do it before it's too late!' and then, as if the effort of speaking had used his last strength, groaned deeply.

Tark shuddered. The wooden stake in his hand seemed unreal; he fought to make sense of the whole situation and could not for his thoughts slid away even as he grasped them.

'Strike!' Tark never knew if the command came from the prisoner or sounded only within his head. As if in a dream, he ran his fingers down the man's sternum, encountering the thickened skin of an old scar halfway down, until he came to the bottom of the ribcage and could feel the rapid beating of the heart beneath. Then he withdrew his hand from the living flesh and moved it to the killing stick, holding the point directly above the place, maybe a finger's breadth below the base of the sternum.

The man gasped, 'Now!'

Tark struck.

Chapter 10.

With dawn, the courage of the Lake Folk returned. In daylight the night-terror seemed no more than a dark dream; their blood-guilt for Eeli, Myee and their children mitigated at last by Tani's death. As if drawn by a single will they made their way back to camp for in the panic of the night much had been left behind, objects which while not necessary for daily life were nonetheless precious: a shell from the lake, a grinding stone passed from mother to daughter over generations, a carved wooden dish that had been a betrothal gift, things significant in memory and irreplaceable. And, too, out upon the bare plain in little family groups or couples, they had felt isolated and vulnerable, had longed for the companionship of the camp. Waking from unquiet slumber to find themselves separated from the clan, fear crept over them, the terror of being lost, and seeing the line of despoiled trees which marked the river (which for most was further away than they expected), they hastened towards it and, in doing so, joined with others as their paths converged.

Then, as their shelters came into sight, the returning people saw something else. Two figures, stretched beyond human dimensions by shimmering heat haze, were also walking towards the huts, heads held high. The taller was obviously a man because he bore a spear bundle on one shoulder; the other a woman for she carried the bag ubiquitous to all women of the tribes. Only gradually did it become evident that the man's body was twisted, that his gait dragged slightly, and then at last they knew him. With cries of joy and relief, the closest began to jog, as if fearful that the couple might sprout wings to fly or else turn invisible and thus elude them.

The two had, of course, seen the approaching figures from far away yet though it had been their intention to seek out the clan, both were assailed by a strange apprehension. Looking all about they found themselves surrounded and when many of the people began to run towards them, they were dismayed; each sought the other's hand and then they stood still and waited, each taking comfort from the presence of the other.

Once they were certain that this was indeed Draa and Mingar however, the people hesitated. This enabled those furthest away to catch up: soon the couple stood in centre of a staring, silent crowd. Face to face with the man who had left because of their obstinacy, and now returned unlooked-for, they were daunted and more than a little afraid, guessing that he would not condone the murder of Tani even though the thin man had been his enemy. Some looked guiltily at their hands and feet and many, whose skin was bloodstained, tried surreptitiously to rub the marks away.

Mingar looked at the hollow faces, recognized the need in the eyes of his people and it seemed to him that he had come full circle: they might have been at the lakeside again, at the very start of their journey. Pity and contempt vied within him for a moment, then he remembered why he had wanted to see them again. Fixing the closest, a young man called Memi, with his gaze (and his eyes seemed to blaze so that those held by them could not easily look away), he demanded: 'Who killed the thin man?'

It was customary that the dead should not be named yet many trembled at his tone. But the young man, who was only a little older than Tark, tilted his head as if answering a challenge and said 'You should be glad, Mingar, not angry. He had nothing but scorn and hatred for you and your kin, therefore be thankful he is dead.'

At these words, many of the bravest in the crowd raised their voices in agreement but more were quiet and avoided Mingar's gaze. Then Draa, sensing that the truth was within their grasp yet might be lost forever if the people were frightened or antagonized, broke in gently but firmly, 'We are not angry, but we miss our son. We hoped the thin man could tell us of his fate. Did he speak of Tark before he died?'

A low wail broke involuntarily from many of the women and the young man's lips tightened as if he were reluctant to say more. But for Mingar these things seemed to confirm his worst fears: the light faded from his eyes and he bowed his head murmuring, 'So he is truly lost to us, the last of Eeli's children, and all my hopes were in vain.'

Though he did not weep nor wail, the crushing weight of his grief was clear for all to see: he seemed to age before their eyes as if his life-force was ebbing at every breath. And Draa also seemed stricken, her head drooped and her hands hung loosely at her sides: the grass bag dropped to the ground. But then Memi said, 'He may still be alive: the thin man said only that he fell into a great river and was swept away. Maybe he swam to safety for he was a good swimmer. Do you not remember how we used to play and race in the waters of the lake? He was boldest and swiftest of us all!'

Into the minds of all the listeners, for whom the great lake had been at the very centre of their lives, memories crowded in at these words: the splash of water mingled with children's laughter as they frolicked and dived, slick and lively as eels while the men fished far out where the waters were met by sky and the women sat on the shore, weaving reed baskets and talking with one eye on the youngsters lest they come to harm.

Draa pictured children playing in the shallows. They scooped water in their hands and threw it high into the air, catching the sun's rays in fleeting rainbows. In the far distance, dark flecks were all that could be seen of the fishermen standing tall and straight in their narrow craft with net or spear in hand. Then one boy broke away from the leaping group of children and, with a shout and a wave, plunged into the water and began to swim with hard, fast strokes, straight out towards the centre of the lake. The other children ceased their play to stare after and some swam in his wake but these soon gave up and turned back while the boy swam on, never deviating from his course nor slackening his strokes. Soon his head was no more than a small dot then it was lost altogether against the broken, shimmering surface of the water.

This picture was so clear and bright in Draa's mind, it came as vision rather than memory: as far as she could recall, Tark had never swum so far or so swiftly. (Though he had often dared others to race him to the boats, they had never done so for fear of incurring their fathers' wrath). And since dreams and visions were highly regarded among the tribes both for foretelling the future and understanding the past, she was filled with hope. She needed no proof: she knew certainly as if he were standing beside her that Tark was still alive.

She raised her head and met the gaze of the young man who had inspired her vision: they exchanged a smile of perfect understanding. Then, loudly and clearly, speaking as if to him but in reality addressing the whole assembly, she said, 'You are right, Memi: it's too early to give up. Tark is still alive: I feel it in my heart. Therefore we must find this river for he will be somewhere along its reach.'

The simple, fervent conviction of this speech acted upon the hearers like cold water on the face of a sleeper. Many in the crowd even shook their heads and rubbed their eyes as if awakening from slumber and when they saw Draa's face, alight with hope, her eyes shining with the ecstasy of her vision, they felt the horror and grief of the night slough away like a shed skin and began to talk excitedly, trying to recall the thin man's exact words, wondering how far it was to the place where the boy had fallen.

Only one man seemed unmoved. Mingar stood silent and downcast. And knowing him of old, Draa did not seek to rouse him at once for she had learned patience through the long years of the Great Dry. Instead she moved to embrace and thank Memi, then, speaking directly to the crowd, she said, 'The journey does not end here after all: we have tried to make our home on the Flowering Plain and the rains have failed us again. But where there is water there is life. We shall set off in search of this river and this time we shall not rest until we find Tark. Eh, and there may be others of our clan there also. Beside such a river must be many places to settle and there we shall make our home.'

These words were spoken with the certitude of prophecy and even ancient Myall, who was craning his head to catch them, clapped his hands in delight. And then Mingar raised his head.

Whatever grief had burdened him, compounded by the manner of Tani's death, Mingar had, by a supreme effort of will, pushed aside. His visage was stern as he looked upon the people yet recognizing the need in their thin, worn faces, seeing the hope that flickered in their eyes, hope that he could quell or kindle with a word, he no longer despised their fickleness, their weakness. He understood at last that the killing of Tani stemmed largely from shame because they had turned against him, Mingar, much as he had assumed the leadership beside the dying lake in an attempt to assuage his own guilt. And it seemed to him also that perhaps they had saved him. Long had he anticipated and dreaded an encounter with his enemy; now, recalling the thin man's eloquence, how he had been able to use words to entrance and beguile, how he had been cunning yet subtle, a liar none could accuse, Mingar was glad in his heart that he would never have to face that keen and malicious mind again. A rare smile broke out upon his face and his hand sought Draa's.

'Together we are strong; scattered and wandering alone, each is vulnerable,' he said. 'Let us travel as a clan as we began. This place is no home: it cannot sustain us. We shall follow this river in the hope it leads to another and we will not stop until we come to the great river the thin man spoke of. Then we shall have water and food at hand, more than we could find upon the plain.'

There was such joy at this declaration, an impromptu dance began and as more joined in, clapping and stamping, the dust rose in a red-gold haze, first around their ankles, then half-way up their calves, then to their knees and thighs and at last waist-high. Then Mingar lifted his hands for many of the children had begun to cough and choke and he wanted everyone fit for the journey.

So the people returned to their shelters exuberant and hopeful, sure that with the return of their leaders all would be well again. Draa shared their optimism for she felt the sense of security experienced by any returning exile, a deep contentment in the presence of kin and friends. She sang softly as she entered the shelter and when Mingar came in she put her arms around to hold him. He submitted quietly to her embrace, leaning his head against hers. Then, weary from the exertions of the night, they lay down and slept.

Between the effects of the draught and the horror of the killing, Tark's memory of his initiation was dislocated and incomplete. Thus it was only on the following morning that he was able to appreciate the true nature of his achievement for he woke in Gullilli's house with Myalah sleeping beside him. As a man, the little hut he had used before was denied him: it was the custom for newly-weds to build a place of their own, one large enough to house themselves, their children and any aged relatives that might need care in the future. With Gullilli as father-in-law, Tark's status was high among the Valley people and the site chosen for the couple was a coveted one, close to the spring yet still within the village, under the very eaves of the forest.

Now, as he watched the dawn light strengthen through chinks in the woven walls of the house, Tark felt both excited and pensive, the first because of the swiftness of his rise, the second because of the manner by which it had been achieved. A lattice of light fell across Myalah's shoulders, accentuating the smoothness of her skin, the delicate bone structure beneath and picking out a thin plaited cord around her neck. From it hung his wedding gift to her, the shell bequeathed to him by Draa in his mother's name, and a pang went through him for Eeli had been the last woman to wear it. He had not yet told Myalah the full history of the talisman lest she be dismayed yet now, thinking of the man he had slain, he shivered, realizing suddenly that his life was but the latest link in an ancient continuum.

'You've a grim face for the first morning of your manhood.' So lost was Tark in his reverie, he had not noticed Gullilli enter the hut. Now as Myalah stirred in her sleep, he felt suddenly defensive.

'I was thinking,' he retorted.

'Ah.' The elder's eyes glinted with amusement. 'On how big to build your house so that it will shelter all the grandchildren you will give Manalah and me?'

Tark did not reply.

The Lake Clan set off from their camp on the Flowering Plain rested and full of hope. Their leaders were restored to them, the thin man was dead and they had a clear path to follow: the river. Though in places the water was no more than a sluggish trickle threading pools where the channel was deepest, it was drinkable. Moreover, they knew that where there was water, there would also be food: they did not fear the way ahead.

Even Mingar was affected by the general mood of optimism.

He had slept deeply and come to terms with the demise of his enemy while Draa had risen and gone round the camp, reassuring and encouraging the people for whom she had become a kind of talisman. Patiently, she listened to their gossip and the warmth of belonging filled her so that when she returned to Mingar, she was content.

It was just past dawn when they left. The sun breached the horizon, a blood-red orb which spread a ruddy light over the plain, turning the broken trees beside the river the colour of flame. But as the sun rose higher the red hue faded and the people turned their backs on the cluster of shelters and the place where Tani's bones lay. To Mingar it seemed that the omen of the bloody sunrise had been fulfilled and their time of fear and hardship also lay behind them.

They walked until midday, sometimes on the banks, sometimes on the dry mud of the river bed, and then they came to a clump of trees. These provided welcome shade in which they drank and sat down to rest and eat. Once the sun had passed its zenith, they continued their journey refreshed and though, at day's end, they were still within hunter's reach of their former camp, they were not disheartened for all understood that they were held to the pace of the slowest.

At the end of the second day's journey they reached the confluence of their river with a smaller tributary. Although the lesser channel was dry, reeds grew thickly within it. The tubers were good to eat and their lush growth meant fresh water was not far beneath the surface. But more than this, Mingar was encouraged by the simple fact of the two watercourses joining: it seemed proof that they were heading the right way.

And yet, despite the abundance of water and food, there was no sign of people in this region. The marks in the soft mud at the margins of the water were all of birds and four-footed animals and looking across the flat plains beyond, there was no thread of smoke from a cooking fire: the landscape was empty of human habitation.

As when they had entered the Flowering Plain, Mingar was concerned at this though he tried to conceal it. But Draa was quick to notice. 'Have faith my love,' she reassured him. 'There is nothing for us behind. The river will sustain and guide us to a new place and maybe Tark will be waiting there.'

For Tark, the days following his initiation and formal marriage to Myalah passed in a blur of activity. Not only was there a hut to build but the couple had received many invitations to elders' hearths, all of which had to be fulfilled. Those first nights they slept in Gullilli's house and it was to this that Myalah attributed her husband's coyness for while Tark was kind and gentle towards her, the marriage had not been consummated.

'Be patient,' Myenah said when, embarrassed and ashamed, the young woman sought advice. 'Customs differ: maybe among his people sex is a private matter. Wait until you have your own place, far from peeping eyes and listening ears. And remember, you are a woman: it is as much for you to seduce him as he you.'

With this Myalah had to be content and in truth, the couple were so tired at the end of those first days, they fell asleep almost as soon as they lay down on the bed that had been set aside for them. For there were small trees to be felled for the frame of the new hut; saplings to be trimmed for poles; branches stripped and woven through the uprights to form the walls. As to the roof, Tark had decided upon the kind of thatch used by his own people which meant the frame needed to be stronger than was usual in the Valley where bark, large leaves and the animal-skins were tied on in a patchwork to keep out the rain. And in addition to this work, there were all the usual tasks of gathering food and carrying water, crafting tools and weaving baskets though Myalah already possessed a fine wooden dish: that was the mark of her womanhood.

During the day, while he was occupied with the hut, Tark seemed happier than at any time since arriving in the Valley but in the evening a brooding, troubled look overcame his features whenever he thought himself unobserved. Often whilst listening to one of the elders relating a tale, his eyes became unfocused and his mind would drift away until some pointed remark brought him back to himself. Then he apologised for his distraction, which he attributed to weariness.

'Myalah's demands too much for you, eh lad?' Nygeli quipped

one evening. 'Or is it the other way round? Better ease up: you've a whole lifetime ahead of you. For her sake if not yours!'

Such remarks had become common since his marriage and they hurt Tark deeply for he felt his failure like a wound. But even as he responded with the kind of flippancy expected of a newly-wed, something in his old mentor's tone resounded in his memory like an echo of the past. It transported him to the terrible moment of indecision during his initiation when the prisoner beneath his hands had begged for death: he recalled that even then the voice had seemed familiar. He stared incredulously at Nygeli but the old man met his gaze with an artlessness that made the idea growing in Tark's mind seem ridiculous. The thing was impossible: that the whole ritual was based on trickery, that it could have been Nygeli acting the role of victim. And yet the man he had slain had been scarred across the ribs as Nygeli was scarred . . .

From habit, Tark's hand sought his talisman, Draa's parting gift, for comfort; missing it, he felt suddenly lost and terribly alone though he was surrounded by friends. And it seemed that Nygeli understood for he said kindly, 'Better go to her then and sleep for I can see you are weary without having to listen to our talk. What is important to the old seems irrelevant to the young I know, though sometimes there is wisdom in it. And it is already late: she will be waiting.'

When Tark reached the half-built hut (his feet had strayed that way though he and Myalah were still living with her family), he stopped and stared at it with something akin to hatred. The plaudits heaped upon him since his initiation, the kindnesses he had received from his wife and her kin, were bitter to him because in his heart he knew it had not been through courage or loyalty to the clan that he had succeeded, but fear of failure. And though he had begun to doubt the veracity of that experience, his guilt would not be assuaged because he had struck in the belief that he was slaying an innocent stranger.

The moon was almost full and the roof-struts of the hut were stark against the lambent sky. Tark shivered for a chill breeze stroked his skin like the fingers of a ghost and a voice seemed to whisper softly: 'When a man's body fails him, he learns to use his head.' Then as he stood rigid, waiting for he knew not what, he thought to glimpse a slight, furtive movement inside the hut.

At first he ignored it for the stillness of revelation was upon him: he saw suddenly that there was another way. In the same instant, he understood why he had come to resent this hut, symbol of his future in the Valley: that future was one in which his children would grow up in the belief that the murder of strangers was not only necessary but right, something he could never condone but was forced to accept. Unless, of course, he left before his unhappiness turned to something more sinister.

'Tark!' Normally he would have recognized Myalah's voice among any in the Valley but so distracted was he and so low and urgent her tone, his mind reverted to the past: he thought Draa was speaking and because this was impossible, it seemed to him that her spirit had come to warn or guide him and he moved towards the sound like a sleepwalker.

'Tark.' As he entered the hut, the voice changed, becoming soft and enticing. Such was its power, he let himself be guided by it until his foot came against a pile of leaves and grass. This had not been there earlier and he stopped, confused. Then a hand grasped his wrist, gently but firmly, in an attempt to draw him down upon what he realized at last was a bed.

'Myalah?' His voice came out as a hoarse whisper though even as he spoke, his eyes were adjusting to the darkness and he saw the smooth line of a thigh and the curve of a breast. 'Myalah – what are you doing here?'

His trance-like state shattered, he did not bother to conceal his surprise and disappointment and she shifted abruptly from what was meant to be a seductive pose, sitting up and seizing his arm with both hands.

'I was waiting for you of course!' she answered fiercely. 'This is our place, isn't it: we can do what we like here? Or don't you want me anymore?'

Something in her tone, a plaintiveness beneath the anger, struck Tark to the core. Up till then he had been ambivalent towards Myalah, seeing her as a childhood friend, sometimes irritating and yet a trustworthy companion in all kinds of mischief, whilst at the same time being in awe of her womanhood, the burgeoning ripeness of her body and the grave tenderness that was sometimes in her eyes when she looked at him. In both cases he had failed to see her as a person in her own right, someone capable of thinking, feeling, even doubting as he did. Now, all at once, he realized how he must have hurt and shamed her by his selfishness and he felt his face flush even as he tried to pull away.

'I can't,' he said lamely. 'You don't understand. It's not your fault.'

She leapt to her feet without releasing her grip and the moonlight fell across her head and shoulders. Her eyes glittered, every muscle of her face was taut.

'You're right!' she spat. 'I don't understand! What's happened to you? I thought you were pleased by our betrothal, that you wanted me as your wife. You were happy before, weren't you?'

He knew he could break her grip with a single blow, turn on his heel and take to the forest, but it was not in him to do it. Trapped, he stared at her and the tension between them seemed to shimmer in the air.

Her brow creased at last and she frowned. 'It's since that day, isn't it?' she said slowly. 'When you became a man? They made you do something against your will and you don't like it.'

The keenness of her perception shook Tark though he should have expected it from Gullilli's daughter. He shook his head slightly but she saw the change in his eyes and a note of scorn entered her voice: 'Fool! Haven't you worked out they're all tricks, the tests they put you through?'

That she should mock him and at the same time fuel his doubts was more than Tark could bear. With a violent jerk he twisted free of her clinging hands and stepped towards the doorway. Myalah did not move but her voice followed him. 'What will you do then? Run away like you did from your own people?'

He had intended simply to walk away but this he could not ignore. Hands clenched into fists he swung round to face her. His aspect was so wild, Myalah was afraid though she stood her ground and did not cower or flinch as he stepped towards her.

'You know nothing about it!' The words burst from him before he had time to think; he stood before her and trembled with emotions he could not have described, still less comprehended. Anger and sorrow were mixed with frustration and desire: he understood only that his world had disintegrated into a jangling confusion of thoughts and feelings which made no sense. 'How could you, stuck in this valley all your life? You've never even met someone from outside before because anyone who comes is killed by your father and his friends. Do you think that's right? They made me do it and it could have been my father or uncle or someone else I knew: whatever they'd done to him, he begged for death. It was awful: I don't want to do it again, ever. That's why I'm leaving. I'm sorry, Myalah.'

'Tark, you can't!' Even as he put a hand belatedly to his mouth, having said too much, Myalah's anger dissolved in a rush of love and pity: there was no doubting his anguish. She stepped closer but he evaded her touch.

'Leave me alone!'

'Tark, listen,' she pleaded. 'Those things that happen in the ceremonies, none of it's real! Don't you think that if a stranger had entered the Valley, we'd all have known? They try to frighten you in order to test your courage. Everyone's talking about how brave you were, that you did better than many Valley-born boys. One of the elders must have pretended to be a stranger and if you shed blood, it wouldn't have been a man's. Think about it, Tark, it couldn't have been! Please!'

He stared, torn between doubt and dawning certainty then, in a voice that did not seem his own, said slowly, 'But even if it was a trick, it makes no difference: I believed it was true. I killed a man because he didn't come from here. He wasn't an enemy: he was a stranger, like me. Don't you see? One day someone will come, perhaps my kinsman or friend, it doesn't matter. I'll be expected to slay him just for entering the Valley. And I won't do it again: I can't. It's wrong!'

'Is that it then?' Her voice shook with exasperation. 'You'll just walk away after all we've done for you? You're my husband, Tark: does that mean nothing? And anyway, you can't leave. There's no way out of here except the river. And if you manage it, you'll break the oath you swore to the Council and that means you can't ever return. If you do, you'll be killed.'

'The river brought me here, the river will take me away,' he replied. 'Forget me, Myalah, wed a Valley man instead. You'll be happier then.'

'No!' she wailed. 'It's you I want. If you're leaving, I'm coming too.'

'Don't be stupid.' He was backing away from her even as he spoke, shaken by the depth of her passion. 'You've never lived outside the Valley: you'd die. Stay here with your people, where you belong.'

He turned abruptly and strode into the darkness between the trees. She stared after for a moment then, silent as a shadow, followed.

The Lake Clan fell once again into the rhythm of travelling, a rhythm that, after a few days, was natural to them as breathing. Long ago, all their kind had been nomads and only the discovery of the great lake had stayed them. Now, with only a vague idea of their destination, they were strangely content for the slow passage of the ground beneath their feet brought its own satisfaction and by keeping to the river, there was always water and food available. They moved steadily, never hurrying, resting out the midday heat and those who had begun to sicken in the camp on the Flowering Plain grew stronger, the children more lively. To them the journey was an adventure with something new, a rock that glittered, a strange animal track, to be discovered every day.

Draa and Mingar, highly esteemed since leading the clan from the dying lake, were now venerated with a respect that verged on awe. Even the few who were jealous of the couple's power, acknowledged their strength and sagacity. And these, though they might doubt the wisdom of the journey, said nothing, telling themselves that if all went awry then blame would fall wholly on the two leaders and then the rest would pass judgement on them.

Travelling at the same steady pace every day, few noticed the landscape change around them for their focus was the river whose waters were the source of life not only to them but all the creatures of that place. But those who looked beyond the dead tree or fleeing animal when they went to collect firewood or hunted for meat saw that the savannah of the Flowering Plain had given way to stark desert: baked earth and salt pans which shimmered in the heat haze like pools of rippling water.

It was flat, this land, so that the eye was easily deceived when it came to judging distance. What appeared to be a distant line of hills might be a dune less than a man in height; a stunted thorn-bush might loom like a great tree, mirages arose frequently, reflecting the line of vegetation that marked the river's course so that it seemed another river flowed where there was, in fact, empty desert. Even lizards and insects struggled to survive there and there were no people save a few wanderers who crossed as swiftly as they could or else left their bones to bleach in the sun and be scattered by the wind.

Although he was careful to conceal it, Mingar was profoundly disturbed by the desert. He had expected the land to become greener as they followed the river downstream, not more arid. Deep within him a secret terror grew that the river would fail as the lake had failed, leaving them stranded. When he looked in the eyes of his people and saw their hope and faith, his heart quailed and all his old doubts and fears re-surfaced: he withdrew into himself and took to walking ahead of the rest so that if, one day, he rounded a bend to find the river bed dry, he would be first to know though in his imagination he never went beyond this moment because the consequences were terrible.

Draa, who shared these fears but likewise would not admit them, watched her husband with increasing concern while the rest simply regarded his apparent diffidence as part of his nature, something to be expected of the wise and great.

The river however, though it sometimes diminished to a trickle and once plunged underground, emerging half a day's walk later in a deep welling pool at the base of what would be, in times of flood, a cascade, did not fail. And in the far distance the monotonous line of the horizon was broken by a dome-shaped feature, the eroded root of an ancient mountain range. Gradually, over days of walking, this grew larger until it dominated the landscape, resolving itself into a mass of hills the colour of dried blood which, though it appeared low because of its extent must, Mingar realized, tower high above the plain. And though the rest looked upon it without trepidation because, like any landform, it was simply something to be traversed or skirted when they reached it, he was affected by a vague disquiet, a kind of dreadful anticipation not of the place but of what he might find there.

Chapter 11.

Tark knew he was being pursued. But so tumultuous was his state of mind, he did not pause to look back. He strode almost blindly along the winding paths until he came to the track to the river and then his pace increased. Myalah followed and although at first she kept to the shadows, she realized quickly that he was either unaware of, or had chosen to ignore, her presence and then she walked openly upon the trail, less than a spearthrow behind.

They were more than halfway to the river when Tark slowed. To anyone watching it seemed as if he were suddenly unsure of the way though the path ahead was clear, dappled by moonlight. In truth, it was a faltering of resolve that stayed him, an overwhelming sense of futility. From the moment he turned his back on Myalah he had forced himself to concentrate on the way, the waiting river and the dry lands that lay beyond but the faint sound of her feet on the path behind had worn at this willpower as water wears at stone. He thought of how his clan had longed for a place like the Valley, green and bountiful; how he had been accepted by Myalah's people; that she had chosen him above all the youths she had known since childhood. All this, now that he was about to reject it, seemed infinitely desirable and it was already his: he had earned it by passing the test of loyalty, a trial in which, if his suspicions were correct, he was free of guilt since he had not really killed anyone.

As these thoughts seethed, his pace slowed even more. Though he had believed he was slaying an innocent stranger, if it was all trickery then surely all this agonizing was pointless? And if Myalah was right in this (and the more he went over the strange dialogue between himself and the 'victim', the more certain he was that it had been Nygeli lying on the slab), it might also be that he would never have to fulfil his oath for the likelihood was that no-one else would cross the desert in his lifetime.

His feet dragged to a halt at last and he stood with his head bowed, hands hanging loosely at his sides in an attitude of dejection. He felt weary to his very bones now that his sense of purpose had faltered; he longed for nothing more than to lie down and sleep. But this far from the village the forest was dangerous: predators lurked in the shadows and snakes and stinging insects were common. He would have to return to the safety of the hut.

So distracted was he, he had forgotten Myalah was behind him. Thus, when he turned and saw her only a few paces away, he started visibly and stared.

She was watching him steadily, standing straight and still in the middle of the path and a shaft of moonlight fell across her. In that pale radiance her body seemed almost to shine and her eyes glittered while in the hollow of her throat the shell talisman gleamed as if a fragment of the moon hung there.

'As your wife, am I not of your people now as well as mine?' she asked. 'And, since that is so, it is my right to go with you to any place and for any reason. I do not think so lightly of you as you seem to of me, Tark.'

So unusual was the gravity with which she spoke and the calmness with which she regarded him, Tark was taken aback. He stood dumb, gaping stupidly and she tilted her head and smiled.

'I know how hard it has been for you, living here,' she continued. 'For you are right: if you came now, a stranger, they would kill you. And that I could not bear.'

He shook his head, not in denial but in a kind of mental anguish he had never experienced before or imagined. Most painful was the irony that while he wavered, her resolve should have strengthened. And he was shaken by her sagacity which was that of a mature woman, not a girl.

'I – ' he began then, seeing the certainty in her expression, held his tongue, resolving never to tell her that he had, in fact, been on the way back to the settlement. And he realized suddenly that if he had returned, he would, in time, have grown to despise himself for his cowardice. Every morning he would have woken dreading that this was the day he would be called upon to slay some hapless wanderer who had strayed into the Valley. He could see himself in time becoming embittered like his father and friendless.

'Tark.' She stepped towards him, frowning. 'I know it will be hard for us outside the Valley but we will find a place, somewhere, where we can live happily. Perhaps we will come across your kin, who knows? For those that fled the Night-Stalkers long ago it was the same: none knew where they would come to or what they would find yet see, here we are!'

This speech, as she had intended, reminded Tark that in truth the Valley people shared the same ancestry as the Lake Clan who had also enjoyed a life of ease and plenty before the Great Dry. And so, instead of arguing, he was forced to acknowledge that she was no more likely to succumb to the hardships of the journey than he. Looking into her face, steadfast and trusting, he felt a thrill through the very core of him: he could no more have denied her than cut off his right hand.

'Come then,' he said thickly, 'if you are sure of this.'

They walked together along the path in the dappled moonlight and only the night-hunters of the air marked their passing.

Despite Mingar's foreboding, the Lake Clan drew steadily closer to the range of hills and he made no attempt to lead them any other way. The river led there and it had become more than a simple watercourse in his mind. It was his road and, because of Tani's hints, almost an obsession. Whatever might lie ahead for him, as portended in dreams and omens only his eyes saw, nothing could shake his belief that the river would lead him not only to the truth of Tark's fate but also to the place his people had yearned for since the beginning of the Dry. In this landscape of blood-red rock, greyish-pink dust and dry earth, he longed for forest, not the thorny, half-desiccated scrub of the desert but the luxuriant growth he remembered from his youth. And while here there was no hint of any green thing except at the river's edge and, as it grew closer, the range was revealed as a barren waste of stone and scree, his faith was unmoved.

It was, however, a belief shared by no-one else, not even Draa who had used the mystery of Tark's fate to rouse Mingar from despair. She did not, however, voice her doubts because as the range rose before them, forbidding in aspect, daunting in its sheer size, the mood of the clan changed. The journey along the river bank had so far been easy but this mass of red rock was so alien to anything they had encountered before, they were afraid.

Draa hoped secretly that when they came to the foothills, the river would go round rather than through them. And to try and make this true, she avoided looking at the range as much as possible, walking with downcast eyes or chatting with the other women to keep her mind from what lay ahead.

But, inevitably, as they progressed, the ground rose around them. Shelves of friable sandstone mounted along both sides of the river, forming slopes that were shallow at first but steepened gradually, forming cliffs that were sheer and high in the distance. Beyond these loomed the main mass of hills, formed of contorted strata which varied in hue from blood-red to fawn. The rock was deeply fissured and in some of the cracks stunted trees and thorn bushes grew.

Walking as was their habit beside the river, the implications of this changing landscape were lost to most. Their concern was the welfare of their children and old folk. But Mingar was sharply aware that the flat space between the river bank and the base of the slopes was gradually lessening. For as the cliffs grew higher they began to converge, forming a steep gorge.

A hard choice now lay ahead: whether to stay close to the water in the hope that there would always be enough space to walk and camp beside it, or to climb the slopes and follow the river's course from the cliff-top. An attempt at the latter now would be more scramble than climb, hard for a woman bearing an infant yet not impossible. But beyond these slopes lay the range itself.

Unable to make up his mind, Mingar continued to lead the clan along the river's edge and tried to ignore the gradual shutting out of the sky as the valley narrowed to a canyon. Daunted by the cliffs, the people drew close together and the children looked fearfully about them, sensing their parents' trepidation. And though trees and bushes grew thickly in places, the ground was scoured by a recent inundation and this increased the travellers' unease because there was no escape should the river rise.

They made camp and spent an uneasy night longing for dawn.

All were hungry for there were no animals to hunt in this place and the river ran too deep and swift for the men to fish from the banks. And in the depths of the night a new terror came upon them: showers of stones fell from the cliffs above, the result of tiny landslides set off by the abrupt change in temperature from baking heat to freezing cold. By chance, no-one was seriously hurt but many were cut and bruised and all were frightened for it seemed to them that the land itself was warning them to go back.

Next day, what Mingar dreaded most happened. The platform upon which they walked narrowed until they were forced to go in single file. No more than a ledge it became and the old folk and young and those that were timid-hearted, clung to the rock wall and edged along, trying not to look at the water flowing swiftly but a step off the brink. At last even this petered out to a tiny, crumbling shelf only a child's foot could have trodden. There was no choice but to go back.

They returned in silence to where they had camped but no-one was prepared to spend another night there, so they went even further back, stopping at last where the valley sides were relatively shallow and the floor was wide and flat. Here, tired and hungry, they made camp, fractious children squabbling while their mothers set up brush shelters and their fathers went to fish from a broad sandy beach beside the river.

Mingar sat on a boulder and watched the activity with a kind of weary admiration for his people's stoicism. He knew they would expect him to choose a course around the range for the sake of the infants and old folk but his obsession would not permit him to forsake the river, even for a few days. And suddenly, as if a voice had spoken to him, he realized what he must do: venture on alone until he had discovered what lay at the heart of the mountain range. Then he could return here to find his people rested and lead them round the hills without the awful uncertainty that would otherwise haunt him, the anguish of not knowing.

But when he suggested this to Draa, she was aghast. 'Were the stone showers not enough?' she exclaimed. 'Let us stay here and rest for a day or two, then leave this place forever. Tark must be somewhere else. There is nothing in the hills but bare stone. You cannot go: we need you here with us!'

He looked at her sadly and shook his head. 'Ah Draa,' he said, 'can you not hear yourself? Use your mouth to better purpose. Look at the river: it is broad and swift and deep: where does all that water go? Not into a barren desert surely? Somewhere close is the green place we have dreamt of and I must find it. For was it not I that made us stay beside the dying lake until it was too late?'

'It was not your fault!' she cried, for his face was stern and set and she knew herself powerless to dissuade him. In fear and exasperation, she sprang to her feet and walked away to join the women who were gathering food beside the river.

Mingar watched as she pulled reeds for their succulent roots, laughing with the others as if nothing was wrong. The light of the setting sun glistened in the water streaming from her hands and arms and turned her skin the colour of flame. It seemed to him that she had never been so beautiful or so desirable and sudden doubt overtook him. Perhaps she was right: it would be madness to attempt the mountain alone, risking death for a wild and baseless dream.

And then, just as his resolve faltered, a young man approached. It was Memi and he trod the ground with a light, firm pace. A large fish hung from one hand, its scales shining red and gold in the sunset, in the other he held his spear.

'This is for you and Draa,' he said, laying the fish on the slab beside Mingar. 'This is a good place: we caught plenty.'

Mingar thanked him distractedly for beside Memi he felt old and weary, the aching of his twisted body (which he had grown to accept as the price of living), more acute. He looked into the young man's eager face and it seemed suddenly unfair that his own son should have run away instead of being here to look after him. He grimaced in an involuntary spasm of bitterness, wanting to be left alone.

But to his dismay, Memi lingered though he no longer seemed at ease. He eased his weight from one foot to the other, his hand clenched and unclenched around the spearshaft while his gaze roamed anywhere but Mingar's face. And realizing the young man was preparing himself for some planned speech or action, the elder forced himself to wait.

The silence stretched between them, the women crouched beside their fires and the smell of cooking rose into the air. At last Mingar's patience broke for he was tired and hungry.

'What do you want?' he asked.

'I heard you and Draa arguing,' Memi said uncomfortably. 'Don't go into the hills alone. Take me with you. I am strong and Tark was my friend. Please!'

'Meaning I am weak?' Mingar growled but Memi continued, 'We can do it, you and I, but it will cause trouble if you go alone. Everyone will think you've deserted them and they'll quarrel until a new leader is found. Even Draa will be powerless to stop it once you are gone. But if I am with you it will be as if the whole clan is a part of it, don't you see? Then they'll be happy to wait here and rest until we return.'

There was wisdom in this though Mingar was loth to acknowledge it. He nodded then said reluctantly, 'There is some truth in what you say but this will be no easy journey and there may be no returning.'

'Easier for two together than one alone,' Memi replied, and his eyes shone.

That evening Mingar called the clan together and told them of his plan. Most were relieved at the prospect of a few days' rest but Draa was tight-lipped and her eyes rested anxiously upon her husband for she had not forgotten his dread of the mountain and feared that if he went there she would never see him again.

That night as she lay stiff and unresponsive in his arms, Mingar tried to comfort her with tender words and caresses. 'At least I will not be alone,' he insisted, 'and unless one of us ventures there, how shall we know where best to go? And if I am proved right and the river leads to the green place we long for, better to float down knowing what lies ahead than to take to the water in ignorance.'

'Float!' she exclaimed. 'Is that your plan? If we stripped every tree in this place and pulled every reed, we could not make enough craft to bear all of us. This is madness!'

'The strongest can hold on and be towed,' he answered stubbornly. 'We have found a way this far, we cannot give up now.

What's happened to you, Draa? Where is your faith?'

He felt her shudder but she did not reply and he did not know what more to say. Silence lay upon the camp, the river rushed past and stars wheeled overhead yet the two lay wakeful, each constrained by fear for the other. And when her tears dropped onto his arm, it took all Mingar's self-control to keep still: they seemed to burn his flesh like fire.

As soon as there was light enough, Mingar and Memi set off into the hills. They carried only one spear apiece, their skin capes cloaked their shoulders and each had tied a pouch containing some of the reed tubers about his waist for there was little hope of finding food or water on the bare slopes. All the clan had gathered to see them off but while Draa had helped Mingar make ready, she would not or could not look him in the eye as he bade farewell and her face was haggard and grey in the cold dawn light.

Once the camp was out of sight Mingar's cares seemed to fall away. His tread was light and firm as Memi's despite his dragging foot and he felt young again and strong. An ancient travelling song spilled from his lips as he walked and Memi glanced at him in astonishment. It was as if the old Mingar, the man he had been before the accident, had returned.

But the broad shelves they trod grew ever narrower and steeper. At length they were forced into single file and each kept his free hand upon the rock face for guidance and security. Soon they were high above the river. The place where the clan had turned back was visible as a narrow slot in a landscape of bare rock and still the strata beneath their feet steepened until they were forced to scramble rather than walk.

Having spent their lives upon the flats where a ridge of sandhills was the highest feature of the landscape, this experience was new to both men. But while Mingar, who was leading, moved with a swiftness which at times was almost reckless, looking about often to gauge their progress, untroubled by the drop into the gorge which grew more precipitous with every step, Memi clung to the rock with both hands and kept his eyes fixed upon his companion. Fear of falling bathed him in sweat and he left his spear far behind so as to free both hands. Only pride and respect for Mingar kept him from giving up and when an eagle flew out unexpectedly from a ledge just above their heads, he cried aloud in terror while Mingar laughed from joy at the bird's effortless flight.

'If only we had wings, eh Memi?' he exclaimed. 'How easy it would be! We could traverse the whole range and follow the river to its end and still return to Draa and the others by sunset.'

Mouth dry, limbs trembling, Memi could only grunt in response and Mingar looked round in surprise. When he saw the state of the young man he was perplexed: after his eagerness for the venture, it did not occur to the elder that he could be afraid.

'What is it?' he asked. 'Are you sick? Where is your spear?'

'I needed both hands for climbing,' Memi stammered, his eyes fixed on Mingar's face so that he would not see the drop into the chasm. 'I'm sorry. I didn't know it would be like this.'

Then, looking deeply into the young man's eyes, Mingar understood at last and pity overwhelmed him. 'There is no shame in being afraid,' he said kindly. 'All men fear something though they may keep it secret. It is in how he faces his fear that a man reveals his true mettle. You have made no complaint and have followed me despite your terror: that is something to be proud of. But I will force you no further. Return to camp and say I sent you with a message for Draa and no-one will think badly of you.'

Memi swallowed hard then, with a great effort, looked back the way they had come. The precipitous drop, the steepness of the path they had already climbed, made his head reel and his stomach lurch. Groaning, he pressed himself closer against the rock and waited while his heartbeat steadied. To go back down alone seemed infinitely worse than going on. Through gritted teeth, he muttered, 'I'll stay with you.'

'When we reach the top, we'll rest,' Mingar said, 'It cannot be much further.' And he turned and clambered on with Memi toiling close behind.

Although it seemed to the young man that the nightmarish climb lasted an age, the sun was barely halfway to its zenith when they reached the cliff-top. Memi flung himself gratefully on the flat rock surface while Mingar turned slowly, his eyes noting every detail of the landscape spread before him.

They were on a massive plateau which was cloven by the gorge from which they had climbed. There was an eastward tilt to the whole massif which was composed of reddish sandstone, the strata forming stripes of varied hue and thickness. Some of these were eroded into fantastic shapes as if wind-tortured trees had been petrified, some had formed spikes and pinnacles, while others had simply weathered smooth. Round stones were scattered upon the surface and these too were a cause for wonder because they varied in size from pebbles to boulders yet all exhibited the same perfect sphericity. Many of the largest had been hollowed out by the actions of wind and water and could, Mingar thought, be used for shelter if the need arose. Towards the west, the massif formed a dome as high again, Mingar estimated, as they had already climbed, but the way looked far easier than the cliff: a steady clamber to the summit.

They rested briefly and ate sparingly of the reed tubers. As far as they could see there was no sign of any living thing, no hint of green nor any movement save a speck of shadow which belonged to a great bird of prey wheeling high above, perhaps the eagle they had disturbed. It fleeted across Mingar's mind that somewhere within the bird's range there must be a supply of food sufficient to support it and this was enough to send him to his feet. He was sharply aware that unless they found water, they had but the remainder of the day to search, then they would have to turn back. And after the effort of climbing from the gorge, he was in no mood for failure.

Memi followed without complaint as Mingar left the cliff edge and began to climb the great slope that rose to their left. The sun was high and the two soon began to suffer from the heat but they set their teeth and struggled on. Thirst quickly became a discomfort, then a torment for they had only a few of the reed tubers left and no hope of finding water in this place of bare rock. And yet, though the climb seemed interminable, they moved steadily up the dome, bent against the slope and the fierceness of the sun's rays and gradually the sun sank and its fierceness diminished. But this made little difference to the pair because the heat radiating from the stone was intense as ever, fanning their faces and bodies until it seemed to them that if there came a time when they could stop and straighten, their skin would crackle and split like a chrysalis.

It was close to sunset when they reached the summit of the dome and here at last Mingar stopped. His limbs shook with weariness and without his staff to lean upon, he would have fallen. Memi, despite his youth and strength was in no better state: his skin, like Mingar's, was grey with dried sweat, his eyes bloodshot and his lips cracked and black with sunburn. Exhausted, he sank to his knees on the bare stone and hunched over, his hands trailing loosely at his sides. Then his nostrils twitched and he snuffed the air.

'I can smell water,' he said, in a voice distorted by thirst.

Here, on the apex of the massif, the rock was criss-crossed with narrow crevices, some of which had weathered into deep hollows that at this hour were filled with shadow. There was no sign of water anywhere, and Mingar looked closely at his companion, worried that the heat had turned his wits.

'The river,' he said, after a long silence. 'It must come from there.'

'No, no!' Memi shook his head violently and crawled to the nearest of the hollows. 'Give me your staff.'

With great reluctance, Mingar handed it over and Memi probed the depression in the rock with the butt end. To the astonishment of both the hole was deep, more than an arm's length and when he retrieved the staff, the bottom quarter was wet. Lying on his belly, scooping out handfuls of the water and sucking it from his palm, Mingar felt weak with relief. When he had drunk his fill, he rolled onto his back and the stone was warm against his skin, the air cool at last for the sun had dipped below the horizon and the sky overhead was a deep translucent blue: soon the first stars would appear.

'Who would have guessed there could be water here?' Memi said joyfully. And then he was silenced for looking out for the first time across the line of the gorge, he saw shadow where no shadow should have been and it seemed to him that he looked upon trees.

'It cannot be,' he murmured.

'What?' With an effort Mingar sat up and his eyes followed the young man's gaze. Yet because of the swiftness with which twilight deepened to darkness, he also could not be certain of what he saw save that the texture of it was different to the bare rock, multiform and soft. A strange anxiety gripped him and his hands twisted together as if in conflict for it seemed to him that what he was looking at must be the fulfilment of part, if not all, his dreams.

Stars glittered in the sky and the two sat in silence, their eyes fixed on the landscape below. And then the moon rose, turning the gorge to black shadow in which the river could be discerned in places as a silver thread. In that lambent light there could be no more doubt in the travellers' minds: what they were looking at was part of a forest.

After that the night seemed interminable to Mingar. His mind veered between hope and trepidation and he could find no peace. Only when a pale glimmer in the east heralded the dawn did he sleep at last, sitting hunched with his knees drawn up to his chest, his cape wrapped close against the night chill. But such was Memi's weariness that his head drooped to his chest almost as soon as the moon had cleared the horizon and he fell asleep where he sat, slumping eventually onto the rock which was still warm from the day's heat.

Memi woke first. He looked first in the direction of the forest, frightened it had been illusion, a trick of the moonlight. But it was still there, darkling in the pale dawn light and he gazed at it in wonder. He rose to his feet so as to improve his view and, in doing so, roused Mingar.

'What can you see?' the elder asked sharply, for in the broad light of day he thought the forest must have been part of a dream. But Memi did not answer. Even as he watched, the distant landscape had grown gradually diffuse as mist formed above the river and rose to wreath the trees. This happened with such slow inevitability it seemed to the two that they were indeed caught in some kind of spell: they stood rapt as the mist flowed up the slopes towards and around them and the sun dimmed. Only then was the spell shattered for the air grew chill and moisture condensed on their hair and skin so that they shivered.

'So this is where the water comes from,' Mingar said at last, speaking with difficulty because his teeth were chattering. 'There must be more then, all along this side of the dome.'

'Maybe.' Memi clutched his cape close about his shoulders and stared into the mist in the direction of the forest. 'But now we have found what we sought, should we not return to camp with the news? Then we can devise a way to reach it.'

Mingar looked at him as at a well-meaning but misguided child. 'Go back?' he asked incredulously. 'No, not yet. To glimpse a few trees is not enough. The river is swift and deep and we have old folk and children with us. And does not your heart yearn to see more ere we return with the tale of what we've found?'

Moonlight had given way to the translucency of dawn when Tark and Myalah reached the forest's edge. The river ran before them, broad and swift, stretching from the bank beneath their feet to the base of towering cliffs of sheer red sandstone. Tark judged these were even higher than the cliff he had fallen down and he saw at once that Myalah was right: they were unscalable. And even if it had been possible to climb them, there was the water to cross first.

He therefore turned his attention to the river which was, in its own way, little less daunting. It was more than a spearthrow wide (and a skilled spearmen could cast a distance of three hundred feet), and though the surface appeared smooth at first sight there were ripples and eddies within the flow; lines of bubbles and standing waves marked where obstacles lay submerged, streaks and swirls where currents met and merged. And the water itself was dark and opaque, brown from tannins washed in from the forest, heavy with sediment carried from distant deserts and savannahs where flash floods stripped the soil in seconds.

Myalah stared at the river with deep trepidation. Without speaking, she bent, picked up a twig and flung it as far as she could across the water. It struck the surface without even a splash, bobbed and was swept away. Within the space of a few heartbeats, a couple of breaths, it was gone.

'We'll be alright.' Tark spoke with a confidence that was partly feigned. 'This river brought me to the valley: it will bear us out again.'

She nodded, her eyes fixed on the swirling eddies close to the bank on which they stood, where the water was shallow yet still fast-flowing. Almost inaudibly she muttered, 'But how?'

Because his mind was occupied with the river, Tark was slow to assimilate these words and when he did, they made no sense to him. Being of a people to whom swimming can as naturally as walking, it did not occur to him that it might be different for others: that a person might not know how to swim was, simply, unthinkable. Now, faced with that very possibility his mind balked, he grasped her upper arm (it was so slender his fingers almost encompassed it), and demanded, 'Do you mean you can't swim?'

Although he had not been gentle, she made no attempt to pull away yet he felt her trembling as if with fever. Her brow creased at the unfamiliar word. 'Swim? I don't know.'

'How can you not know?' In exasperation, he shouted at her. 'Why did you come then? Or have your people learned to fly?'

'Oh be quiet!' Her eyes filled with tears. 'You go, Tark. Even when they realize you're not coming back, they won't hurt me. And I can always send them on a false trail.'

'No.' Calm now, Tark let her go and looked again at the river. To the Lake people, the art of swimming was so much a part of everyday life, he could not remember being taught the skill but he recalled that the smallest children, seeking to match their elders, would sometimes use a piece of wood as a float. 'We'll find a way. And whatever happens, I promise I won't leave you.'

She watched with doubt and fear as he left the river bank and began to search for something big enough to support Myalah yet small enough to handle. But because of the dampness and humidity of the forest, the swiftness of vegetative decay, the wood lying on the ground was already rotten and fell apart in his hands.

Then, from deep within the forest, came the sound of a twig cracking. It might have been only a piece falling from a tree or the tread of an unwary beast but in both their minds the same thought sprang: this was the pursuit close on their trail. And desperation lent Tark strength. Looking up, he saw a dead branch hanging overhead. He leapt, caught it and hung on, calling for Myalah to help because his weight alone was not enough to break it.

She tugged his legs: the bough snapped and they fell together, then scrambled up and dragged their prize to the river. There was no time for a trial: the terror of the hunted was upon them. Pushing the branch before them, they plunged into the water.

The mud bank sloped steeply and the current was so strong, their feet barely touched bottom before they were swept away. Even Tark was astonished at the power of the river: though he had experienced it before, he had forgotten the sheer overwhelming nature of that force. He found himself clinging to the branch with the same desperate strength as Myalah. Glancing at her face, he saw it rigid with a mixture of fear and determination.

The rock walls slid past swiftly on one side, on the other was the forest, green and tangled, the vegetation overhanging the water's edge and rare mud banks and beaches where the river bent. In such places alone, Tark realized, was there any chance of landing but the branch was being carried inexorably towards the centre of the river: once there he doubted the two of them together possessed the strength to break free. And with every moment his fear grew that they would weaken and drown before the river slowed or grew shallow enough for them to wade ashore.

In an attempt to steer the branch towards calmer water, he began to kick hard. Myalah looked at him in confusion but at his urging joined in though it was clear from her wild eyes and fixed expression she was close to panicking.

What Tark had not anticipated was the sheer difficulty of manoeuvring a long object against so strong a flow. Up till then they had floated passively without trouble. Now, as they tried to force their way back across the river, the branch twisted and bucked like a live thing and between the effort of holding on and kicking, Tark's strength ebbed rapidly. Beside him, Myalah's head craned out of the water, her fingers gripped the wood white-knuckled but her kicks were feeble and spasmodic: she had no energy for more.

The river bent in a wide meander and the cliffs seemed to rush towards them but on the forest side there was a shoal on the inner curve of the bend where sediment had collected between floods, slowing the flow. Here the surface of the water was broken and Tark instinctively steered towards it, kicking with all the strength that remained to him, aware that this might be their only chance. Gradually, the branch edged towards the shallows. They made one last supreme effort and then there was gravel beneath their feet, the edge of a bar that sloped gently out of the water.

They staggered through the shallows, pushing the branch until it grounded and then they fell to their knees for all strength had deserted them and their limbs felt heavy and boneless as clay. Myalah's hands had locked round the branch as if clinging to life itself and it was many minutes before, at her begging, Tark was able to prise them loose. Then they clawed their way up onto the top of the bar where there was a patch of soft, dry sand.

Here they collapsed side by side and the lap of water all around, the soughing of leaves from the forest soothed and comforted them. Despite the warmth of the air, they shivered in the aftermath of fear and, inevitably, moved closer and clung to one another in relief at having escaped both their pursuers and the river. And then, as warmth returned, a new, fierce hunger awoke in them, each to explore and possess the other: it coursed though their blood like fire and would not be denied.

Lost in rapture, they were not aware of uttering the cries that rose above the sounds of water and forest and afterwards fell asleep, all thought of danger effaced.

Chapter 12.

As soon as the mist began to swirl and lift, Mingar and Memi set off down the slope, heading towards the point that would bring them closest to the forest. The way was easy for the most part, the rock smooth beneath their feet, and they moved swiftly. Gradually the mist dissipated, blue sky appeared above and the sun's rays warmed them. And when at last they stood on the edge of the precipice once again with the river churning far below, the landscape was revealed to them for the first time in the full light of day.

What they saw astounded them. The forest was set like a green jewel in the mass of red rock, ringed by cliffs on all sides. More a massive bowl than a valley it seemed, yet its span was far greater than a man could walk in one day. In the very centre the trees were wreathed in a grey-blue haze but otherwise the air was clear. Birds of many kinds were there in great numbers and the two looked at one another and smiled for this meant the forest must be rich in flowers and fruit, an abundance of food.

The mist still lingered over the river however and Mingar was impatient for it to lift for he wanted to see what kind of landing places there might be upon the far bank. He crawled to the very brink of the cliff while behind him Memi quailed at his recklessness and concentrated on the haze in the middle of the bowl for there was something about it that disturbed him.

It was pleasant lying there in the sun for the full heat of day had not yet begun. Mingar kept his eyes on the line of the river and waited. Soon swiftly flowing water could be glimpsed through rents in the vapour, then the edge of a gravel beach. A breath of wind made the mist swirl and dissipate and there, far below, Mingar saw two figures.

They were lying on a patch of sand, naked, limbs entwined and motionless as if drowned save that no surge of the river could have stranded them in so tender an embrace. As he stared, Mingar rose to his feet for there was something about the two that sent a lancinating pain through his very core though whether it was joy or sorrow he could not tell. For it was as if he had been transported to the very beginning of things when, according to the legends of his people, one man and one woman had been formed of earth and water, strong in themselves, possessed of the beauty and carelessness of youth. And then, as the young woman shifted slightly and raised her head, the head and shoulders of her partner, which had been obscured by her long hair, was revealed and a hand seemed to close around Mingar's heart. He stared and his vision blurred with the concentration with which he tried to focus, then the young man, roused by the woman, leapt suddenly to his feet pulling her with him and they were gone, slipping under cover of the trees like shadows.

A deep groan escaped Mingar, the kind of sound a man makes when a spear is pulled from his chest and his life is about to leave him. He sank to his knees and swayed and only Memi's courage and quick hands saved him from going over the brink for the young man lunged forward to drag him back, momentarily forgetting his terror of the drop.

'What is it – are you sick?' he asked for the elder's face was stricken and his eyes started from his head as if he had seen a ghost.

'Tell me you saw them too.' Mingar's voice was low and forceful. He reached out and grasped Memi's shoulders so hard that the young man winced. 'It was Tark, I am almost sure of it. Yes, it must have been him. What kind of father would not know his only son?'

Memi did not answer. His attention had been focused exclusively on the distant haze, which he had come to realize was hearth smoke: he had seen nothing of the lovers far below. And it seemed to him that obsession had at last turned Mingar's mind for the elder's wild eyes and desperate demeanour were those of a madman. Then, seeing the doubt and dismay in his companion's visage, Mingar let him go and crawled to the very edge of the cliff. There, his hands resting on the crumbling rock, he looked down and yelled with all his strength: 'Tark! Come back! Tark!'

The cry echoed against the towering cliffs and he waited, rigid so that every muscle stood out clear beneath his skin, his eyes fixed on the narrow beach at the edge of the forest. But there was no answering shout, nor did any figure venture out from the trees. He waited on, unwilling to believe that Tark would hide from or ignore him but as time passed and nothing happened, an unreasoning anger overtook him; he raised himself slightly, cupped one hand to his mouth and cried, 'Useless boy, go your own way then! Does it mean nothing that I have come all this way to find you?'

There was no response. The river flowed and the shadows shrank beneath the trees as the sun rose higher: the last shreds of mist had vanished. And now a mixture of doubt and shame assailed Mingar, he wondered if what he had thought to see had been a trick of the light and shade next to the water or whether he had momentarily fallen asleep on the cliff edge and it had been a dream. And his disappointment was so profound, he ground his teeth and beat his fists upon his head as if to dint the image of the lovers from memory.

'Mingar, stop!' Appalled and frightened, Memi reached out and grasped the elder's ankle, lest in his anguish he throw himself over the cliff. At that touch, Mingar shuddered and held himself so still, Memi thought he was in the throes of a fit. But then the elder's ribs moved as he took one breath, and another. At last he raised himself and sat back on his heels and his face was calm, masking the turmoil within.

'Let go, Memi,' he said. 'I am better now. Tell me, what did you see?'

'I was watching the haze,' Memi said uncomfortably. 'It is hearth-smoke, in the middle of the forest. There are people living there.'

Mingar frowned and his gaze followed the young man's pointing finger to where thin threads of smoke rose into the sky, clear against the trees and encircling cliffs. And the sight evoked such conflicting emotions within him, he could not think coherently. One hand went to his mouth and he bit savagely at the knuckles while the other clenched and unclenched on his thigh. For if the valley were occupied it made what he had seen commonplace, a young couple slipping away from the settlement to conduct their lovemaking in private, proof that Tark was not only alive but living life to the full. Yet while one part of his dream had thus been fulfilled, the other was, if not negated by the smoke, damaged by it. For so secluded and rich a land was not likely to be shared lightly by any kind of people and Tark's refusal to acknowledge him only exacerbated Mingar's fears.

'But if it was Tark, then the people of the forest should welcome us,' he murmured. 'It may be that the young woman is his wife and we are kin.' He paused, then added strongly, 'We have found what we sought, Memi. Let us go back now and tell the clan!'

He got to his feet and wrapped his cape around his shoulders for protection against the burning sun. Memi handed him his staff, smiling because it seemed to him that all was now resolved. But it was not him the elder had been trying to convince.

While Mingar agonized over the identity of the young man he had seen, for Tark there was no such lack of certainty. Roused from a slumber as deep and satisfying as he could remember by Myalah's abrupt movement and her hiss: 'Someone is watching!' he had only a fleeting glimpse of the man standing on the cliff edge but it was enough. There had been no time in that first moment of panic to wonder how and why his father should be there but there had also been no doubt as to his identity: that thin, twisted body could belong to no other. And Mingar's shouts simply confirmed what Tark already knew though Myalah was reduced to terror by the naming of her husband by what had appeared to her as a kind of spectre. As the echoes of his last despairing cry were swallowed by the noise of the river, she clutched at Tark, her mouth drawn down in a rictus of fear: 'Who is it?'

'Mingar, my father.' Somehow, speaking these words increased the sense of unreality that had assailed Tark since that first, terrible instant of recognition. 'How can it be? Him, here?' He stared at her with wild eyes. 'I don't understand!'

She moved closer meaning to hold and comfort him (and her flesh tingled at remembered pleasure), but he pulled away with a curt 'There's no time for that now!' and she shrank at his harshness.

'Perhaps I was dreaming.' One look at Myalah's face destroyed this faint hope and his eyes went to the talisman that hung between her breasts. 'It's no good: you saw him too, didn't you? Crippled as before, yet something must have changed to bring him so far.' And the young woman was shocked by the bitterness in his face and voice as he added, 'I never told you my father was a fool and a coward, did I? He stood by while his enemy trampled my mother and sisters to death. That shell was all that remained of her. And he let them chase me away: if I hadn't fled they'd have killed me too. And now here he is!'

Myalah was silent though her heart was wrung. Tark turned to look at the towering cliff where Mingar had stood and murmured, 'When I was little I thought he was a great man; as I grew older I feared for him until, at last, I despised him for his weakness. What should I feel now? And what shall I do?'

Without warning he stepped forward and smashed his fist against the nearest tree trunk, looking at his hand after as if amazed at how it hurt. And Myalah watched, torn between love and fear, for she knew in her heart that Mingar's arrival, the very contingency they had planned to escape, changed everything.

'Maybe he'll go away,' Tark continued musingly. 'Yes, for he called me worthless: why then should he seek me still? And yet why should he have come so far? Surely not for my sake alone. There must be others with him.'

Wholly absorbed in this inward struggle, he sank to his haunches, picked up a piece of stick and jabbed it distractedly in the dirt. In pity, Myalah crouched and laid an arm tentatively across his shoulders, half-expecting he would shrug it away. But he did not.

'We can still go,' she said at last, unable to bear his silence. 'Maybe he, too, will doubt what he saw. And anyway, how can he enter the Valley? You were half-drowned when we found you and you are young and strong: he is a cripple. We should leave, now!'

Too deep in his perplexities to perceive how she was trying to protect him, Tark shrugged her arm away.

'What, and let him be killed by your people if he reaches here alive?' he asked. 'Would you do so in my place, Myalah? If we go now I'll never know what happened. Yet if I let him come without warning him, it will be the same as if I slew him with my own hands.'

She sat back on her heels and stared at him, appalled. 'But what is the difference?' she cried. 'It was an ill chance that he saw and knew you and you him: had we slept under the trees instead of upon the beach, he would be none the wiser and we would be far away. Forget it, Tark. After all, did he not forsake you?'

He looked at her and it seemed to him that all the differences between his people and hers were encapsulated in these words. And so his answer, which to her seemed unnecessarily provocative, was, in fact, meant as a simple question: 'And could you forget? If I had stood there, or Gullilli, could you walk away? I do not think so, not if you are the person I thought I married.'

She was ashamed then and bowed her head while a deep flush mantled her neck and shoulders. 'Then what must we do?' she asked. 'For we are as one now Tark and therefore Mingar is my father as Gullilli is yours. But that does not change the law of my people.'

He let out a sound that was like a groan and she raised her eyes in alarm. But to her amazement, instead of being despondent, Tark's face was alight with hope.

'Myalah!' He took her face between his hands and kissed her brow. 'You're right! We are one: the Lake Clan and the Valley People! We can change the law! We'll wait for my father to arrive, then we'll lead him and his companions to the village. Under our protection, who would dare harm him? After all, the Valley can provide more than enough for all our people. Why should mine not share it? With Gullilli and Nygeli on our side, we cannot fail!'

'Tark, you do not know my father!' she protested but he was deaf to the warning inherent in her tone. And realizing the futility of arguing while he was in this mood she said no more, for being Gullilli's daughter she understood well the single-mindedness of men.

Inspired by new hope, Mingar walked at a great pace along the cliff which, he guessed, was the quickest way back to Draa and the rest. The sun rose to its zenith and they paused to eat the last of the reed tubers in the scant shade of a rock ledge set a little way back from the brink. In the distance a small patch of forest was still visible and Mingar's heart sang because it seemed to him that his people were at last coming to journey's end, not merely the trek from the Flowering Plain but one that had begun at the very start of the Great Dry, when the elders had realized they must abandon the dying lake and find a new place to live and he, in his stubbornness, had denied it.

As he mused, a strange urgency gripped Mingar, a sense that if he did not act now it would be too late. And he longed to see Draa's face when he told her the news, that not only had they found a new green place but that Tark was living there with a young woman. Memi had already stretched out in the shade to sleep away the hours of heat but Mingar shook him roughly saying, 'Come on, if we hurry we shall reach camp by nightfall. This is no time to rest!'

Reluctantly, Memi clambered to his feet and followed as the elder strode away, heedless of the crumbling cliff edge, the terrifying chasm but a single step from where he trod, the heat which smote them from beneath and above. All these things exacerbated Memi's dread of what was to come but he forced himself on even as the ground began to slope steeply and the path plunged down across the cliff face.

Mingar did not falter as he began the descent but he moved his staff from his right hand to his left and felt the bare rock as if for guidance. He drew swiftly away from Memi who was half-paralysed with terror. The younger man edged his way down, his face to the rock, clinging on with both hands, his eyes fixed straight ahead lest by chance he glimpse the drop to the river and fall.

When he was halfway down, it occurred to Mingar to check on his companion's progress. He stopped and looked back and there, high on the path behind, was Memi, his progress so slow as to be almost imperceptible.

The elder knew he should wait for the young man to catch up but, for once, his impatience would not be stayed. He turned and hurried on, for in the distance he could see smoke from the camp. And the gradient of the path had eased: instead of a sheer cliff to his right there was now a steep rocky slope where the strata had slipped, and the ledge he walked upon had widened.

When he reached a place where the ground was almost level, he turned to look back and although he could no longer see Memi because of the curve of the cliff, he cupped his hands to his mouth and shouted encouragement. At the rate the young man was descending, he reckoned that he, Mingar, would be in camp before Memi reached the base of the cliff.

High up and far away as he was, Memi heard Mingar's shout but could not distinguish the words. Thinking that the elder was in trouble, he let go the rock face and, with infinite care, turned to face the path he had yet to tread. With a supreme effort, he forced himself to look down.

Such vertigo seized him in that moment, his senses reeled and he staggered. One foot trod air: he clutched vainly at the rock and fell. He screamed in terror and despair as his body bounced against shattered edges of stone but by the time he hit the river, he was past feeling anything.

Mingar heard Memi's screams and a cold hand seemed to grasp his heart. He rushed back until he reached a place from which the cliff path was visible but, as he expected, it was empty. Nor was there any sign of the young man in the swirling waters: he had already been swept far away.

Stunned, Mingar turned and made his way slowly back towards the camp. He knew there was nothing he could do: Memi was gone, but he rued the lack of compassion by which he had left the young man behind instead of helping him. And the news he bore was now tainted with bitterness for it had been dearly bought.

Thus it was that when he walked at last into camp, Mingar's face was grim and sad and though his people gathered round him, none asked what had happened because they were afraid. Draa was beside the river with the other women, busy tying reeds into bundles, and when she saw her husband, she rose slowly to her feet for tragedy was written clearly in his features. And secretly she rejoiced, believing that he had failed in his quest and there would be no need for the rafts she and the rest had begun. It was only when he was close that she realized he was alone.

'Memi is lost,' he said, pre-empting her question. 'His foot slipped on the cliff and he fell. He may still be alive: I do not know.

The river swept him away and we must follow.'

An outcry of mingled grief and amazement arose in which Draa's voice was the loudest for she feared a new obsession had taken root in his mind with the failure of the old. But he held up one hand for silence and when he spoke, his voice was stern and clear.

'Though Memi may be lost, my news is not all woeful,' he said. 'For he found what we have long sought. In the very heart of the mountain is a green bowl filled with forest. Around it flows the very river we stand beside and though it is broad and swift, there are gravel bars and sandy beaches where we can land. And though we saw hearth smoke rising from the middle of the forest, it is my belief that we can live there in peace for we and the people of the valley are kin.'

At this a ripple of excitement ran through the crowd and even those most affected by the loss of Memi ceased wailing for the dream of a bountiful green place to live in was embedded deep within their psyche. But they assumed Mingar's claim of kinship with the valley people meant no more than the ancient ancestry shared by all the tribes of the great flat land. Only Draa, who knew Mingar best, suspected he had not told all for he could not quite meet her eyes and so when the hubbub had died down a little, she drew him away, saying he needed to rest. Then, when they had reached their shelter and he had eaten and drunk the food and water she gave him, she sat back on her heels and regarded him with mingled love and sorrow.

'What else happened on the mountain?' she asked. 'And how did Memi come to fall? He was young and childless, barely come to manhood: why were you not there to help him?'

Dismayed by the keenness of her perception, Mingar avoided her gaze and stared fixedly at his hands which were clasped in his lap. They seemed gnarled and knotted at the roots of an ancient tree, the hands of an old man he thought suddenly, and a pang went through him.

'I saw Tark,' he said heavily. 'He was with a young woman. I'm sure he saw me but they fled into the forest and though I called, he did not answer.'

Draa stared at him, astounded by the news, confounded by the manner in which he had imparted it. And as Mingar continued to scrutinize his hands, doubt grew in her mind. She asked sharply, 'Did Memi see them?'

'He said not: I do not know,' Mingar replied. 'Maybe he had his own reason for denying it though Tark was his friend. But they were there!'

Now he lifted his head to look at her and his eyes blazed: there was no doubt this was the truth, for him. Yet Draa could not quell the suspicion that Mingar had somehow engineered the young man's death lest he dispute this story. Though even as this thought crystallized, she realized it made no sense since Mingar had not spoken of Tark before the people.

'I believe you,' she said at last. 'Maybe Tark did not know you, perhaps he couldn't hear you above the noise of the river. But are you sure your own eyes were not mistaken? It might have been another young man and hope turned him into your son.'

'It was Tark!' Mingar insisted in a low, pained voice. 'And I am sure in my heart that he knew and deliberately ignored me. What have I done that he should hate me even now?'

'Ah Mingar, do not revisit the past, it will heal nothing,' Draa said. 'You are weary: lie down and sleep. And I will see how work is progressing on the rafts, now we have somewhere to go.'

She left him and he heard her voice amid the distant chatter of the women but though he yearned for the oblivion of slumber, it was long in coming.

Memi's body was taken swiftly by the current. He floated face down, limbs asprawl as he had hit the water, an impact which had broken his neck though many of his other bones had shattered during the bouncing plunge down the cliff face. Before Mingar reached the point where he could see back along the river, the corpse had been swept beyond his sight for the channel bent sharply before beginning the wide curve that encompassed half the Valley.

Here, where the flow slowed a little, Memi's body revolved in eddies caused by submerged blocks fallen from the cliff. Gradually it drifted across the river. The water shallowed and the corpse grounded at last on a gravel bar overhung by trees. Memi's brow ploughed into the pebbles and then little wavelets drove his body lengthwise against the beach, lapping gently so that his hair moved as if caressed by a light breeze and one hand lifted and fell in a simulacrum of life.

But he was dead and as the sun's heat struck his flesh, flies began to swarm. It was their buzzing that alerted the man fishing a little way downstream.

As they made their way back to the village, Myalah begged Tark to think again for with every step she grew more certain that he would only condemn himself by speaking for Mingar. All her life she had loved and respected her father for his steadfastness and integrity but now, she realized, these very qualities would force him to uphold the Law. Only ignorance or naivety could account for Tark's stubbornness in her mind and as he strode on, apparently deaf to her pleas, she gave up and followed in resentful silence.

But Tark was, by no means, sure of his course. He was simply doing what seemed best because his other choices, to leave, pretending he had never seen his father, or stay and face the prospect of having to slay his own kin or himself be slain, were equally revolting to him. He knew he was taking a huge risk in opening his heart to the elders but he could think of no alternative. He was certain that Mingar would try to find him.

Far sooner than he had expected, the half-finished hut came into view and his pace slowed. Only at that moment did he understand fully the sacrifice Myalah was prepared to make for him, forsaking the settled life she was used to for the uncertainties and danger of a nomadic existence; he recalled how she had almost drowned in her determination to stay with him and a pang of regret and sorrow smote him: almost he relented. But then he remembered the man lying beneath his hands on the stone slab, the horror of the killing, and he shook his head (as if to dislodge doubt), and strode on, making straight for Nygeli's hut because his mentor would at least listen, even if he disliked what he heard.

The scarred elder was with a group of young men sharpening spears by the central hearth but when he saw the couple he rose and went to meet them for it was clear from Tark's bearing that he had some grave purpose. And yet from their lack of self-consciousness towards each other Nygeli could tell that the rift between the two was healed: there was a kind of sheen upon them, a bloom of youth that made him feel old and weary.

'So then,' he said when they were settled inside his hut, and there was a kindly smile upon his usually grim features. 'What brings you here? Have you nothing better to do than while away the bright morning with me?'

'We need – I need your help,' Tark said and the urgency of his tone wiped the smile from Nygeli's face. 'Something has happened that I dreaded and I do not know what to do.'

A look of puzzlement settled upon the elder's countenance and he leant forward, spreading his hands in a gesture of peace. 'Speak then, and if you wish it, be sure your words will go no further. But I do not know what I can do that Gullilli could not, for he is more powerful than I, and your kin.'

'Listen and you will understand,' Tark said heavily and he launched into an account of the encounter by the river though he did not say why he and Myalah were there or give any hint of their intention to leave the Valley.

It was then, watching the elder's expression change from incredulity to outrage, that Tark realized the enormity of what he was proposing. Nygeli was too wise to interrupt at first but as Tark explained how Mingar and his companions (assuming there were any), should be welcomed, he raised his right hand for silence and shook his head grimly from side to side. And the flow of Tark's words faltered and dried up.

'Tark, you do not know what you ask,' Nygeli said. 'Or if you do, you are more foolish than I had thought. You know the law: you have bound yourself to it. If your father enters the Valley, he must die. There can be no compromise. It is this custom that has protected us for so long: for us there is nowhere else.' He paused, then added sadly and with great circumspection, 'Tark, we were merciful towards you because of your youth: do not make us regret that decision. For with every word you speak it seems to me we made an error that may cost us our lives, perhaps the Valley itself.

And if you will heed the counsel of your old teacher, it would be best to pretend ignorance of this matter. There are those that envy you, who think you a usurper, perhaps even a spy: a trickster whose whole stay here has been a ruse to gain our trust while you prepare for the coming of your own people. Give them reason to believe this and they will slay you, have no doubt. Not even Gullilli can help you then.'

'But it's not true!' Myalah, who had been sitting unobtrusively at Tark's right, could not contain her indignation. 'It was me who saw his father high on the cliff. And we were leaving, that's why we were by the river. So how could Tark be planning to bring his people here?'

'Leaving?' Nygeli's brow creased in a deep frown and he looked piercingly into the young man's face. 'For what reason?' His tone was suddenly stern and suspicious. 'To leave the Valley is impossible. You could never return.'

'I did not mean to return,' Tark said and there was such misery in his voice and countenance, the elder pitied him. 'It was to escape this very chance that I was going.' He hesitated, then added quietly, 'I saw my mother and sisters murdered and my father stood by and did nothing. But I am not like him.'

There was a heavy silence while Nygeli pondered these words. 'It is not the same,' he pronounced at last. 'No. And you need to think hard before deciding what to do next. I have grown to think of you as my son yet were you my own flesh and blood, I could not endorse either your leaving the Valley or your proposal. I doubt you even understand what you have already done by opening your heart to me. Indeed, were you Gullilli himself or any of the great ones in the past, it would be the same. For sedition, there is only one punishment, and that is death.'

Tark sat silent and these words struck like stones. But Myalah moved restlessly and her eyes glinted as her gaze locked with the old man's. She said deliberately, 'They would not dare.'

'Because you are Gullilli's daughter?' Nygeli smiled faintly but it was a smile without mirth, only irony. 'You know better, Myalah. To protect the Valley, they will cast you into the crack along with Tark. You are a woman now: behave as one, not like a spoilt child.'

Tark shuddered, realizing the true nature of the stone amphitheatre with its fissures and stench of decay: it was a place not only of ceremony but punishment. He said slowly, 'Then you will betray me because I trusted you?'

'I did not say so.' Nygeli sighed and it was as if a flame had died within him, he seemed suddenly old and tired. 'You put a harder choice upon me than you face yourself. My heart would act more as a doting father's than an elder's, though my head warns I may rue my decision bitterly ere the end. Therefore take my advice and leave now, await your father beside the river and bid him go away. And I will do my best to excuse your absence here. But if you refuse or your father will not listen, do not expect more of me. I am old and weary and my powers fail. This alone can you be sure of: neither Gullilli nor Myenah nor any of the Council will countenance mercy in this case. The law that protects the Valley cannot be revoked.'

From his face and voice it was clear that nothing Tark or Myalah said would make the old man change his mind. And yet there was no anger in Nygeli's countenance as he looked upon them. Sorrow was in his eyes but he made no attempt to stay them as they rose and backed out into the bright sunshine.

'See!' Myalah was careful to keep her voice low though she could not wholly keep a note of triumph from it. 'Did I not warn what would happen? If my father hears of this, he will call a council and they will condemn us. We must do as Nygeli says and leave now, while we have the chance. Otherwise it may be too late.'

'Nygeli will not betray us,' Tark said flatly. 'But I am no longer minded to go to Gullilli. We shall return to our own place and rest while we think on our next step. It will take my father at least a day to reach the riverside from where we saw him I would guess: we have a little time.'

Chapter 13.

In the riverside camp that night ceremony was conducted to mark Memi's passing for there was no doubt in Mingar's mind that after such a fall the young man must be dead. The funeral fires burned brightly, sending showers of sparks into the sky where, the clan believed, the ancestors resided. By the lurid flame-light bulky shapes were visible upon the riverbank that had not been there before. These were the craft painstakingly constructed from reeds and every animal skin that could be spared. More like massive floats than rafts they were for the plan was that only the weakest would ride upon them; everyone else would cling to the grass ropes that bound them together. And Mingar, who had conceived more elaborate craft to bear them to their new home, was forced to accept these since there was no wood available to construct rafts, nor time to fashion enough reed punts to bear the whole clan.

When the dancing and singing were at their height, Mingar slipped away and sat on a boulder a little outside the camp. He was filled with a strange mixture of elation and foreboding as he reflected on the day's events: the discovery of the forest, the chance sighting of Tark, the loss of Memi. He looked up at the stars and wondered whether, at that moment, Tark was doing the same. And then he mused upon what they would say to each other when they came face to face and he smiled, trying to reconcile the young man he had glimpsed, well-muscled and sleek, with the skinny boy he remembered who was always whining that he wanted to leave the dying lake and go away with his friends.

'You have found your own friends now, eh boy?' Mingar muttered, thinking of the nubile grace of the young woman upon the sand. 'If they are all like that, what a place this forest must be!' And chuckling quietly to himself he made his way back to join in the feast for it seemed to him that aside from grief, there was much to be thankful for.

Next morning Tark was woken by a tumult from the centre of the village. Beside him, Myalah was sitting up, listening intently. She was so tense, her body rocked to her heartbeat. Tark held his breath and waited and the thumping of his own heart muffled his hearing. The same dread gripped them both: that Mingar had already entered the Valley and been discovered.

Their fears appeared to be confirmed when Myalah whispered at last, 'I think they've found a dead man by the river, a stranger. He is being brought back now so the Council can decide what to do. Tark, what about us? We must leave now or it will be too late!'

But after her first words, Tark was not listening. A dull heaviness had descended upon him at the thought of his father dead. The thing seemed impossible: only yesterday he had seen Mingar alive, a sighting that had shattered all his plans. Now it seemed that all his agonizing, all his efforts to make the right choice, had been futile. He said slowly, 'We cannot leave until I know who it is.'

His mouth shut in a firm line and realizing she was powerless to change his mind, Myalah did not answer. But she was listening still as the hubbub died down and at length she said, 'They say it's the body of a young man, tall and strong-looking though very thin. His bones were broken as if he'd fallen from a great height.' She hesitated, then added reluctantly, 'They say he is much like you to look upon.'

'What – he has two legs, two arms, a head and a penis?' Tark exclaimed. He was relieved (yet in some way he did not fully understand, disappointed), that the dead man was not his father: even a blind man could not have mistaken Mingar's gnarled, twisted body for a young man's. But he did not underestimate the danger he and Myalah faced. Whoever this was, their situation was unchanged.

'If we are not leaving, then we should join the rest,' Myalah said. 'If we stay away, they will grow suspicious. But Tark, please be careful.'

So profound was their dismay, none of the Valley folk noticed the couple's arrival, nor, it seemed, had any marked their absence. Gullilli had sent a band of young men to help bring the corpse back for appraisal: it was necessary, he said, to be sure this was indeed an intruder and not some hapless hunter or fisherman of their own people. For it was the nature of their lives even in the Valley that only rarely was the whole clan gathered together: someone was always off gathering food or on the hunting trail. And sometimes a person would simply slip away when the desire for solitude grew strong (though they might be regarded with some suspicion upon their return). Tark thought his father-in-law glanced sternly in his direction as he tried to reassure the women that all was well but Myalah grasped his hand and he returned the elder's gaze steadily though his heart quailed at the thought of what would happen should Nygeli betray them.

'It will be some time before they return,' Gullilli declared at length, realizing that reasoned argument was making no difference to the women's distress. 'Therefore go: there are children to mind, food to gather and prepare. As for the men, it would be as well if we made sure our weapons are sharp and close to hand.'

These last words had the opposite effect to his intention for the women began to wail as if he had declared war. Gullilli shook his head and strode through the crowd, straight towards Tark and Myalah. Anger was written clearly on his features and the couple waited fearfully lest Nygeli had already unburdened himself and Gullilli was keeping quiet in order to save face. But instead of accusing or berating them, the elder simply asked if they had seen Nygeli that morning.

Tark scanned the crowd automatically though he knew if Gullilli could not see someone it was certain they were not there: he possessed keen and penetrating vision.

'I saw him yesterday,' he said, 'I haven't seen him since.'

Myalah gripped his arm so fiercely at this, Tark thought her fingernails must have broken the skin but Gullilli said merely, 'Ah well, no doubt he will be here when they bring the dead one in' and then he walked away, heading for the relative peace of his hut.

As Gullilli expected, when, a little while later, a group of young men came jogging up the track from the river with the corpse slung from a pole they bore between them, Nygeli joined the waiting throng. Whence he came, Tark had no idea for he simply appeared as if sprung from the shadows beneath the trees. He did not approach the couple but Tark felt his gaze keenly as if the old man had touched him. Nygeli's visage was grey and haggard and there was a look upon it that filled Tark with dread: a mixture of sorrow and grim expectation.

The bearers whooped triumphantly as they entered the central court, like hunters at the end of a long and successful chase and the people crowded round to see the body (like crows, Tark thought with disgust). Their clamour was only silenced when Gullilli shouted for quiet and pushed his way through. To Tark's dismay, Nygeli followed, though he moved stiffly, as if reluctant. Then the crowd closed again, blocking corpse and bearers from the couple's view but even a brief glimpse had sufficed to convince Tark that the man had not belonged here. The limbs were long and lean, the skin darker, as of one who had lived a much harder life than any of the Valley folk, and his apprehension deepened.

Myalah was still clutching his hand: he drew her close and whispered, 'Let us go: no-one will notice for a while,' and they stepped quietly away. But it was too late.

'Tark!' It was Gullilli. 'Where are you? Come here!'

Tark knew he had no choice. He let go Myalah's hand and made his way through the crowd, many of whom recoiled as if contact with him would somehow contaminate them. It was as though all the time he had spent in the Valley counted for nothing and he was a stranger again. But he barely had time to realize this, when he came to the body and all else fled his mind.

Still tied to the pole like a slaughtered beast, Memi lay on his side, his neck crooked unnaturally, his flesh torn and bruised by his fall. Tark had to suppress a cry of grief and outrage at the sight. He knelt, ostensibly to examine the corpse more closely but in reality to hide his face lest it betray his feelings.

'Do you know him?' There was no trace of suspicion in Gullilli's tone: it was simply a question, most likely intended to allay the doubts of Tark's detractors. But for Tark it was then that reality slipped into nightmare and he realized the impossibility of his situation: that whatever he did, it meant betraying people he loved. He hesitated, sensed the attention of the crowd sharpen; his mouth was dry; his tongue stuck to the roof of his mouth: he could not speak.

'Tark,' Nygeli's voice was stern. 'You belong in the Valley now: you are one of us. If you knew this man, that is no crime but if you knew him and keep silent, it is a different matter.'

Slowly Tark raised his head. He looked into his old mentor's face and there was such sadness in Nygeli's eyes, his heart was wrung. And he found himself saying, 'Once, long ago, I might have known him. But that was beside the Lake, when we were boys. I do not know how or why he came here. And he has already paid the price.'

The outcry that followed came like the screeching of parakeets to Tark's ears. His eyes were still locked with Nygeli's, seeking help. But the scarred elder turned his head slowly from side to side like one in despair or great pain, and asked calmly, 'Are you sure?'

Afterwards, Tark realized that the ambiguity of the question was deliberate, to give him time to consider the implications of what he had already said. But fear and grief confused his mind. In a voice barely audible above the noise of the crowd, he replied 'He is dead, what difference does it make? Once he was my friend but I cannot tell what he is doing here. I haven't seen him since the day my home was destroyed. What do you expect of me?'

'I? Nothing more,' Nygeli said and he turned and shuffled away as if weary of the whole issue. Tark watched until he was lost to view and he was assailed a by a profound sense of loss wholly different to his grief for Memi, one he did not understand. Then the crone, Myenah, pushed her way forward until she stood beside Gullilli and her eyes were bright and malicious as she looked from the corpse to Tark and back again.

'Let us treat this carrion like any other stranger,' she said. 'Cast it into the crack, let it be swallowed up as if it had never been. Yet maybe we should watch the river lest there are others. It is strange that another of Tark's kind should come here but who knows how far he floated down the river? Most likely he knew nothing of the Valley before he died.'

'That is wisely spoken,' Gullilli said. 'And lest any still doubt Tark's loyalty, he shall have the honour of pushing this trespasser, this nothing, into the earth and he will join in the watch along the river. If others come, they will not find us unprepared. Let every man have his weapons ready.'

Memi was dead: he could not know what was happening, nor feel anything, nor care. This Tark told himself repeatedly as he and other young men of the village dragged the corpse face-down along the path to the stone pavement by means of a rope attached to the dead man's ankles. After them walked the elders, all save Nygeli who could not be found, but the women and children stayed behind. Tark had made sure Myalah was with her mother and aunts for her face betrayed her distress and he was afraid of what she might do or say in his absence.

By the time they reached their destination, the battering and scraping it had received had all but separated the dead man's flesh from his bones. When, on the very edge of the rock platform, they halted and turned the body over, Memi's visage, once so full of life and good to look upon, was unrecognisable and Tark had to swallow the vomit that rose scalding in his throat.

'Wherever you came from and for whatever reason, take this message to the spirits of your people!' Gullilli cried in a loud and terrible voice and he spat full into the ruined face, lifted his right foot and stamped with bone-crushing force, obliterating all that remained of Memi's features. Then, to Tark's horror, all the elders joined in, each choosing a different part of the body to desecrate. As they spat and stamped, a wild keening issued from their lips. It rose to an eerie howling which echoed against the rock walls and made Tark's head reel. He clapped his hands over his ears in a vain attempt to shut it out and all the time his dread increased lest he also be expected to take part. But when the body was reduced to a trampled sac, they stepped away, their feet befouled with blood and nameless filth.

'You, Tark!' Gullilli's words came in short, panting gasps. 'Drag this carrion to the cleft and cast it in. For you are one of us.'

Only his love for Myalah and the knowledge that if he were dead or injured he could do nothing to help his father, lent Tark the composure and fortitude to obey. No-one moved to help as he picked up the trailing rope and tugged upon it though it was still some way to the first cleft and Memi had been taller and heavier than himself. Soon all he could think of was finishing the hateful task. Sweat dripped into his eyes and the muscles of his legs and arms strained as the corpse lodged against irregularities in the stone pavement, the breath rasped in his throat and the sun's heat beat down upon him: he thought he would never make it. And then, just as his strength was about to fail utterly, he felt a waft of cool air against his face, air that bore the taint of decay, and the cleft yawned at his feet.

As Tark dropped the rope and stood still to recover his breath, the rest swarmed to join him.

'Into the dark, into the cold!' they chanted and their faces were distorted into masks of hate and the naked lust for violence. Even Gullilli was affected by the frenzy: as Tark stepped away from the brink lest they pitch him into the cleft by the force of their onrush, the elder grasped Memi's ankles and danced backwards a little, dragging the corpse as if it weighed no more than a child.

'Come Tark, this is your victory!' he called and Tark, as he knew he must, bent and took the wrists, hard and dead as sticks. Between them they swung the body once, twice, thrice and each time it reached the chasm's edge, a shout swelled from the throats of the onlookers.

Then, on the fourth swing, Gullilli shouted 'Now!' and the corpse was flung out into the air and dropped into the cleft. And Tark had to fight hysteria because his mind jerked back to a game he and his friends (Memi amongst them), had played beside the lake, taking turns to be swung high above the glittering water and then let go, the winner being the one who reached the furthest, landing with a satisfying splash away from shore.

The juxtaposition of such happy memories with what he had just done made Tark shudder and he longed to slip away into the forest and hide. But his ordeal was not over. With a blood-curdling scream, Gullilli began to prance at the very ledge of the fissure while, from somewhere behind, someone beat a hollow log for a drum. And the young men who had, hitherto, waited under the eaves of the forest, ran forward to join the elders in what, Tark realized suddenly, was a war dance.

His people had no such tradition, nor had Nygeli taught him, but Tark joined in as best he could, stamping and whirling, his voice raised in a wordless howl. And a kind of ecstasy took hold: his will was subsumed with the others in a frenzy whose lust was for blood, the blood of any stranger that dared set foot in the Valley, trespassing on their earth, their water, sullying the world with their presence. It was a fierce, red urge that possessed Tark, a need to rend and tear: like some of the others, he bit savagely at the insides of his wrists and revelled in the taste of the blood that sprang beneath his teeth. In the joy of it he forgot who he was, knew only that he was young and strong, invincible, immortal: he could spit upon his enemies and they could not touch him and his enemy was anyone he was told to fight because nothing, even sex, could surpass this intoxication of the senses which precluded thought and negated self.

When the drumming ceased, Tark, like the others, stood as if stunned, running with sweat, limp with exhaustion yet his mind reeling still in the aftermath of ecstasy. Gullilli was first to recover: he watched the younger men with satisfaction, then said sharply, 'Come!' and led the way back across the stone pavement.

After the merciless heat of the stone amphitheatre, entering the cool green darkness of the forest was like plunging into deep water. It dissipated all but the last remnants of the trance and Tark found himself weak and shivering. Gullilli and the others strode along at a great pace and Tark fell behind for he was exhausted in body and in mind. Gradually the feeling grew upon him that he was not alone: there was that indefinable prickling sensation between his shoulder-blades he had felt so often during Tani's long pursuit. And his steps slowed for his first thought was that Myalah must have followed the procession a certain distance and was hidden close by, having waited for his return.

But when he turned to look behind, it was not she that emerged from the green shadows. Nygeli stepped out onto the path and his dark, unfathomable eyes settled on the young man as if to read his very thoughts. Under that gaze, Tark felt inordinately uncomfortable for Nygeli neither moved nor spoke, he simply stood there and after a while he sighed deeply, turned on his heel and walked slowly in the direction of the stone pavement.

Shaken, Tark watched the old man until he disappeared from view and had he not been desperate to see Myalah and know that she was safe, he would have gone after. But he told himself that he could visit the old man later and made his way in the opposite direction, hurrying now because the others were far ahead.

Wilful as usual, Myalah had not stayed with her mother but was waiting in the half-finished hut at the forest's edge. Her face was drawn and anxious and she let out a cry when she saw the state of him.

'Aiee, what have they done?' she moaned when at last he reached her. Her hand went to his right shoulder and only then did he feel the hurt where the rope attached to Memi's ankles had bitten deep into the flesh: the horror of what he was doing followed by the ecstasy of the war dance had made him immune to pain.

'Let me tend it.' She tried to take his hand, to draw him inside the hut, but he snatched it away. Now he knew she was safe, the fear that their secret might be discovered was sharper than ever: with each passing moment, Mingar's arrival in the Valley came closer.

'Leave it.' His brusqueness was not aimed at Myalah, it was more that the sight of her had restored him fully to himself, nullifying the effects of the dance and the ritual beside the cleft. He realized that in that state of bloodlust he would have slain his father without hesitation and shame overwhelmed him at how easily he had succumbed.

'Tark, please.' She took his face, smeared with blood and dust, between her hands and he submitted dumbly to her caresses, his hands hanging loosely at his sides. And his apparent indifference dismayed Myalah: she drew back exclaiming, 'What happened? What's wrong?' her voice shrill with an mixture of anxiety and exasperation.

Any answer he might have given was precluded by a sudden noise from the centre of the village, voices raised in ululation akin to the howl of scavengers squabbling over a carcass. It was a sound meant to inspire courage in the warriors of the Valley and fear in their enemies and Tark shuddered. It reminded him of the war cries that had preceded the dancing yet this seemed even more terrible because the women had joined in, keening like the kites and buzzards that wheel over a battlefield.

'It's only noise,' Myalah said, forcing calmness on herself because she saw panic flicker in the eyes of her lover. 'It will be over soon. They are always like this when there's an alarm. There's nothing to fear.'

Tark disagreed but he did not have the heart to say so. Yet he knew that if their cover were to be kept, he must join Gullilli and the rest before they missed him.

'I must go,' he said. 'Otherwise they will suspect me, even though I did what they wanted.'

'Then I will come with you.'

Mingar knew it was not far in distance from the camp to the gravel bar where he had seen Tark but he misjudged the speed and strength of the river. Soon after dawn he and Draa marshalled the clan on the riverbank where the floats were drawn up. In the clear morning light the surface of the water was smooth and glassy, reflecting the cliffs and the cloudless sky with such perfection as to appear opaque, giving no clue as to the ferocity of the current. But as soon as he and some of the other men waded in (and within a couple of paces, they were waist deep), the flow almost swept them away. They clutched at each other to keep their balance and their dismay was mirrored by those watching from the bank. It seemed madness to wilfully commit the whole clan to so uncertain and dangerous an endeavour.

Only Mingar was undaunted though even he realized how fragile was the chance of landing so many on a small shoal which was, moreover, on the other side of the river. He shouted for the first of the craft to be pushed into the water and this was done though the float was large and unwieldy and almost knocked those waiting to receive it off their feet.

And now the main flaw in Mingar's strategy was evident. It was taking the combined strength of all those already in the water to hold this one craft against the flow: it would take the resources of the whole clan to load and launch it safely. His plan to go down the river as a flotilla was clearly impossible.

As he stood there, fighting the current and the sheer bulk of the float, his resolve faltered. For hope and inspiration he looked at Draa but her eyes were fixed on him in the same agony of fear and apprehension as the rest. Then anger overwhelmed him, a rage exacerbated by shame because in what should have been his moment of triumph, he foresaw only failure. He ground his teeth, trying to think of a resolution that did not come, feeling the constant battering of the water and the tug of the craft sap his strength. The others hanging onto the ropes, beside him and on the bank, began to shout but with the noise of the river and the banging of his heartbeat in his ears, he could not make out their words.

And then Draa, seeing her husband's anguish from the wildness of his eyes and the rigidity of his features, which were set in a kind of snarl, gathered all her courage and stepped down onto the craft. It bucked under her weight, throwing her onto her hands and knees but she quickly sat down and slipped her feet under one of the loops of rope tied onto the bindings for that very purpose. Once settled, she smiled reassuringly at Mingar, then extended her hands to help others aboard.

Her example and the fact that the craft, held as it was, did not tip or sink, sparked panic among those on the bank who now feared being left behind more than drowning. They rushed forward and scrambled down to join Draa, some of the women clawing at others, some throwing their infants to those already on the raft. Children's screams rent the air; the craft tipped alarmingly and one of the men standing in the water was knocked over: only the quick hand of his neighbour saved him from being swept away.

'Stop! Stop!' Mingar's shouts were in vain. Already the float was crowded. It settled deeper in the water and began to list ominously as desperate women and children jumped on top of those already aboard. And then, inevitably, the weight became too much. The craft tipped violently, spilling a third of its human cargo into the water, tugging those that had tied the anchor ropes round their waists off their feet and dragging them with it as it drifted away from the safety of the bank.

Mingar stood aghast amid a mass of floundering people and watched numbly as the craft moved out into the main flow, revolving in the current's grip. Shrieks and cries for help clamoured in the air both from those in the water and those being carried upon it but he was deaf to all. His eyes were fixed upon Draa who sat in the middle of the float with many of the others clinging to her as if she possessed the power to save them. As she was borne away, it seemed to him that his heart was being torn out.

Then, gradually he became aware that while he stood as if stunned by the disaster, others were acting to mitigate it. Someone yelled his name, then another craft was pushed into the water. This one was smaller than the first and therefore lighter and easier to manoeuvre. Mingar caught one of the ropes and helped hold it steady while the remaining people climbed aboard but his attention was focused on the first raft. This was picking up speed and would soon be swept round the first bend. There was no time to lose.

'Quick!' He urged those still on land, many of whom had scrambled there after being thrown off the first raft and now stood trembling from the shock and terror of their unexpected immersion. 'Get on or we may never see the others again!'

These words provoked another frantic rush for many families had been split in the chaos, a child or parent being stranded on the float that was being swept away. Soon only those holding the ropes were left upon the bank.

The first craft disappeared round the great meander and a wail arose from many of those on the second for it was as if their comrades had been wiped out of existence, swallowed by the unknown. But Mingar, though the raft was desperately overloaded and rode so deep that those at the edge were sitting in water, shouted for the men on the bank to jump in and himself pushed the craft out into the main channel.

Tark squatted wearily in the shade fringing the gravel bar where only a day ago he and Myalah had made love. His whole body ached from the exertions of the morning and he was plagued by flies which swarmed to feed on the blood oozing from the rope-wound across his shoulder. His eyes were bent on the furthest reach of the river, the point at which his father would come into view (if, indeed he came at all), though so dazzling was the play of sunlight on the swirling surface, he doubted he would spot a swimmer's head until it was much closer.

As he waited, everything that had happened since glimpsing Mingar on the cliff seemed unreal yet there was no doubting the solidity of the spear-shaft on which he leant, nor could he deny the trust Gullilli had put in him. Yet he was not alone. A short distance back along the path Matah, his former rival, stood. Renowned for his swiftness, he was waiting for Tark to give the alarm. Then he would run to the village where the warriors were ready.

A fish jumped mid-stream, a flash of silver, and the fierce scream of a hunting eagle seemed to pierce Tark's brain for the steady rushing of water had lulled him into a kind of reverie. And then, his senses alerted by the bird's call, he thought to catch human voices amid the noise of the river, faint at first but growing steadily louder and clearer.

Without being aware of it he had risen to his feet and moved forward, out of the concealing shadow, drawn by the voices which, he was now convinced, were real and not some trick of the running waters. Next moment the first of the floats, so laden with people the craft itself was barely visible, appeared round the bend and Draa, who was scanning the bank for the landing place Mingar had described, saw him.

'Tark!' Their eyes locked across the rapidly diminishing stretch of water between them and each felt a jolt, a shock of recognition, though Tark's was one of dread, Draa's of unmitigated joy. And then Draa encouraged the swimmers at each corner of the float to redouble their efforts and make shore for the current ran swiftly and they were in danger of being swept past.

Then Tark knew he must act. At any moment Matah might hear the voices and come to investigate: as soon as he saw the strangers he would think Tark had betrayed the Valley and sprint to raise the alarm. And impelled by the simple conviction that this must not happen, Tark suddenly turned on his heel and moved with a hunter's stealth into the forest for he knew he must somehow silence his companion though he was unsure how this could be achieved.

As it happened, Matah was asleep, worn out by the exertions of the morning. He sat with his back against a smooth tree trunk and his face was serene. When he saw this, Tark laid his spear carefully on the ground and picked up a hunk of rotten wood. This he used as a club, bringing it down on the young man's head with enough force to stun though not, he hoped, to kill. Matah slumped sideways but made no sound and Tark flung his weapon away and dragged the unconscious man a little way off the path. He had nothing with which to bind him but he hoped that when he woke, Matah would be disoriented for a while, thus buying time.

Panting from dragging his comrade, an effort that stretched his already strained and aching muscles and sent pain shooting down his arms and back, Tark retraced his steps, picking up his spear as he went. By the time he reached the riverside, the first float had grounded on the gravel bar and the second had just come into view. The people crowded on the beach all stood watching with their backs to the forest and they jumped up and down and shouted encouragement to those desperately trying to steer the second craft towards them.

Their noise and complete ignorance of their danger made Tark angry. He pushed his way into the throng, seeking Draa, ignoring the amazement his appearance caused for some, looking to see who was shoving them, stared as if at a ghost. He did not pause until he found her, standing knee-deep in the swirling water, her eyes fixed on Mingar who had joined the swimmers trying to guide the second raft.

'Be quiet!' He grasped her shoulder and pulled her round. 'The Valley people will kill us if they find us! Stop them shouting!'

She stared, open-mouthed, then regaining her composure, called for silence though a new outcry had begun with Tark as its object. The crowd did not obey until Tark yelled suddenly, 'Do you all want to die?' and then the shock of his unexpected presence and the urgency of his tone quietened them. Gradually the float moved towards them and Tark and some of the other young men waded as far as they dared to meet it. Only when his feet touched gravel and hands reached to haul him out, did Mingar realize that Tark was there.

'My son!' The habitual grimness of his features was transformed by joy: he embraced Tark and Draa came forward and joined in, laughing and crying at the same time. And their happiness was echoed by other families reunited after the terror of the short river-voyage. But as the noise rose around him, Tark pulled away from Mingar and again called for quiet and this time there was something in his voice and face that checked the people's joy for he alone seemed distrait among the throng.

Indeed, while the rest celebrated, Tark felt only dismay which he struggled to conceal. He was acutely aware of their danger but more than this, a strange kind of self-consciousness discomfited him. In the time he had been in the Valley, he had almost forgotten how hard life was outside. Worn by their long journey, the bodies even of the young pared by necessity to stringy muscle and bone, their skins dry-looking and dark compared with the sleek golden-brown Valley folk, his kin now seemed strange to him. And they, looking upon him, wondered at the fullness of his flesh, the swelling of his muscles beneath skin as soft and flawless as an infant's and then they gazed at the lushness of the forest and many laughed aloud in sheer relief for it seemed to them that they had reached the fabled land of plenty. Some even reached out to touch Tark as if the evidence of their eyes alone was not enough. But the contact awoke the fear that up till then he had tried to quell. He stepped away and the sudden wildness of his gaze made Mingar ask, 'What is it?'

'You cannot stay here!' Even as he spoke, he was looking into the shadowed darkness of the forest, half-expecting to see Gullilli and his warriors approaching. 'I told Draa: the Valley people will slay us all if they find you here. I was set here on guard. I knocked my comrade senseless and came to warn you. But he will wake soon.'

A murmur of dismay arose as this speech was relayed to those who stood or sat beyond hearing and women grabbed children that had begun to explore further along the river bank. And Mingar, who had believed in the fulfilment of his dream with the blind fervour of a fanatic, shook his head in disbelief saying, 'But we are kin, or was she I saw with you not your betrothed?'

'She is my wife,' Tark replied, 'but we have no time to talk. Either we must hide deep in the forest and decide what to do or you must take to the river again and hope it bears you past the other look-outs without loss. We cannot stay here.'

The effect of these words was painfully clear. Draa and Mingar exchanged uncertain glances, then Mingar said unhappily, 'I do not understand. Are you sure of this, Tark? We have done nothing to earn the enmity of these Valley people. Surely we should go to them and claim the bonds of kinship? How could they then hate us?'

With an effort, Tark forced patience on himself, remembering his own incredulity when Myalah first told him of the Valley custom. Yet with each passing moment, his anxiety increased.

'Perhaps the children might be spared,' he said starkly. 'They suffered me to live because I was still a boy. But everyone else will be killed. That way they think to preserve the Valley and everything in it. It is their custom and they will not countenance change. Therefore, if you want to live, help me now. We must bind my companion then you must find a hiding place away from the river, for that is guarded. And conceal these craft as best you can. Make a camp and I will find you there.'

'But Tark –' Draa reached out to grasp his wrist but he twisted away and strode swiftly through the crowd into the forest. Mingar came after, limping heavily in his weariness and with him two others with lengths of rope they had untied from a raft. As they walked, Mingar's mind seethed with questions but sensing Tark's desperation, he knew this was not the time.

Matah was just stirring when they reached him. He groaned and groped for the lump on his head where he had been struck. Hearing people approach, he vainly tried to sit upright. As his senses returned, his eyes fixed on Tark in dazed bewilderment.

'Wha-' he began but before he could say more, he was gagged with rope, his arms wrenched back and bound by Mingar's companions who, once he was trussed, lifted him and bore him away, twisting and struggling to no avail.

Tark watched guiltily as Mingar and the others disappeared into the green forest-shadow. Then he turned and hurried along the path to the village for he wanted to be sure that Myalah was safe.

Chapter 14.

The settlement was quiet. The men sat resting in the shade while the women and children went about their usual tasks as if nothing extraordinary had happened. No-one seemed to notice Tark as he crossed the open court, making for Gullilli's hut. When he reached it, he found Myalah there with her mother and grandmother but there was no sign of her father.

'Tark, we did not expect you so soon!' Myalah came to greet him open-armed and smiling though it seemed to him that her eyes were somehow guarded. 'Is something wrong?'

'All is quiet,' he said. 'I left Matah by the river: there seemed little purpose in both of us staying. I came back to eat and rest, then I'll relieve him at sunset.'

Myalah nodded but the crone, who was hunched by the hearth like an ancient crow, frowned and spat into the fire.

'No-one else in the Valley would be so foolhardy,' she remarked sourly. 'You're defying the elders, had you thought of that? Don't let Gullilli find you here, that's all I can say. And you can rede it as warning or threat.'

She crossed her arms and began to rock back and forth, eyes half-closed. A faint murmur came from her lips and Tark stared, wondering if she meant to put a spell on him.

'Come, Myalah,' he said for he felt an urgent desire to speak with his beloved alone, 'we will go to our own place.'

He turned to go but Manalah, who had been watching him in silence, said unexpectedly, 'No, daughter, stay here. I want to be sure you are safe.'

There was a quiet determination in her tone that alarmed Tark: when he turned to face the women he found that they were looking at him intently save Myalah who stood beside her mother with downcast eyes.

'How is she threatened by being with me?' he demanded angrily.

'She is my wife. Come, Myalah, I am tired.'

To his astonishment, she did not move or speak and it was the crone that answered, saying 'She is staying here and it is better so. Until the danger is past, we should all be together. But if you want to sleep in your own hut, go.'

At the end of such a day, this was too much for Tark. Fist clenched, he took a step forward and so fierce was his expression, the old woman shrank. But Myalah still stood dumb and her mother moved protectively in front of her.

'Tark, go away and sleep, then come back when you feel better,' she said.

Thwarted more by Myalah's silence than the others' intransigence, Tark pushed past and reached to grab his wife's arm, to force her if necessary to go with him. But at that moment a shadow darkened the doorway and Myalah looked up in sudden dismay.

It was Gullilli and Tark's heart sank when he saw his father-in-law's grim expression.

'What are you doing here?'

Realizing how weak his reason for returning would seem, Tark answered as if he had misunderstood. 'I came to fetch my wife,' he said. 'But these women are trying to prevent me.'

'Myalah is safe here,' Gullilli said. 'But that is not what I meant. Why have you betrayed my trust and deserted your post? Do you not understand how dangerous your position is? There are many who would have cast you into the crack along with the body of your onetime friend, doubting your loyalty to the Valley. Do not give them cause to act. And think: on his own, Matah cannot keep watch and raise the alarm. Have your wits deserted you?'

Beneath his father-in-law's sternness, Tark detected sympathy, the last thing he had expected. It redoubled the shame he felt at what he was doing: he could no longer look Gullilli in the eye. With an effort he said, 'I am sorry, I should not have come here. I will return at once since the village is safe.'

'Why should it not be?' Gullilli squatted beside the fire and pushed a smouldering twig into the heart of the blaze. 'I have checked all the look-outs on the river and they have seen nothing.

But they are all downstream of you, Tark. Eh, you have saved me a walk after all: you were the last and you also have nothing to report?'

Unable to trust his voice, Tark shook his head, then stammered, 'All is quiet. Let me take some food for the pair of us and we will keep watch through the night. There's no need to send anyone to relieve us.'

'Very well.' Gullilli smiled and there was no longer doubt in his eyes. 'Go then. And do nothing else to make me question the trust I have put in you, my son.'

Tark waited outside while the women made up a small pack of fruit and the pounded seed-cakes that the men took to sustain them on hunting trips. It was Myalah who brought it to him and though she did not speak as she handed him the food, her eyes met his with a look of quiet desperation that smote his heart. He stared back for an instant, then turned on his heel and walked away for he was still angry at how she had defied him.

When he reached the landing place, it was deserted and there was no sign of the rafts. This worried Tark until he realized that the people had used every skin in their possession to make the floats, skins that they would need for clothing and shelter. However, by allowing them to destroy their means of transport, Mingar had committed his people to the Valley and then Tark cursed as he followed their trail along the river bank.

A faint scent of woodsmoke prickled his nostrils but despite this he was within the camp before he realized it: he had forgotten how simply his people lived upon the road. They had kindled their cooking fires in shallow pits and lay or sat so still in the dappled shade as to be almost invisible. Many were asleep, the rest were silent, as if waiting. Their eyes followed Tark with an odd detachment, as if they had forgotten who he was.

Draa and Mingar were under a tree at the far end of the camp, Mingar reclining with his head in Draa's lap, she sitting with her back against the trunk. She let out a little cry when she saw Tark and they scrambled to their feet. But they did not approach, they simply looked and let him come to them. Now, without any emergency to demand action, Mingar did not know what to say to the son he had sought so long. And Tark, looking upon his father, was similarly affected. So much change had been wrought in both since their parting on the day of the cataclysm they were like strangers: there was an awkwardness between them neither knew how to overcome. Face to face, both were reminded of how Eeli and Myee had died, how Mingar had done nothing to protect them or Tark. And their recent encounter when Mingar had spied the couple beside the river was also sharp in their minds.

Watching them, Draa realized that if she did not intervene, this reunion, which should have been an occasion for joyful celebration, might turn swiftly to woe. Without looking at Mingar, she stepped forward and embraced her foster-son saying, 'We have journeyed far to find you, now is the time to rejoice. Let the past lie behind us since it cannot be changed. Whatever happens, we are together again and that is more than we hoped for.'

Inwardly Tark squirmed with embarrassment at her artlessness though he submitted willingly to her embrace. But then Mingar, who had watched and listened with envy, said deliberately, 'Draa is right: there are things between us that are best forgotten or at least laid aside. But this you should know at least: the thin man is dead.'

It had been so long since Tark had thought of his old enemy, it was a moment before he realized who his father was referring to. And he almost laughed for without Tani he would never have found the Valley. But he was loth to admit this so he said merely, 'He tried to kill me many times and failed' and left it at that, for in the face of their current danger what had happened in the past seemed irrelevant.

'That was not the tale he told but we guessed it,' Draa said and there was both compassion and admiration in her gaze as she looked upon the young man, so much more mature in body and mind than the boy she remembered. And Mingar said 'You have done well, Tark, and I am proud of you' and his voice trembled as he spoke.

Such praise was almost unprecedented and Tark stared, torn between tenderness and contempt, for he could not forget how his father had reviled him in the past. And something of this conflict must have been evident in his expression because Draa said suddenly, 'Come now son, sit down and tell us your tale, how you came here and of the people of the Valley. We have yet to decide what to do.'

These words restored Tark's sense of imminent danger: he looked round wildly and said, 'Why are the men not making spears? Then at least you can defend yourselves. Did you not listen to me beside the river?'

Mingar's brow creased in perplexity but before he could speak, Draa put a hand on his arm though her eyes were upon her foster-son. 'Hush, Tark,' she said quietly. 'We have heard what you said and our hearts are dismayed but all are weary. When they have rested, the men will make weapons, they'll do anything you ask of them. Yet before we decide our next step, we must know more of this place and its people. Therefore do not be angry but tell us what we need to know. The rest can wait.'

'Very well.' Forcing restraint on himself, Tark sat on a nearby tree-root while Draa and Mingar settled on the ground before him. 'But it will make hard listening.'

With that he launched into an account of his life in the Valley, how the people had succoured him and how, in return, he had been initiated into their clan. And though he saw incredulity and disgust grow in the faces of Draa and Mingar, he spared them nothing and described how Memi's remains had been desecrated and how the law of the Valley was immutable so that not even Nygeli, his friend and mentor, would contemplate change.

'But how can this be?' In Mingar's outrage, Tark recognized his own when he first heard of the custom of the Valley. 'We have done no harm to this place or its people! What would happen if everyone did the same? It makes no sense!'

Tark spread his fingers in an age-old gesture of peace. 'I am telling you how it is here, that's all,' he said wearily. 'I do not argue it is right though I have sworn to uphold that law. I'm trying to make you understand.'

'I understand,' Mingar said grimly, after a moment's silence. His eyes left Tark's face and surveyed the makeshift camp, the tired people who looked to him for leadership. His hands clenched and his face-muscles hardened so that his visage looked more than ever like something hewn from wood or stone. 'What you mean is that we must fight for the right to stay or leave before we are discovered. And there is no chance of compromise, even if you took me to their elders alone and unarmed?'

His conversation with Nygeli had convinced Tark that any attempt to broker a peaceful outcome would be futile. He replied starkly, 'When they set eyes on you, they will slay you: that is the law.'

Silence fell between them and Draa looked from one to the other in dismay.

'We must leave then,' she said at last. 'For we are not fighters and there are few of us. It was folly to destroy the rafts so quickly.'

'Whatever you decide, it must be now,' Tark said. 'For the river is guarded and warriors are waiting in the village. And they are many, well-armed and fierce. They will give no quarter.'

An awkward silence descended upon them, none knowing what to say. Somewhere deep in the forest a twig cracked and Tark leapt to his feet, heart pounding, for despite his apparent calm, he was in a state of high anxiety. He crept a little way into the trees and stood poised to listen but there was no other untoward noise and nothing to be seen save a flock of small birds foraging in the undergrowth.

When he re-joined the others, Mingar was on his feet, staring into the forest but he was reliving the moment he had first seen the Valley, a green island in a sea of barren rock. He thought of the ancestors, who had been driven from their homeland by the dreaded Night-Stalkers who were hungrier and fiercer than they. And musingly he murmured, 'But we are hungry too.'

Only Draa heard these words and they filled her with alarm. She reached out and took Mingar's wrist as if to physically restrain his thoughts but he snatched his arm away.

'Why should we run away?' Mingar said. 'These people have no rights over us: the land does not belong to them. If we attack at night, surprise will give us the advantage!'

He strode round the camp, urging the men and boys to make spears and clubs, the women and children to collect stones for missiles while Draa and Tark watched in appalled silence. The people scrambled to do Mingar's bidding, their fear lessened by his certitude and when he was satisfied that all were busy, he began to question Tark about the village and the numbers of warriors they would encounter. But Tark refused to speak.

'Answer me!' Mingar's face was distorted by rage. 'You are my son: you have no choice but to obey! Or would you see us slain by those you call your friends?'

Tark shivered. 'My wife and her family are in that village,' he pleaded. 'What do you expect of me? If you refuse to leave, I will betray those I love whatever I say or do. And I came to warn you, not to wage war on my kin.'

'It is their law that has forced us to this,' Mingar said grimly.

With his intimate knowledge of the forest, Nygeli had followed Tark undetected. When he reached the riverside his worst fears were realized for the gravel bar was marked with many footprints and it was unguarded. But instead of returning to the village to raise the alarm, he followed the trail into the forest. For he had come to love Tark as a son and was reluctant to betray him.

As he picked his way carefully between the trees the old man mused over his last conversation with Tark and Myalah and he almost regretted his hardness, realizing he had done nothing to help them. Yet neither had he revealed their secret though this was in itself an act of treason, the first time in his life he had broken the law of the Valley.

'Maybe I have lived too long,' he thought sadly and then he stopped this contemplation for he thought he heard voices ahead.

A twig broke under his foot just as he came within sight of the camp and Nygeli cursed softly to himself as Tark jumped to his feet and moved forward to investigate. But so still was the old man and so well did his scar-seamed body meld with the colours and textures of the trees in that dappled light, he was all but invisible. When Tark gave up and returned to the man and woman with whom he had been talking, Nygeli crept forward for a closer look.

As he did so, he was aware of a profound sorrow gathering within him for he knew that whatever happened, the coming of these strangers marked change. Life in the Valley would never be the same again.

It was clear to him that from their attitude towards each other, the couple with Tark must be his father and foster-mother but Nygeli was struck most by their physical appearance. Their bodies seemed weathered and tough as rawhide; their faces were honed by hunger so that the shapes of the skulls was evident. And when the man (whose back had been twisted by some past injury), limped around the camp, giving orders to the people sitting quietly beneath the trees, a thrill of fear, something he had not felt for more than a generation, went through the elder for he understood suddenly how fierce these intruders might become, how urgent their need for all that the Valley had to offer, which his own people took for granted.

'We are many and better armed but even the children here look as if they can fight,' Nygeli reflected. 'We must strike swiftly if we are to be sure of winning.' And yet though he knew he should set off at once to raise the alarm, that the very future of his people depended on him, he hesitated.

For as the men and women scrambled to do the twisted man's bidding, he saw Tark's face. It was stricken, the look of one close to despair and then, for the first time, Nygeli began to question the law he had believed in all his life, that had seen many innocent men and women tortured and killed, people he now realized were no different to his in their needs and desires save that they came from beyond the confines of the Valley. And he recalled how avidly he had listened to Tark's tales of that world where the horizon stretched vast and limitless in all directions rather than being walled in by massive cliffs, where there was an infinite variety of places: terrible deserts; green forests; grassy plains; lakes and coasts; watercourses broad and shallow with intricate mazes of channels; torrents deeper and swifter than the river he knew. And looking upon these people who had travelled across desert and mountain to reach the Valley, he was filled with regret that all their experiences, all their stories, would die with them for the sake of a law designed to protect those afraid to venture beyond the boundaries of their own rock-rimmed existence.

As he thought these things, Nygeli moved closer to the glade, drawn by curiosity and a growing desire to be acknowledged by Tark though it was still his intention to protect the Valley. And these conflicting needs confused the old man who, before Tark's arrival, had lived with simple certainties. He crept to the very edge of the camp, his hand against a tree, one of the ancients of the forest, moss-hung, festooned with orchids and other parasitic plants, and his eyes fell on Matah who lay bound and gagged on the opposite side of the glade.

In that moment, as Nygeli stared in shock (for he had forgotten Tark's companion), Draa looked round and saw him.

Startled, she let out a low cry and her hand went to her mouth for so singular was the old man's appearance he seemed more like some spirit of the forest than a person of flesh and blood. This illusion was heightened by Nygeli's immobility for they stared at one other as if transfixed. And each saw something unexpected in the other's eyes: beneath Draa's fear, compassion; a kind of pleading in the old man's.

Bu the moment was swiftly lost. Alerted by Draa's cry, others looked and saw the newcomer. Cries of anger and surprise rang out and a hail of missiles, lumps of wood, stones, clods, sticks filled the air even as Tark leapt before his mentor shouting 'No!'

A chunk of rotten wood had hit Nygeli on the shoulder, knocking him to the ground. He sat dazedly, clutching the place and tears sprang to his eyes. Yet it was not pain that made him weep.

'Nygeli!' Tark's voice dragged the old man from self-pity; the young man's hands felt him over, checking for injuries. Finding none, he sat back on his heels and regarded his teacher with wonder. 'Are you alone? How did you find us?'

'I followed you,' Nygeli said simply and his eyes went to where Matah lay struggling against his bonds. 'What are you doing here, Tark?'

By now the whole clan had gathered to see what was happening and a murmur arose at the sight of the old man, more ancient than any among the Lake people though he was not the eldest in the Valley. Yet while some admired his courage in entering their camp alone, others called for him to be made captive or killed as a spy and still more thought him witless and wanted to drive him away. But Mingar, seeing that this old man was of great significance to Tark whatever else he might be, called for silence and waited for the intruder to explain himself.

'These are my people,' Tark said quietly as he helped Nygeli to his feet. 'And so they are yours also. Do you understand now why I came to you for help?' He bent to kiss the old man's shoulder, an age-old sign of homage from a son to his father or grandfather among the Valley folk, (a gesture which smote Nygeli to the heart), and led him forward.

The introductions were, necessarily, brief yet long enough for Mingar to recognize power in the old man's self-assurance and to feel a stab of envy at the easy relationship between him and Tark while Nygeli, looking upon the leader's twisted body and fierce mien, recalled how this man had been described as a faithless coward. And Draa, seeing how their eyes locked as if each was testing the other, was filled with foreboding though she guessed that she and Mingar were deeply indebted to this old man because of Tark.

'You do not understand your danger,' Nygeli said after an awkward silence. 'You must leave, now! Tark and I risk our lives by being here: once you are discovered you will all be killed. And you must decide what to do with your hostage for if he is freed to bear witness against us, we will pay for your escape with our lives.'

'We cannot leave,' Mingar replied and he shrugged as if the elder's words were of no account. 'Nor are we minded to. For we have sought long for a place such as this and we will fight for it if we have to. No, we will not leave. And since you speak of hostages, old man, why not join your comrade? We have no other use for you.'

So terrible were Mingar's voice and aspect as he spoke these words, Nygeli did not argue. Casting a long, meaningful glance at Tark, he shuffled across the clearing and sat quietly beside Matah who, exhausted by his struggles, now lay still. Then Mingar, ignoring Tark's stricken expression, said 'Bind his hands and feet and gag him well for is it not the old crows that have the loudest voices?' And when Tark hesitated, he shouted, 'Are you deaf? Do as I say! Was this not what you wanted: a father you could be proud of?'

For an instant as he stared into his father's eyes, eyes that were narrowed and inflamed with passion, Tark was ready to retort that

Nygeli was more of a father to him than Mingar had ever been. But perceiving that in his present mood Mingar might murder Nygeli in a fit of jealous rage, he forced control on himself and obeyed. As he tied his mentor's wrists, he whispered, 'Forgive me, Nygeli, none of this is what I wanted. I should have listened to you and left with Myalah. I am sorry.'

'It is I that am sorry,' Nygeli answered drily. 'I allowed you, a stranger, into my heart and for that we shall all suffer. I am sorry to have lived to see this day.' And with these words he submitted to the gag and closed his eyes.

The sun sank behind the ring of cliffs and shadow spread over the forest. In her parent's hut Myalah helped prepared the evening meal but anxiety made her clumsy and at length her mother told her to go and fetch water from the spring since she was no use by the fireside. Resignedly, Myalah took the waterskin and made her way through the village. Since the afternoon had passed without incident, the atmosphere of dread had largely dissipated and the men gathered in the courtyard now sat or lay at their ease while the women and children brought food.

As she passed, some of the young men called out, asking if Tark had deserted her and, if so, which of them would she choose but she ignored them and hurried on for twilight was deepening. Yet when she was beyond range of their voices and the smells of the village she felt strangely lonely and vulnerable.

It was simply the possibility that strangers were close that made her nervous she told herself for she knew this path well and her feet were sure upon it. But in her heart she knew it was the uncertainty of her situation, the danger she and Tark were in, which preyed upon her mind, that and a sharper anxiety for Tark himself. She did not understand the purpose of his visit that afternoon though his distraction had been obvious enough. Unless he had come to bid farewell.

As this thought struck her she stopped in her tracks. Suddenly everything made sense: Tark had wanted to see her one last time before leaving the Valley, forsaking her despite his promise. And this realization, simple and devastating, wiped all else from her mind. With a cry of dismay, she dropped the waterskin and sped back along the path, taking the fork that led to the river, running with the grace of a wild animal, her hair flung out behind like a shadow.

When she came to the river she made her way to the gravel bar where she and Tark had made love. By the time she reached it, she was panting and her body glistened with sweat. In the starlight the river seemed oddly sinister, flowing blackly past like a torrent of blood. Filled with foreboding, she looked down and saw that the sand on which she stood was pocked with footmarks of all shapes and sizes. Her hand went involuntarily to the shell talisman that hung between her breasts and her heart beat so wildly she felt faint. There was no doubting the significance of the footprints but there was no sign of what had happened to Tark and Matah.

'Oh where are you?' she cried. She no longer believed Tark had run away, therefore he was either dead or had colluded with the strangers, betraying the Valley for the sake of his blood-kin. And a terrible apprehension gripped her for recalling their argument with Nygeli, she realized there was no course open to the newcomers but violence, to strike before they were discovered.

'No, it must not be.' She climbed back up the riverbank and then, seeing the place where Mingar had led his people into the forest, hesitated. She knew she should return to the village at once but if he were still alive, her warning would condemn Tark to death. Warily she left the path and picked her way along the trail left by the strangers. Soon, a little way ahead, she saw a red glow and knew she had found their camp.

By sunset even the children of the Lake Clan understood their danger. Mingar had made sure everyone had eaten so as to regain their strength and nearly all had some kind of weapon at hand. Only the very old and the infants were being left behind while the rest went to attack the village. As the light began to fade, Mingar ordered all those accompanying him to blacken their faces and bodies with charcoal and while the youngest indulged in wild antics as if it was a game, to many of the adults it took on the grave significance of a ritual, acting both to calm them and to focus their minds on what lay ahead. For though they were by nature a timid and peace-loving people, the intransigence and unfairness of the Valley law had incensed them and their hunger for the bounty that lay all around was greater than any fear.

Even Tark, torn as he was by his love for Myalah and his obligations to those that had helped him during his time in the Valley, was affected by the fervour. He remembered his outrage when he had learned of the Valley custom; the horrors he had endured so that the Valley people would accept him; how he had been forced to desecrate Memi's body. And the anger that had smouldered deep within him since those first days was fanned at last to a raging fire. He recalled how he had tried to argue against that law to no avail though by his betrothal to Myalah, his clan and the Valley people were, by any normal custom, united, and how at last they had decided to leave the Valley rather than face the calamity that, through chance, was now upon them. And then bitterness melded with his anger and his face became grim: he went to where Nygeli lay and crouched beside the old man saying 'If you had done as I asked and called the council together, perhaps this bloodshed would have been avoided. We are kin, not enemies!'

Gagged as he was, Nygeli could not answer but his eyelids quivered and his body became rigid with tension.

'It is the law of the Valley that has caused this!' Tark said and then he rose and went to join Mingar who was assembling his force for the journey to the village.

Had Gullilli and his men witnessed that muster, they would have laughed, first in disbelief that anyone would have the audacity to challenge them with a group that included women and children; secondly from contempt, for ill-armed and half-starved as they appeared, the Lake Clan seemed pathetic rather than frightening, easy meat for a well-armed warrior band. But though they numbered only forty, Mingar's people were desperate, fierce and resolute, knowing they had but one chance: to attack under cover of night using surprise as their main weapon. And Mingar told them that as the law of the Valley was merciless and uncompromising, so they too must be ruthless, slaying all that resisted, even women and children. Only one person was to be spared at all costs, Tark's wife

Myalah, who could be easily identified since she wore Eeli's shell talisman around her neck.

At the mention of that name many sighed and Tark shivered, remembering his mother's gentleness. But Mingar, grim and imposing in the lurid firelight, held up a hand for silence and said solemnly, 'All we have said and done in our lives has led to this moment. We have found the place our forefathers sought long ago, eh ever since the Night-Stalkers drove them from their homes, but we must fight to gain it. Let us strike hard then. And let no-one be afraid!'

They waved their weapons and followed him and Tark between the trees. By now the moon had risen and by its light they slipped like shadows through the forest, the charcoal they had rubbed into their skin rendering them almost invisible for it absorbed rather than reflected that pale radiance. In the camp a few old women comforted the babes and toddlers and Matah struggled against his bonds but Nygeli lay motionless, staring unblinkingly at the stars.

All was quiet in the village. The warriors lay sleeping around the central fire while the women and children had retired to their huts. Any sense of danger had dissipated with the coming of night for it was deemed impossible for strangers to attack during darkness since they could have no knowledge of the layout of the village or even of its existence.

Only in Gullilli's hut was there any trepidation and this was due to Myalah's absence. For she had not returned from her errand fetching water and while Gullilli assumed she had gone to find Tark, he was irked by her disobedience. Only the pleading of the women prevented him setting off after her, to force her home like a naughty child.

'You may be her father but she has a husband now,' Myenah said. 'And she has always known her own mind. Let them alone: whatever they are up to, Matah will guard Tark's post for he is young and ambitious, eager to be noted by the elders. Lie down and sleep for who knows what tomorrow will bring?'

To keep the peace, Gullilli allowed himself to be persuaded though Myalah was his favourite daughter. He lay down on his pallet and closed his eyes but sleep was long in coming.

Stealthily, Myalah crept closer to the camp, moving from tree to tree though as she drew near, she realized the place was almost deserted. A few old women sat huddled around a small fire with children sleeping in their laps. But though other spots of red marked more fireplaces, these were unattended. There was no sign of Tark.

Perplexed, Myalah squatted in the shadow of a massive tree to think. It seemed inconceivable that Tark should have betrayed the Valley without warning her yet if the strangers were not on the way to the village, where could they be?

Resolved to follow them she rose to her feet but a convulsive movement in the shadowed space behind the old women caught her eye. It was the jerky, restricted paroxysm of some wounded or restrained creature and the young woman paused, staring. A cold had seemed to grasp her heart as she realized that what she had taken for sections of a fallen tree were two captives lying bound or maimed upon the ground.

Her first thought was that these were Tark and Matah who must have been captured before they could raise the alarm; her second that she must rescue them. Treading with the utmost care, she retraced her steps into the cover of the forest and made a wide loop so as to come upon the prisoners from behind.

When she was close enough to identify Nygeli, whose face was stark in the dappled moonlight, she was certain he must be dead for his eyes stared glassily and he did not move. With an effort she quelled the wail that rose involuntarily in her throat and fixed her attention on the other who was obviously alive for he writhed and strained against his bonds with the mindless tenacity of a trapped wild animal.

She saw at once this was not Tark who retained the leanness of his people; when she recognized Matah, she moved to his side, trusting that the old women would not look round and secure in the knowledge that even if she were discovered, she could easily elude them.

When he saw who was crouching over him, Matah's eyes glittered, he shuddered and then lay rigidly still while her fingers worked to untie the ropes, all of which had been tightened by his struggles. He hissed with impatience as she fumbled with the knots and tiny though the sound was, it broke Nygeli's reverie. He turned his head and seeing Myalah was filled with a dreadful prescience, for he remembered what Myalah had long forgotten, that Matah, of all her suitors, had been hurt most by her betrothal to Tark, the outsider. That envy would now, the old man was sure, be exacerbated by Tark's treachery and he struggled against his bonds with a ferocity that surprised Myalah and aroused her pity though she was full of joy that he was alive after all.

'Lie still and be patient: I will come to you soon,' she whispered and then he gave up for he knew his efforts were in vain.

At last Matah was free. He lay still for a moment then sat up, rubbing the places on his wrist and ankles where the ropes had chafed. There was something in his expression that dismayed Myalah yet she asked softly, 'Where's Tark?' even as she turned to help Nygeli.

A spasm crossed Matah's face. He groped upon the ground and his hand fastened on a chunk of wood. He rose to his feet, trembling. Nygeli saw him loom over the crouching woman then he struck her a blow on the head that sent her sprawling. As she tried to crawl away, Matah seized her ankles and dragged her back, dazed and helpless.

'Where's your precious husband now?' He struck her again, this time across the back as she struggled to rise and she collapsed face down in the dirt.

The sudden commotion panicked the old women. They jumped to their feet, grabbing as many infants as they could. Then they scurried into the forest, herding the terrified children before them, hushing them with hoarse whispers.

Their departure licenced Matah's lust. He fell upon Myalah, biting and tearing at her flesh: she shrieked as if she were being stabbed. His hands closed upon her throat to silence her. She heaved and shuddered: he pressed harder. Then she relaxed, but he did not stop.

Only after he was spent and lay limp and panting upon her, did Matah realize what he had done. He turned his head and met

Nygeli's appalled gaze.

'Don't think you'll bear witness, old man.' Nygeli watched helplessly as Matah tied the discarded rope into a noose. For an instant he thought of undoing the gag but there was nothing he wanted to hear from the elder's lips so he slipped the rope round Nygeli's scrawny neck whispering: 'This is all your fault: you took the usurper under your protection; you made him a man, you gave him Myalah when she should have been mine! You're as much a traitor as Tark and now you will pay for it!'

Nygeli did not struggle, he just looked as the young man flung the rope over a branch and his eyes were full of tears. Then Matah hauled with all his strength, hoisting him into the air. Nygeli jerked and kicked for a while, then only twitched and at last was still. When he was satisfied the old man was dead, Matah tied the end of the rope to another tree and set off into the forest after Tark.

The old women hiding in the undergrowth waited until his footsteps had died away and then they crept out, ushering the toddlers before them. Seeing the hanging body they stared in dread but the sight of the young woman, beautiful and pathetic as a broken-winged bird, affected them profoundly. The boldest of them knelt and stroked Myalah's head then, finding the talisman, began to keen for she knew who this must be.

Chapter 15.

It was deep night when Tark and Mingar reached the edge of the settlement, the clan jostling at their heels. Through the gaps between huts, the central court was visible, its great fire sunk to a heap of glowing embers. The sleeping forms of Gullilli's warriors lay around the hearth and Tark sighed. There was no sign of any guard: the village was at their mercy.

'Are you ready?' Mingar hissed. His charcoal-smeared body blended with the darkness but his eyeballs and teeth glistened in the moonlight. He looked exactly as Tark had always imagined the Night-Stalkers and a momentary terror gripped the young man, a fear rooted in those long-lost nights when he and his sisters had listened to the tale of their ancestors. And then he thought confusedly, 'But I am the same!' and the weight of the smooth river-stone he held in his left hand seemed suddenly insupportable while the spear in his right was brittle and strange.

'Tark!' His father's voice, harsh and terrible, restored him to the present. It was too late now to turn back or attempt a compromise. His tongue seemed like a block of wood in his mouth as he answered; cold sweat bathed him. Then they were moving into the settlement, their blackened skins and stealth protracting the illusion that they were but nightmarish shadows until the moment they howled their war cries.

The attack was over more quickly that Tark had expected yet it seemed to him that this night could have no ending, that dawn would never come. Flames leapt high beneath the sky and smoke blotted out the moon and stars for a while: most of the village was burning. By that lurid light blood glistened blackly on the bodies scattered around the compound, dead of the Lake Clan mixed with those of the Valley folk. Beside the central hearth sat a group of prisoners. The women and children wailed and cried ceaselessly while the men among them sat in sullen silence. Many clutched wounds. All were stunned by the magnitude of the disaster, unable to believe that a group of half-starved strangers could have wrought such swift destruction. And when they saw that the attack was led by a cripple and that Tark had betrayed them, shame and anger exacerbated the bitterness of defeat.

Tark and Mingar went round the whole settlement, making sure all the huts were empty yet while his father was still in a state of battle-joy, Tark was racked by anxiety. Though he had seen Gullilli and Manalah among the prisoners, there was no sign of Myalah.

'Hai! The valley is ours!' Mingar cried when they returned to the centre of the village and his people yelled in acclamation and triumph, the children's voices shrill as those of kites, then began to dance around the fallen. But Tark, who alone amongst his clan had not been overtaken by bloodlust, stood watching with a feeling of detachment, of unreality. He felt as if it were all happening to someone else, though he was bleeding from many wounds.

'Tark!' So like his beloved's was the voice, he went weak with relief and joy. Then he realized it had come from within the group of captives. Reluctantly he made his way towards them. The stained earth seemed to heave beneath his feet.

'Here!' Alone amongst the prisoners Manalah held her head high though one eye was swollen shut from a blow to her face. Gullilli lay with his head in her lap, his knees drawn up and his hands pressed to a gaping wound in his belly from which a foul stench arose. As he stood looking down at them, Tark felt only shame.

'Where is Myalah?' Manalah's voice was sharp. 'Tell me she is safe. I don't care what you and your people do to us but she is your wife! Or was your love for her only pretence, like all the rest?'

'How can you – ' Tark began for her words evoked a piercing pain at the very heart of him, a hurt more profound than any of his physical wounds. But then, seeing the fear behind the accusation in her eyes, alarm leapt within him like a dark flame: he bent over the two demanding, 'What do you mean? Wasn't she with you last night?'

She looked at him and her mouth worked in distress but no words came out. And then Gullilli, whose face was a mask of pain, groaned and whispered 'She went to fetch water at nightfall and did not return. We thought she'd gone to the river to find you.'

Tark's answer was written so clearly on his face, Manalah bowed her head while Gullilli grimaced and his hands clenched until the knuckles stood out white beneath the layers of blood and filth. And Tark gazed around wildly, fighting for control because having left Myalah with her family it had never occurred to him that they would let her out of their sight. Now, as he saw the dancing victors, the bodies scattered wherever he looked, he realized the magnitude of his folly for Gullilli could have had no idea of the danger they were in and that was his, Tark's, doing.

At last Manalah raised her head, distraught. 'It is my fault,' she moaned, 'I did not think any harm would come to her. Where can she be?'

Then, with a terrible prescience, Tark thought of the camp with only a few crones to guard it and the captives lying bound side by side. He imagined Myalah following the trail from the river, how horrified she would have been to find Nygeli and Matah prisoners, how she would have gone at once to help. And since it was impossible that at least one of these two would not have sped to the village to raise the alarm or join in the fight, he was certain some calamity had befallen them all.

Barely had this thought crystallized before he was moving. He snatched up a discarded spear and limped painfully between the burning huts towards the river path, Manalah staring after in bewilderment.

Matah reached the edge of the village when the fighting was at its fiercest. So far beyond his worst imaginings was the scene that met his eyes, he could not comprehend it. He leant against a tree and watched the destruction of his home as if in a dream, incapable of movement, even of coherent thought. The stench of the burning filled his nostrils and the screams and wails of the wounded and dying seemed to pierce his skull yet somehow it all seemed remote.

Slowly, he slid down the tree, his legs unable to support him for the blows to his head and his struggles to escape had weakened him even before he had been overtaken by the frenzy which had left him exhausted. Only his hatred of Tark had given him strength to reach this far: now, seeing his enemy triumph, he was overwhelmed by a sense of futility. Though he felt no remorse for killing Nygeli, whom he regarded as a traitor, he had begun to regret assaulting Myalah for he realized confusedly that if she had known of the attack, she would never have released him. And it had long been his secret hope that if misfortune befell Tark, she would choose him.

Maudlin tears squeezed between his eyelids as he remembered how he had yearned for her and how cruelly she had spurned him for Tark and he wrung his hands and shuddered at the memory of what he had done. Then he groaned and rolled his head from side to side like a wounded beast for he knew that whatever happened, that deed could never be atoned.

In his haste, Tark passed Matah without recognizing him. Slumped as he was, he appeared like many others of the wounded and dying to be seen around the ruins of the village and in the flickering firelight, only close scrutiny would have identified him. But Matah knew his enemy at once and the sight lent him a kind of frantic energy. He jumped to his feet and waited until Tark was a little way ahead, then followed, moving as stealthily as on the hunting trail.

It seemed to Tark in his weariness that it took half the night to reach the camp but when he found it, time no longer mattered. The old women, fearful of the spirits of the dead, had built the fire to a bright blaze but dread had kept them from touching the corpses. Thus, at first glance, all appeared normal. Only after his eyes had adjusted to the brightness did Tark notice Nygeli's body hanging in the air behind the crones and, a little beyond it, the figure of a young woman sprawled face down on the ground.

He stared while his brain tried to assimilate what he was seeing. Shadows wavered as the flames leapt, lending a semblance of animation to the two so that Nygeli seemed almost to dance at the rope's end while Myalah appeared to twitch in pain. The spear dropped unheeded from Tark's hand, the forest and stars reeled and still he stared. It made no sense: it could not be.

Then a child huddled at the old women's feet looked round and saw him. So terrible was his visage, streaked with charcoal and blood, the whites of his eyes gleaming, the child shrieked, thinking an avenging ghost had come. And from the crones a dreadful wailing arose for they also thought they saw a spirit: they clutched the children close and waited, paralyzed by terror.

The noise shattered Tark's reverie. He sprang across the clearing, ignoring the women and children, and knelt beside Myalah, stroking her skin and hair, whispering her name, desperately seeking the faintest sign of life. But she was already cold and did not stir even when he bent to her ear and begged her to wake in a voice that rose to a shout. Then, with a huge effort, he gathered her in his arms and sat holding her though her limbs were stiff and awkward and her head inert as a boulder against his shoulder. And it seemed to him that all joy had fled from his life; he sat there numbly, deaf to the whispering of the crones who, having recognized him at last, now twittered together like bats, their fear replaced by pity.

When Matah reached the edge of the camp he was so tired his limbs shook and he was barely capable of coherent thought. He leant against a tree and watched Tark cradle Myalah's body and it seemed to him that to see his enemy in such anguish was more satisfying than slaying him could ever have been. And yet to fully gratify himself he needed to see Tark's face, to feast upon his agony. He moved closer, ignoring the crones, unaware that in the flaring firelight he was fully visible.

'Aiee! The rapist, the murderer!' One of the old women heard his dragging footfalls, looked round and saw him. The others began to screech abuse and the children screamed as the old women scrambled to their feet. Matah had eyes only for Tark: he stepped further into the clearing even as the crones swarmed towards him, arms outstretched, groping as if they were blind, their fingers curled into claws. The children clung to one another in abject terror for it was as if their ancient guardians were possessed, their wasted bodies animated by some terrible and merciless spirit of vengeance.

Too late did Matah understand his danger. So frail and timid had the old women seemed, he had simply dismissed them, assuming they could be brushed aside if they dared touch him. But now, as their fingers grasped his hair and arms, he realized he had underestimated not only their strength but his own weakness.

He screamed as they clawed his flesh and plucked at his genitals but they had worked themselves into frenzy and he knew he could not long withstand them. They kicked his legs until he staggered: as he fell he shrieked for help.

That cry, shrill and desperate, jerked Tark to the present for it had the same piercing quality as Eeli's when her killers closed upon her. When he saw the heaving gaggle of old women, intent as vultures upon their victim, it seemed to him that events had somehow come full circle except that this time he could prevent a death. He laid Myalah gently upon the ground and lurched to his feet.

'No, stop!' He began pulling the crones away with all the strength that remained to him and so like Mingar's was his voice, they obeyed though for an instant, seeing their fixed eyes and bloodstained hands, he feared they might turn on him.

'See to the children,' he commanded, then knelt beside Matah who lay curled like a foetus, his skin torn and bleeding, one hand thrust between his legs, the other clamped over his face. He had stopped screaming but a faint intermittent whimper escaped his lips and his whole body quivered in terror.

'Matah, you're safe now.' As yet the knowledge that this was the violator and killer of his beloved, the murderer of Nygeli, was nothing to Tark but dull fact: he felt no desire for vengeance. And when Matah at last moved his hand from his face, Tark recoiled in horror, then pitied him for the old women had plucked out his eyes: one hung halfway down his cheek, the other was gone, the socket a mess of writhing muscles, welling blood.

'Don't let them touch me!' Matah whined. He rolled onto his hands and knees and crawled brokenly away from the firelight. Tark made no attempt to stay him, he simply watched until the darkness of the forest had swallowed him and then he returned to Myalah while the crones replenished the fire.

Quiet descended upon the camp, broken only by the occasional sputter of green wood burning and the moan of a sleeping child. But it seemed to Tark that night had entered his very soul and for him there was nothing left but to wait beside the body of his beloved until the darkness took him also. Yet when it came, it was not the nihilation of death but the merciful oblivion of sleep.

A little before dawn, one of the old women woke to the snarling and thrashing of carrion-eaters nearby. She listened intently and threw more fuel on the fire until sparks streamed towards the stars and the flames were high and bright. The disturbance came from the direction in which Matah had crawled and the crone hugged herself in glee for it seemed to her that justice had been done.

For those in the village, dawn crept across the sky as if reluctant to reveal what lay below. Smoke from the smouldering huts still billowed across the ruins with every breath of wind and it was foul with the stench of burnt flesh for many had been trapped inside as the flames took hold. Bodies lay where they had fallen for Mingar had not permitted the captives to tend their fallen, nor had those of his own people been moved. After the elation of victory his fighters had quickly succumbed to exhaustion and lay sleeping wherever they found themselves, often within touching distance of their victims.

Waking to so dismal a scene, their bodies stiff and smarting from wounds and exertion, the people of both clans gazed around as if stunned, unable to come to terms with this new reality. For the vanquished, defeat was bitter and incomprehensible; for the victors, the triumph that had carried them to ecstasy in the night now seemed strange and daunting. They looked wonderingly at the destruction they had wrought and the green mass of the forest and the encircling walls of rock menaced them, as if a horde of enemies might be waiting there.

But whatever the future might hold, hunger and thirst were the immediate concerns of the leaders who woke to that slow dawn: Mingar, who through all the chaos and fighting had somehow remained unscathed and Gullilli who, though mortally wounded, was the only figure of authority left among the Valley people for Myenah, the crone, was dead. To these two the demands of the clans were addressed and while he was powerless to help, Gullilli told the survivors not to despair for he sensed these invaders were uneasy in victory and he still nursed a secret hope that Tark would help those he had betrayed. And before the sun had cleared the tops of the surrounding trees, Mingar sought him out, for he had relied on his son to explain where water was to be found and food gathered yet Tark was nowhere to be seen.

As soon as the two leaders met, each recognized authority in the other for despite his pain Gullilli's dignity was not impaired while Mingar neither gloated nor scorned his enemy but regarded him with a kind of stern forbearance. Draa, who stood beside her husband, was filled with regret as she looked upon Gullilli, guessing he would die before sunset. And it seemed Gullilli sensed this also for instead of waiting for the victors to speak first, he demanded, 'What do you want? You have destroyed my home and my people: can you not let me die in peace?'

'First you must tell us where water is to be found, and food,' Mingar said. 'And if you are their leader, give us surety that the rest of your people will submit. Otherwise we have no choice but to kill them all. And tell me what has happened to Tark, my son. He has not been seen since the fighting ended.'

'Your son?' A spasm of inexpressible bitterness crossed Gullilli's face. 'Your son? So he meant to betray us from the start! How long has it been, truly, since you discovered the Valley and planned this together?' And Manalah moaned softly and said, 'He went to find Myalah, our daughter, and they have not returned.'

Then Mingar was silent. He looked around the ruined village, the people who, vanquished and victors, seemed bemused, still bloodstained and weary from the fighting, and sudden rage gripped him that any of this should have been necessary. He crouched and leant forward until his head was close to the wounded man's, then said fiercely, 'You are wrong: Tark urged us to leave. Your law forced us to this though by rights we are kin. The old scarred man came to find him: we took him captive lest he warn you of our presence, knowing that if we were discovered you would slay us all. But it was only two days ago that I saw Tark: until then we did not know he was still alive.'

Gullilli's head rolled in agony. When he was still again, he whispered, 'We spared him for his youth and he has destroyed us. Why should we help you? Nygeli loved him like a son.'

'Leave us!' Manalah broke in unexpectedly. 'Whether you speak the truth or not, what difference does it make? You may do as you wish since the Valley is yours. Maybe Myalah and Tark have run away together.'

Her hands went to her mouth as she realized the implications of her words and Draa was overwhelmed by pity.

'I do not think Myalah knew anything of this,' she said gently. 'Tark sought to protect her as best he could. He told us to look out for a young woman wearing a shell talisman about her neck and to spare her and her kin. That shell belonged to his mother and her mother before and so on to the generation that fled the Night-Stalkers long ago. He would only have bestowed it on one he truly loved for it was very precious to him.'

As she finished speaking there was a stir amongst the other prisoners and at the same time a new and penetrating sound could be heard, an intermittent keening. It drew Mingar to his feet for it seemed to portend something terrible.

Between the ruined huts a procession came into view. First came a rough bier of branches borne by six crones who, emaciated and doddering, looked close to death themselves. Beside them tottered children, ushered by another old woman burdened with infants, two were slung at her sides and she carried another in her arms. After them came Tark bearing Myalah. He stumbled often in his weariness but had refused to allow anyone else to touch her.

Even here, where there was already so much death and misery, this sight aroused wonder and pity in all who saw it. The children looked at once for their kin and though there were some joyful reunions, others stood bewildered for no-one called to them. These were shoved unceremoniously out of the way as the old women shuffled into the centre of the village and laid the bier down. Then a murmur of outrage arose from the captives when they saw Nygeli's body. His bonds and the gag had been removed but there was a purple-black ring around his neck from the noose and his face was distorted by the agonies of asphyxiation.

Tark's visage betrayed nothing of his feelings as he entered the village he had helped to destroy. His eyes, sunken and bloodshot, scanned the prisoners and when he saw Gullilli and Manalah he staggered towards them, ignoring Draa and Mingar who were staring at him as at a stranger. Beneath the blood and filth that caked his skin and hair he seemed to have aged years in the space of a single night.

When she saw Tark and what he bore, Manalah restrained the cry that rose to her lips and shielded Gullilli's face with her hand to protect him from the truth. But the gesture was futile. When he reached them, Tark laid Myalah down as gently as if she had been alive. Then his legs folded beneath him and he sat numbly, his gaze blank and unfocused for he had reached the uttermost limit of his endurance.

Drawn by pity and curiosity, a crowd gathered round to see what would happen next and the crones that had carried the bier elbowed their way to the front for they were witnesses. All the Lake Clan were there, the wounded helped by their companions, sensing that this moment was pivotal in deciding the future not only for Tark but all of them. And Draa and Mingar waited for Tark to speak because without knowing the cause of these deaths, they knew not what to say.

But Tark was silent. It was Manalah who reached out with her free hand (the other was still shielding her husband's face), to touch their daughter as if to confirm the evidence of her eyes. Her tone low and wondering, she said at last, 'We sent her to fetch water and when she did not return, we thought she had gone to find Tark by the river. How is it then that she is dead? And Nygeli, the wisest of us all, why has he been hanged? The world has turned to madness. Would that we had died last night rather than live to see this day!'

'It was Matah,' Tark said and his voice was flat, devoid of emotion. 'We made him captive along with Nygeli so they could not raise the alarm. Myalah must have found the camp and tried to rescue them. But she released Matah first and he attacked her then murdered Nygeli to prevent him standing witness. And yet there were witnesses and they have avenged his crimes though I, for one, take no comfort from his death.'

Manalah said nothing but her head sank to her breast while Gullilli stirred restlessly beneath her hand. And Draa, shaken to the core not only by Tark's appearance but the manner of his speech, was compelled to kneel and embrace him with the tender compassion of a mother. Yet he was inert as a lump of wood in her arms, as if he also had died and only seemed to be alive.

'Tark,' she said fervently, 'you cannot die with the dead. You have brought her home: you can do no more for her. And we need your help for you alone understand these people and ours. You and she made us kin: let that be her legacy.'

Tark shuddered: he did not want to acknowledge the present, even less contemplate the future. And then Gullilli, with a supreme effort, managed to raise himself high enough from Manalah's lap to see his daughter. A great cry of anguish burst from his lips and he fell back as one struck a mortal blow, mouth open, eyes fixed and staring.

'Aiee!' Manalah bent over her husband, thinking the shock had killed him and as if her wail had been a signal, all the women raised their voices in lamentation for there was not one person in all the assembly that had not lost someone in the fighting or the fires. The cacophony returned Gullilli to his senses: his eyes sought Manalah's while with one hand he groped for hers. When he found it she fell silent for she sensed he was concentrating all his strength for one final effort: his mouth worked and he tried to speak.

But though she was quiet, the rest continued to mourn. It was Mingar who, seeing the dying man's struggle, suddenly turned on the crowd and yelled for quiet. So unexpected and violent was his interruption, they were shocked into silence. It was so profound that Gullilli's voice, though weak, came clear for all to hear though such was the dreadful expectancy engendered in all who heard, it seemed almost as if a spirit were speaking from beyond the grave.

'We should have carried out our law when Tark came,' he said. 'But we did not and so it has destroyed us. For if we had welcomed these strangers as kin, my daughter and all those others would still be alive. And I would have seen the children of Tark and Myalah grow up, the peoples of Lake and Valley joined as one. But now it is too late.'

His eyes closed, his mouth closed in a bitter line and Manalah had to restrain a cry of grief for her heart was wrung by his despair. But Mingar, deeply affected by this speech (not least because he understood what it must have cost so proud and grim a man to make), said: 'What is done cannot be undone: the dead are dead and regret will not return them to life. Revoke your law and let there be no more killing. Though we have slain many, more have died according to your custom over the years and they were innocent of any crime, even as your daughter was guiltless. Then some good can come of this bloodshed though it would have been better if we had not been forced to it.'

Gullilli was silent: it was unclear whether he refused to answer or could not. His visage was corpse-like and he did not respond when Manalah bent low and whispered in his ear. Then the crowd murmured restlessly. The captives were especially anxious for they knew that had their positions been reversed, they would already be dead. And faced with so many who looked to him for leadership, Mingar's old anxiety returned and his resolve began to falter.

All this time Tark had sat unmoving and silent beside the body of his beloved but gradually his grief gave way to anger. For while he had been prepared for many deaths in the confusion of the fighting, the manner in which his mentor had been murdered and the rape and killing of Myalah were both unexpected and, it seemed to him, unfair. And, in part, he blamed Myalah herself for had she obeyed him and stayed with her mother he was certain she would still be alive. He looked upon the corpse with bitter eyes and resentment seethed within him even as the noise of the crowd impinged upon his senses. He raised his head and saw his father's distracted gaze and then his rage could no longer be contained. He rose to his feet and stepped forward and so terrible was his aspect, Mingar quailed.

'Is this what you wanted?' Tark shouted and he waved his arms to take in the restive crowd, the blackened ruins of the village, the dead about which clouds of flies swarmed as the heat of the day increased. 'I tried to do what was right but it would have been better if the two of us had run away. Yes, even though you and the rest of our clan would be dead, your bodies flung down to join Memi's. Yet these Valley people are also my kin. What else could I have done?'

Some impassioned was his outburst all were moved by it though the reactions of the two peoples were different: outrage on the part of the Lake Clan; fear on that of the Valley folk. Yet more profound than these was pity for whichever clan they belonged to, Tark in that moment seemed to embody their own grief and pain. But Manalah raised her head and said bitterly, 'We cared for you and gave our daughter to be your wife and this is how you repay us! See, Gullilli is dead and he was the last of the Council: in him the law and stories of our people were enshrined. Now there is nothing left!'

She clenched her teeth and began to rock back and forth but no sound escaped her: her anguish was contained. And then Tark's rage dissipated: he knelt beside her and looking upon Gullilli, who seemed old and shrunken in death, said quietly, 'He was a great man, wise and strong within the bounds of the Valley, and he was as a father to me. And since the law of the Valley is dead, let there be no more killing. We shall make new laws.' He paused to take her hands between his own. 'Manalah, my mother, do not despair. Mingar, my father and Draa, my foster-mother will take care of you. And from this moment let us live as one people, sharing the Valley. For we have each done only what we deemed necessary and, through grief, maybe we shall come to hope.'

As he listened, pride swelled within Mingar for it seemed to him that Tark had come through passion to wisdom and his own self-doubt was annulled by his son's strength. And Draa put a hand on Tark's shoulder and said firmly, 'You are right, we have come close to destroying what we travelled far to find. Yet is it not from the ashes of the old that new life springs the strongest? If Manalah and her people agree, let us rebuild here together. As one people we shall be all be wiser than before.'

Then she and Tark helped Manalah to her feet and a murmur of assent and relief arose when the captives saw her face for it was no longer full of despair but calm.

'Let there be peace between us,' she said. 'For which of us in Tark's place would have done differently? There is nothing to be gained by more bloodshed, nor in seeking vengeance for the dead will not be restored to life. And, long ago, our ancestors fled the Night-Stalkers together.'

'For your wisdom and magnanimity you will be long revered, Manalah,' said Mingar and he addressed the assembly, telling them that the prisoners were free and that they should fetch food and water, then all could begin the work of tending the dead. 'And when we have mourned the fallen as is fitting, then we can rebuild what we have destroyed. But henceforth strangers will be welcomed, not condemned.'

'That is good,' said Manalah and while no voices were raised in rejoicing (for all were thirsty and hungry and there were many dead lying close by), those sitting next to one another exchanged glances and smiled though they might be strangers who had fought each other in the terror and confusion of the night. And Tark embraced his mother-in-law and they looked upon the bodies of Gullilli and Myalah and wept and now, instead of bitterness in their hearts, there was the stillness of acceptance.

Over the next days, the people of both clans worked hard together. To help meld the two into one, Mingar and Manalah had agreed that all the dead should be burned on a single pyre built from the wreckage of the village. In the centre of the great platform Gullilli and Myalah were laid side by side but Tark took the shell talisman from his beloved's neck and gave it to his mother-in-law for safe-keeping. Only as the flames leapt did celebrations begin for, as Draa had said, grief does not last forever and the end of mourning marked the beginning of a new life for all.

While the people were busy re-building, Tark guided Mingar around the Valley, showing him the spring, where the best fruit was to be found, the paths to the river and watering places where animals could be ambushed. But he avoided the stone pavement, in part because he was ashamed of the customs it represented but mainly because he did not want to be reminded of the day he had dragged Memi's body there and flung it into the chasm, nor of the killing he had enacted as part of his initiation.

Inevitably, the day came when Mingar asked to see where his companion of the mountain lay for by now the journey of the Lake Clan had become an epic tale. And though he could have asked any of the surviving Valley men to lead him there, it was his son, who had been Memi's boyhood friend, he wanted as his guide for he had no idea of the true significance of the place or of Tark's horror of it. Proud as he was, Tark could not bring himself to admit his reluctance to his father and so agreed to take him on the morrow. And Mingar smiled and went away satisfied.

That night though, in the little hut he had built single-handedly on the site of the one he and Myalah would have shared, Tark could not sleep. He thought of all that had happened since his arrival in the Valley and a piercing loneliness filled him. For while both Mingar and Manalah had implored him to stay with them, he could not bear their company for long: his mother-in-law's because he was constantly reminded of his beloved; his father's because of the tension that existed between them, rooted in the past, that neither knew how to acknowledge or assuage. As he lay on his pallet of freshly cut leaves, staring blankly at the roof, it seemed to Tark that of all those now calling themselves Valley folk he was the most unfortunate for he had lost what was dearest to his heart yet gained nothing in return. And when he imagined his future in the Valley, with some other woman, esteemed in his own right yet living always in his father's shadow, he knew he could exist comfortably enough yet there would always be something lacking, the passion and resolve that had lent him strength to endure his terrible journey and survive here. And thinking this, he ground his teeth and tears of frustration and longing sprang to his eyes for he was young still and strong and he knew that the world was not bounded by the rim of red rock that enclosed the Valley.

The night passed, measured by the steady thudding of his heartbeat in his ears, yet no resolution came. At last he lapsed into a reverie in which images of his past: the terror of his flight from the dying lake; his encounter with Tani's hunters on the salt flats; the plunge into the river that had brought him to the Valley, flowed like a tale. And last he saw Myalah as she had been on the day they attempted to escape the very circumstance which had, in the end, resulted in her death, and he realized he would never find peace if he stayed.

As if in a dream he rose and flung his cape around his shoulders against the night chill. Walking through the village, his sense of unreality was enhanced by the stillness and quiet. The only sounds were his own soft tread on the beaten earth and the call of an owl from deep within the forest. He paused outside the hut shared by

Manalah, his father and Draa and bent to lay his palm flat on the threshold in a gesture of farewell. No-one stirred but it seemed to him that if they had, he would have been invisible to their eyes for he felt curiously remote from the village and everyone in it, as if, in spirit, he had already left.

The central fireplace where days ago the great pyre had burned, was visible as a few glowing embers but though the remains of Gullilli, Nygeli and Myalah, all of whom he had loved, had been consumed there, he did not pause for nothing of them remained save in memory. And as he took the path to the river, leaving the village for the last time, he felt no regret but instead a surge of joyful anticipation. This time he was choosing his journey of his own free will and though he knew not where it would lead, that was in itself a kind of freedom impossible in the closed life of the Valley.

At last the smell of fresh water came to his nostrils and he saw the glint of it between the trees. The gravel bar lay before him, still pocked with footprints yet when he reached the patch of soft sand where he and Myalah had made love, he crouched for a moment as if it were possible to recapture something of the rapture they had shared before the fateful moment when she had looked up and seen Mingar watching from the cliff. The dry sand was soft and cool against his palms as he rested upon them for an instant and he understood then that he could not bring her back. Yet a day would come when he could think of her with joy rather than sorrow.

Even as he thought this, he straightened and walked towards the river. Its surface reflected the starlight so that it seemed opaque, a torrent of quicksilver between the black walls of rock and forest. The rush of it filled his ears and for a moment he hesitated, remembering its power. But he felt no fear this time as he made his way into the water. Compared with the chill of the air, it seemed warm and welcoming, caressing his skin like a lover. It lapped his thighs, his waist: the current encircled and tugged at him. He slipped into its embrace and let it bear him away.

Also by S. Pitt:

Trouwerner

Korunah's Gift

Fen-wolf

Cromwell's Promise

Four Wonders

Find out more at:
<u>www.spittbooks.com</u>

www.ingramcontent.com/pod-product-compliance
Lightning Source LLC
Chambersburg PA
CBHW030929210726
48290CB00007B/2131